LETTER TO SURVIVORS

GÉBÉ (Georges Blondeaux; 1929–2004) was a fixture of the French press for almost fifty years. He was best known as a cartoonist, but he was also an author, lyricist, screenwriter, and dramatist; a maker of short films and photo-novels; and a beloved editor and nurturer of new talent. From 1970 to 1985, he was the editor-in-chief of *Charlie Hebdo*. He returned when the weekly was reborn in 1992 and served as the editorial director until his death.

EDWARD GAUVIN has translated more than three hundred graphic novels, including Blutch's *Peplum* (NYR Comics). His work has won the John Dryden Translation prize and the Science Fiction & Fantasy Translation Award and has been nominated for the French-American Foundation and Oxford Weidenfeld translation prizes. He is a contributing editor for comics at *Words Without Borders* and has written on the Francophone fantastic at *Weird Fiction Review*. Other publications have appeared in *The New York Times*, *Harper's*, *Tin House*, *World Literature Today*, and *Subtropics*.

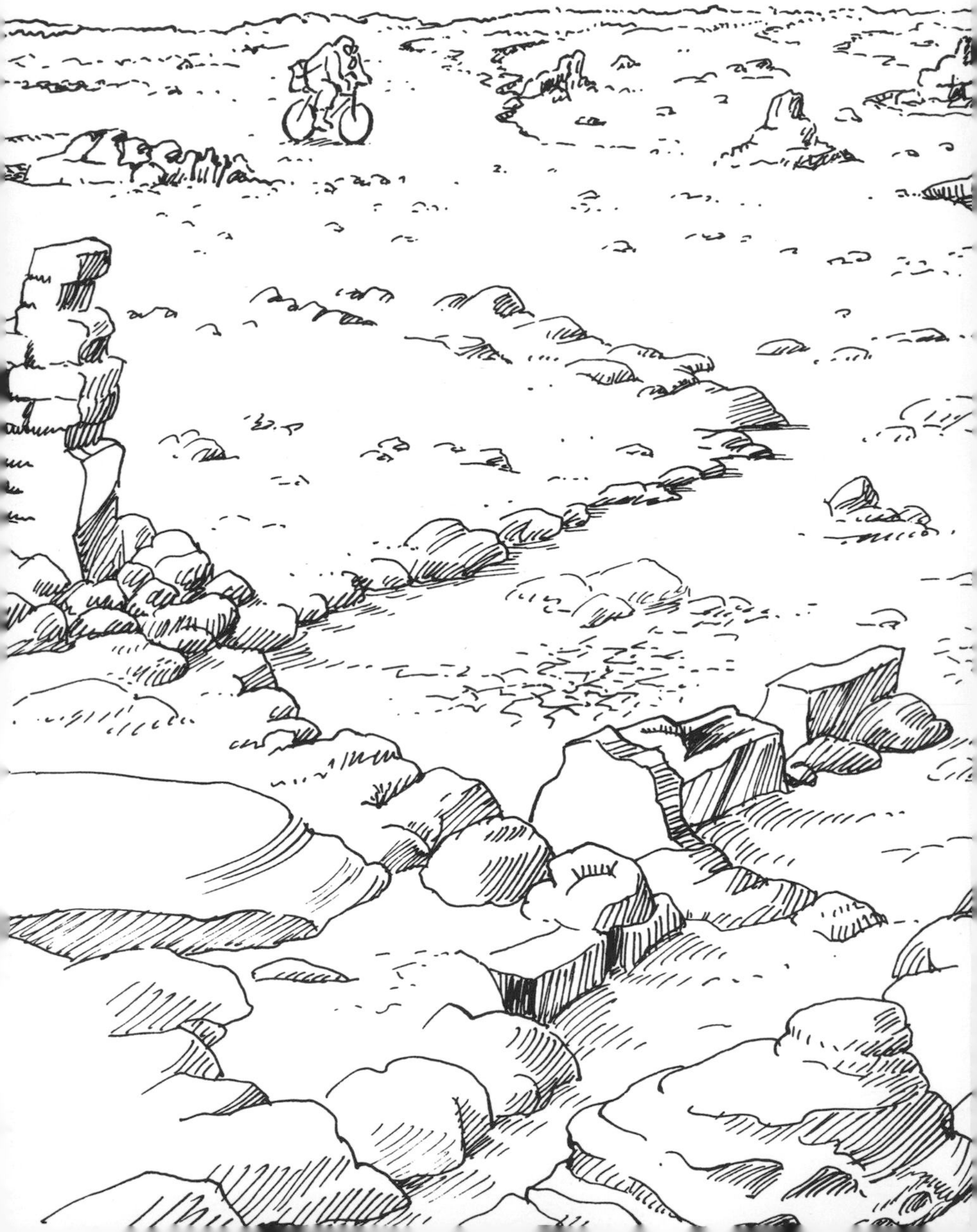

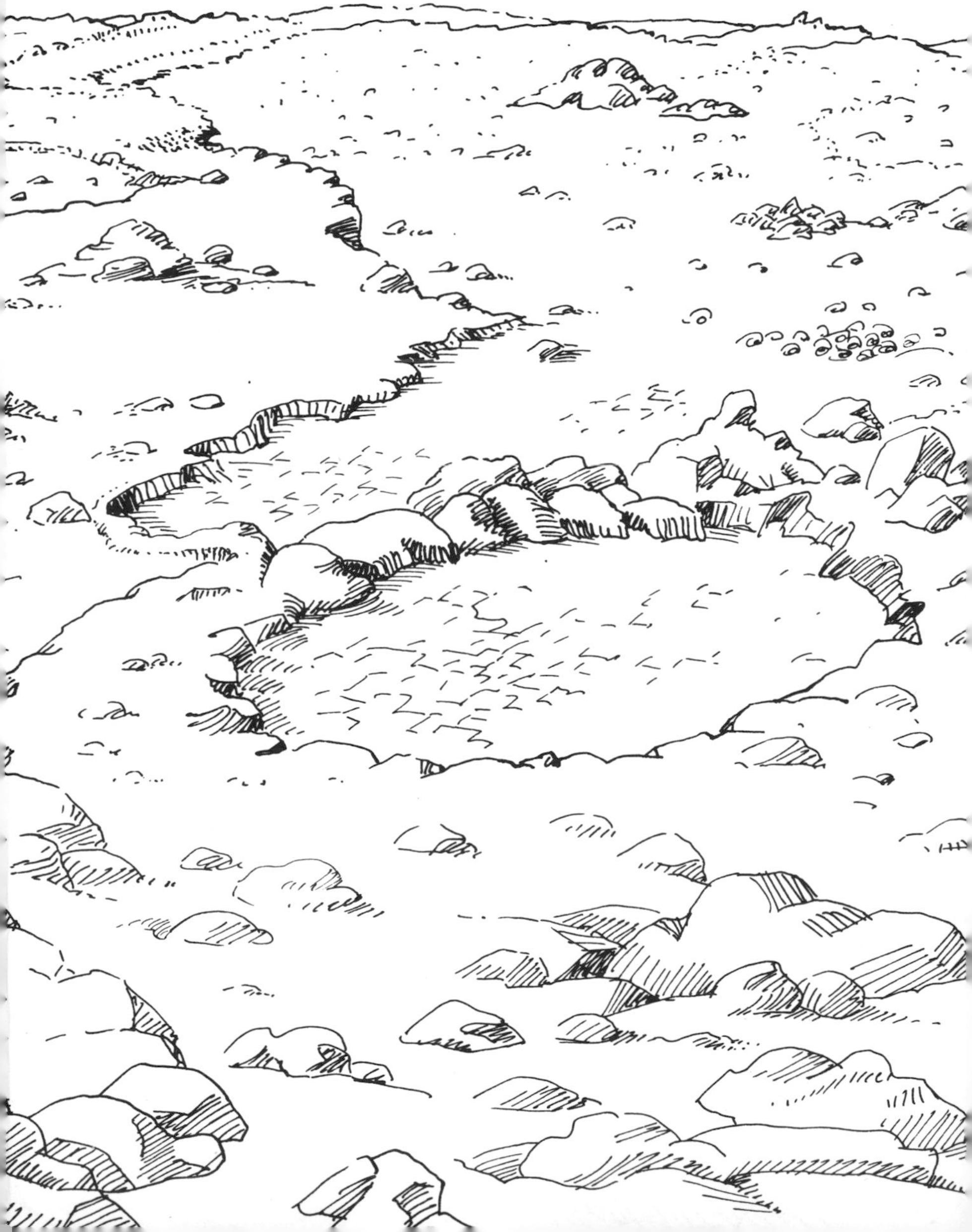

THIS IS A NEW YORK REVIEW COMIC
PUBLISHED BY THE NEW YORK REVIEW OF BOOKS
435 Hudson Street, New York, NY 10014
www.nyrb.com

Cover design by Lucas Adams.

First published in French as *Lettre aux survivants* by Albin Michel (1981).

Library of Congress Cataloging-in-Publication Data

Names: Gébé, artist, author. | Gauvin, Edward, translator.
Title: Letter to survivors / by Gébé ; translated and with an introduction
  by Edward Gauvin.
Other titles: Lettre aux survivants. English
Description: New York : New York Review Books, [2018] | Series: New York
  Review Comics
Identifiers: LCCN 2017051740 (print) | LCCN 2017052616 (ebook) | ISBN
  9781681372419 (epub) | ISBN 9781681372402 (paperback)
Subjects: LCSH: Graphic novels. | BISAC: COMICS & GRAPHIC NOVELS / Science
  Fiction.
Classification: LCC PN6747.G4 (ebook) | LCC PN6747.G4 L4813 2018 (print) |
  DDC 741.5/944—dc23
LC record available at https://lccn.loc.gov/2017051740

ISBN 978-1-68137-240-2
Available as an electronic book; 978-1-68137-241-9

Printed in China
10 9 8 7 6 5 4 3 2 1

LETTER TO SURVIVORS

by GÉBÉ

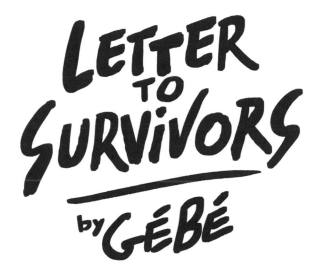

TRANSLATED AND WITH
AN INTRODUCTION BY
EDWARD GAUVIN

ENGLISH LETTERING BY
FRANÇOIS VIGNEAULT

NEW YORK REVIEW COMICS · *New York*

INTRODUCTION

THERE IS AN Henri Cartier-Bresson photo of a fivesome from above and behind—all of them rather *bon vivant*, not to say portly—on the sloping banks of the Marne. Around them in the grass, on newspapers and a rumpled blanket, lie the ruins of a picnic, even as one fellow in a Borsalino and suspenders pours himself another glass of red. Leisure comes off the image in waves, like warm summer air. In the late 1930s, when he took the picture, Cartier-Bresson was coming off Surrealism's influence into a decade of political engagement that would see him working for the communist press. Between 1936 and 1938, he produced a series of photos that caught citizens of the Parisian region celebrating the simple joys afforded by the first paid vacations: one of the great political victories of the *Entre-deux-guerres*, that short-lived interwar period during which modern France's mythical reputation for the good life was largely forged, much of it thanks to the even shorter-lived Front Populaire (a coalition of the Communist, Radical, and Socialist parties with the Workers' International), which with the Matignon Agreements in 1936 secured such complementary legal fundamentals as the right to strike, the right to unionize, and the forty-hour work week.

Simple joys, our common human right to them, and the playful, even surreal shifts of perception that might bring them closer, would become presiding themes in the work of Georges Blondeaux. In 1936, he was seven, the only child of working-class parents in a suburb of

Paris. Just over decade later, he joined the SNCF, France's national rail service, as a draftsman and design technician, and a decade after that, the first single-panel editorial cartoons signed jaggedly but inimitably "Gébé" (the French pronunciation of Blondeaux's initials, "G.B.") began to appear: first in the SNCF's house organ, *La vie du rail* (Life on the Rails), back from its wartime hiatus, and then in periodicals from the mainstream (*Paris-Match, Le Journal du dimanche*) to the fringe (*Radar, Bizarre*).[1]

But it was not until 1960 that Gébé went "off" the rails, quitting his industrial job and fully embracing his calling as an industrious anarchist. In the years to come, he was to exercise his gift for whimsy and satire, absurd yet urgently humane, in everything from cartoons to prose fiction, radio plays to photo-novels, movies to song lyrics. He claimed to love nineteenth-century Russian literature, American science fiction, and Scandinavian theater. He penned a hit song for Yves Montand that manages to link political assassinations, Czech phenomenologist Jan Patočka, and clubbing baby seals. "The true anarchist," wrote Pacôme Thiellement in a posthumous appreciation, "does not make: comics, literature, paintings, music, or cinema. The true anarchist makes anarchy in comics, literature, paintings, music, or cinema."

In 1953, Guy Debord had spray-painted his famous "Never work" on the banks of the Seine. To hear Gébé himself tell it, he woke up one fine spring morning toward the end of the same decade and said, "No! Today I stop selling, at a three-hour round trip from here, eight hours of my life on a daily basis." By the next year, he had joined the crack squad whose creation would change the face not just of satire but journalistic freedom in France: the infamous *Hara-Kiri*. In its motto, taken from an outraged reader's letter, the magazine inspired by Harvey Kurtzman's *MAD* proudly branded itself "stupid and mean."[2] Its early roster was a Who's Who of scathing French humor: founders François Cavanna and

---

1. Rumor has it that shortly thereafter, the young cartoonist lucked into a miracle commission that turned into a major disappointment: an adaptation of Raymond Queneau's *Zazie in the Metro* for serialization in the daily *Paris-Presse*. An editorial change of heart left him with ninety pages enthusiastically completed well ahead of deadline but never to see the light of day.

2. The infamous "bête et méchant," also translated as "dumb and vicious," or even "nasty and brutish."

Georges Bernier (a.k.a. "Professeur Choron"), Fred, Reiser, Roland Topor, Cabu, Willem, Wolinski, Lob, Delfeil de Ton. To *Hara-Kiri*, Gébé contributed cartoons, prose faux-reportages, and sketches for photos later staged with live models as color covers. "What that fellow was able to convey in his spare, deadpan lines!" the excitable Cavanna crowed in his memoirs. "His brain hummed away by itself in its own little corner like a superannuated yet highly subtle machine whose gears had been lovingly oiled." The more mordant Choron claims that the draftsman's exactitude could always be detected in his style.[3] But for Gébé, such tight-winding was the springboard to greater heights of lunacy— locating, like Bergson, comedy in the machine gone haywire. Rigor of art and argument lent his humor its off-kilter power, the sense of madness bristling in the schematics. When the *Hara-Kiri* weekly was shut down a scant decade later for mocking the death of General de Gaulle, its successor *Charlie Hebdo* sprang up almost immediately, while the *Hara-Kiri* monthly marched on with Gébé as editor-in-chief.

Hara-Kiri, if not central to the May '68 protests, had a definite hand in goosing a prudish France into a more permissive media era. Gébé and several *Charlie* comrades began branching out, publishing in the long-running comics revue *Pilote* (home of *Astérix* and *Valérian*), as well as the short-lived, incendiary rag *L'Enragé*.[4] But, riding the high of post-'68 enthusiasm, Gébé was preparing his own call for change, markedly more fanciful than his fellows'. Could his categorical "No!" be extended to all humanity? "Stop everything. Think. It's a good thing!"[5] became the cheery motto of his daffy utopian comic strip *L'AN 01* (Year 01), which first appeared in October, 1970, in the pages of *Politique Hebdo*. "There was," he wrote in a later afterword on its origins, "the idea, bracing as salt air, of vacationers who, having spent their sojourn reflecting, were firmly resolved not to go back to things as they were.

3. Gébé would make a point of pushing this tendency to the point of self-parody in his 1992 fable of an entirely mechanical society, *L'Âge du fer* (The Iron Age).

4. Founded by Jean-Jacques Pauvert (1926–2014), the first to openly publish de Sade, and later the publisher of Bataille, Dalí, Breton, and *The Story of O*. "This paper," declared the first issue, "is a paving stone. It can be used as a fuse for a Molotov cocktail. It can be used to hide a blackjack. It can be used as a makeshift gas mask."

5. "On arrête tout. On réfléchit. Et c'est pas triste."

And the jubilation I felt welling up, steadily overflowing into everything."

What is it with French revolutions and rebooting the calendar? With *L'AN 01*, Gébé went from being the cog that quit the machine to impishly tossing grit in the gears, a wrench in the works. What he proposed was both modest and radical, literal and metaphorical: "a step to the side." What would happen if we all took a step sideways? Lines would no longer match up with windows, rifles would fall down for lack of recruits, laborers would no longer be at their places on assembly lines, and at the bar, "you'd have to sip from your neighbor's cup: no harm done!" Such implacable extrapolations of consequence along the lines of whimsy were a signature move, practiced derailments (*déraillement*) akin to Situationist subversions (*détournement*).

If, as a thought experiment in utopia, *L'AN 01* seems overstuffed, well, "you need a lot of utopia to start with," Gébé advised, "because it cooks down." The book brims with suggestions too outlandish to be taken literally (except when acted out by readers) backed by intentions too serious to be taken as anything but (except when meant in jest). Its population lives on noodles, and its department stores have become museums, but its stakes are the life and death of society and the soul. In his repudiation of violence, his refusal to choose between "the weapons of production" and "the weapons of revolt," his faith in sovereign imagination ("Imagination calls us only to imagine"), and his pursuit of joy as the only true awakening, Gébé recalls Raoul Vaneigem, the hero of whose 1967 classic *The Revolution of Everyday Life* (the poetry to Guy Debord's theory) was "the man of survival ... ground up in the machinery of hierarchical power ... the man of absolute refusal."

Over the course of the next three years, *L'AN 01* would become a transmedia event *avant la lettre*, a collective film in which Gébé invited people across France to freely participate, supplying prompts for scenes in his comics pages for *Charlie Hebdo*. The eventual result—a real movie, including sequences directed by Jacques Doillon and Alain Resnais, and featuring over three hundred actors, from Coluche and Miou-Miou to the *Hara-Kiri* staff and the first film appearance of

Gérard Depardieu—was a minor hit. The *L'AN 01* strips were collected in book form by *Hara-Kiri*'s parent Les Éditions du Square, which also published Gébé's cartoons and photo-novels.

We all know what happened next. The oil crisis. The Cold War came back. The '70s became the '80s, even in France. In 1981, the government shuttered its Ministry of the Quality of Life, founded less than a decade earlier. Les Éditions du Square folded, taking *Charlie Hebdo* and *Hara-Kiri* with it. The intermittent *Zéro*, a magazine from the pre-*Hara-Kiri* days of Cavanna and Choron, was resurrected with Gébé as editor-in-chief, lasting a mere year. Gébé turned to writing prose novels. But before that, he gave us one slim, disillusioned volume composed from a pained rage at the imminence of global immolation, the dystopian *Letter to Survivors*. True humor is never far from suicidal.

American science fiction is hard science, European science fiction is hard humanities; so goes the stereotype. And in keeping, *Letter* is short on how-to, long on how-did-it-ever-come-to-this? If *L'AN 01* was a Whole Earth grab bag of poetic tactics to awaken the imagination, in *Letter to Survivors* it was as if a disillusioned Stewart Brand had put out a special follow-up issue wholly devoted to fallout shelter living. Instead of gung-ho can-do and helpful tips, *Letter* serves up mockeries of advertisement and fragments of familiar genres. Gébé gives us a series of vignettes nested in a postapocalyptic postman's narration. In his short fiction, Gébé was fond of parodying popular genres, from mystery to pastoral to fairy tale. Here, we find a torpid story of love and detection by the seaside, a bucolic idyll of Sunday walks and country cafés, a magic lantern show: time-honored settings likely to stir in readers memories of family outings and childhood holidays. Each strays further back in time, seeming to follow the specious narrative of nostalgia, wherein the good old days are made to glow gold through the alchemy of longing. While *L'AN 01* exhorted us to leave our jobs for the natural state of leisure, in *Letter* such opportunities are severely curtailed; these evocations are but reminders of loss. The past is a trap, and the present a wasteland.

The postman's inscrutable goggle eyes and filter snout visually echo Gébé's early breakout character, the inhuman prankster Berck (a homophone of *beurk*, the French for *ick* or *blech*), a dwarfish, potbellied, errant, and imperturbable id of simple desires who eats fresh fish and flowers. Both Berck and the postman are equal-opportunity offenders (though the postman is unionized) with a bit of Renoir's Boudu about them, reminding us through wile and casual havoc of our best instincts, bringing a new meaning to the words "masked hero." The postman's mission is to introduce a grain of sand into the oyster of the bunker, grit enough to agitate. Through him, Gébé means to awaken us to indignation, to the intolerability of our circumstances, the extent of our passive and successive amputations. Though the worst has not yet happened, so many of us live as if it were at once impossible and inevitable, in a state of willful ignorance and spiritual resignation. Witness the mother's alcoholic disintegration, hitting rock bottom in a bomb shelter. A few deft lines are enough to render her bitterness, and yet her pinched face recalls more than any other family member's the abstract visage (geometrical and hardly idealized) that is arrested by the dual smells near the gazebo in the fondly remembered town square (see p. 13). By the defeat of our hopes and dreams, we have been driven underground already, but Gébé wants to get us back to a place where, out of rage, we might begin to dream again. "We'll be waiting for them right outside their five-star bomb shelters," the trapped mother of Gébé's nuclear family vows. "They'll expect to get butchered but all we'll do is spit at their feet."

By 1992, Philippe Val had resurrected *Charlie Hebdo*, and Gébé was brought on as managing editor. The revolution, back in fashion, spent the decade resting on its laurels and canonizing its survivors. Shortly before his death in 2004, the pivotal indie comics publisher L'Association began reprinting Gébé's greatest hits, and a decade later came a retrospective exhibit. But the genial anarchist and cartoonist's cartoonist, who by temperament shunned the limelight, remained a name for those in the know, never quite achieving the renown of his more overtly political comrades like Wolinski or Cabu—often to the surprise of the same. At the news that critic Jean-Charles Vidal had proclaimed him a genius, Gébé is said to have exclaimed, "*Merde!* Don't let it get around, or they'll can me!"

Over thirty-five years after its initial publication, this letter from one era of staring down the missile silo has reached another, none the wiser. Armageddon, nuclear and non-, is timely again and its aftermath more popular than ever, if also smacking faintly of nostalgia, an almost nihilistic longing for the prophesied doomsday that never came to pass. It is hard to tell real panic from the retro-postapocalyptic. It has been almost midnight for such a long time.

—EDWARD GAUVIN

LETTER TO SURVIVORS

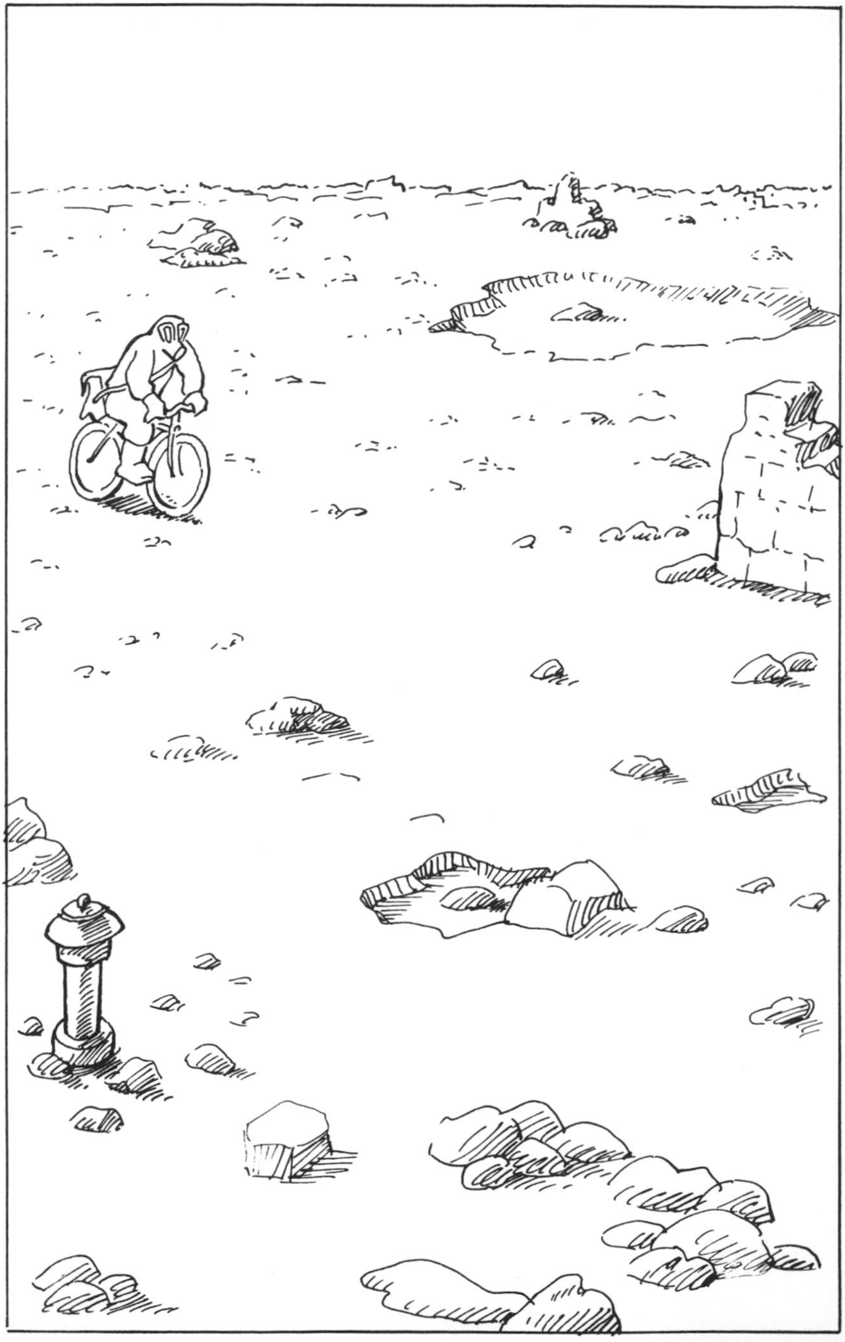

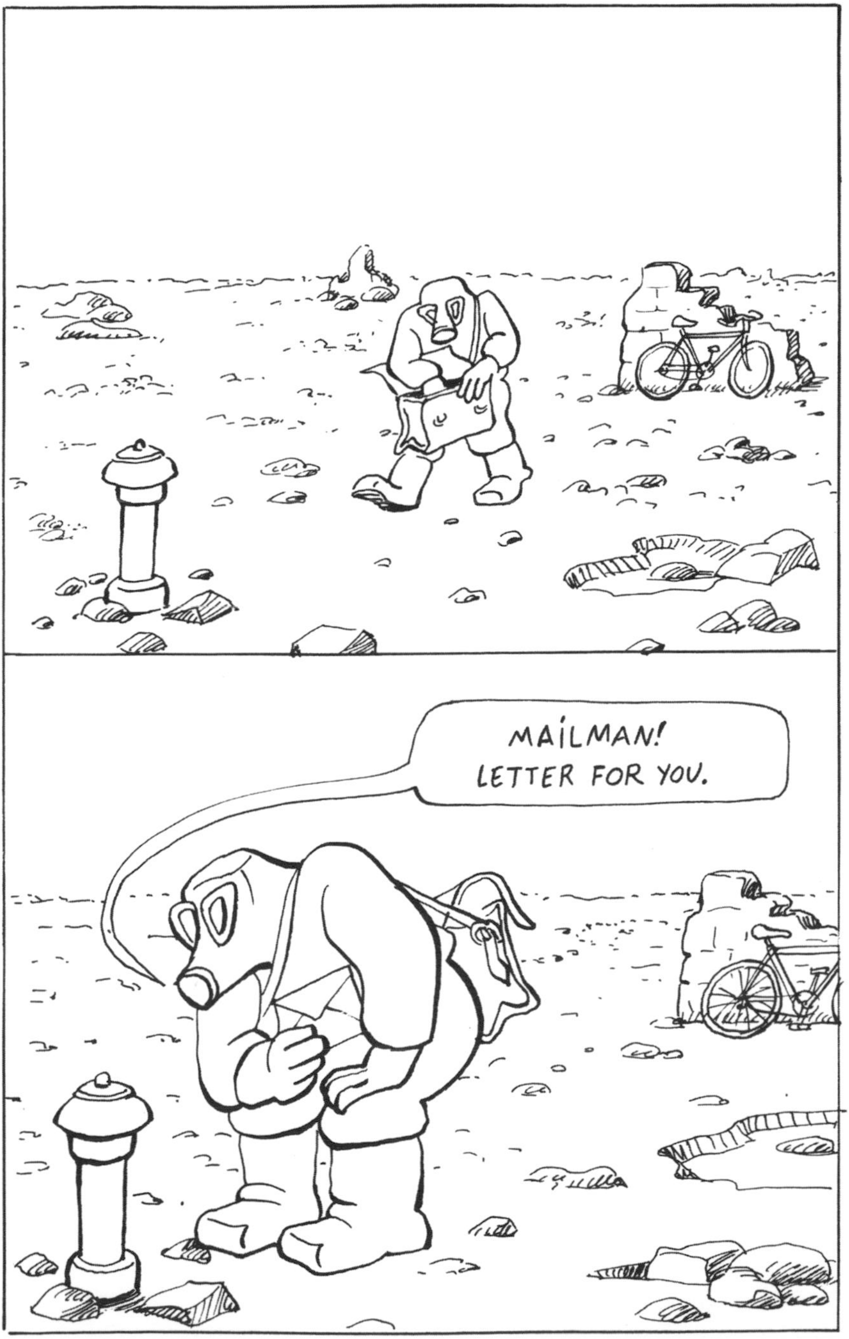
MAILMAN! LETTER FOR YOU.

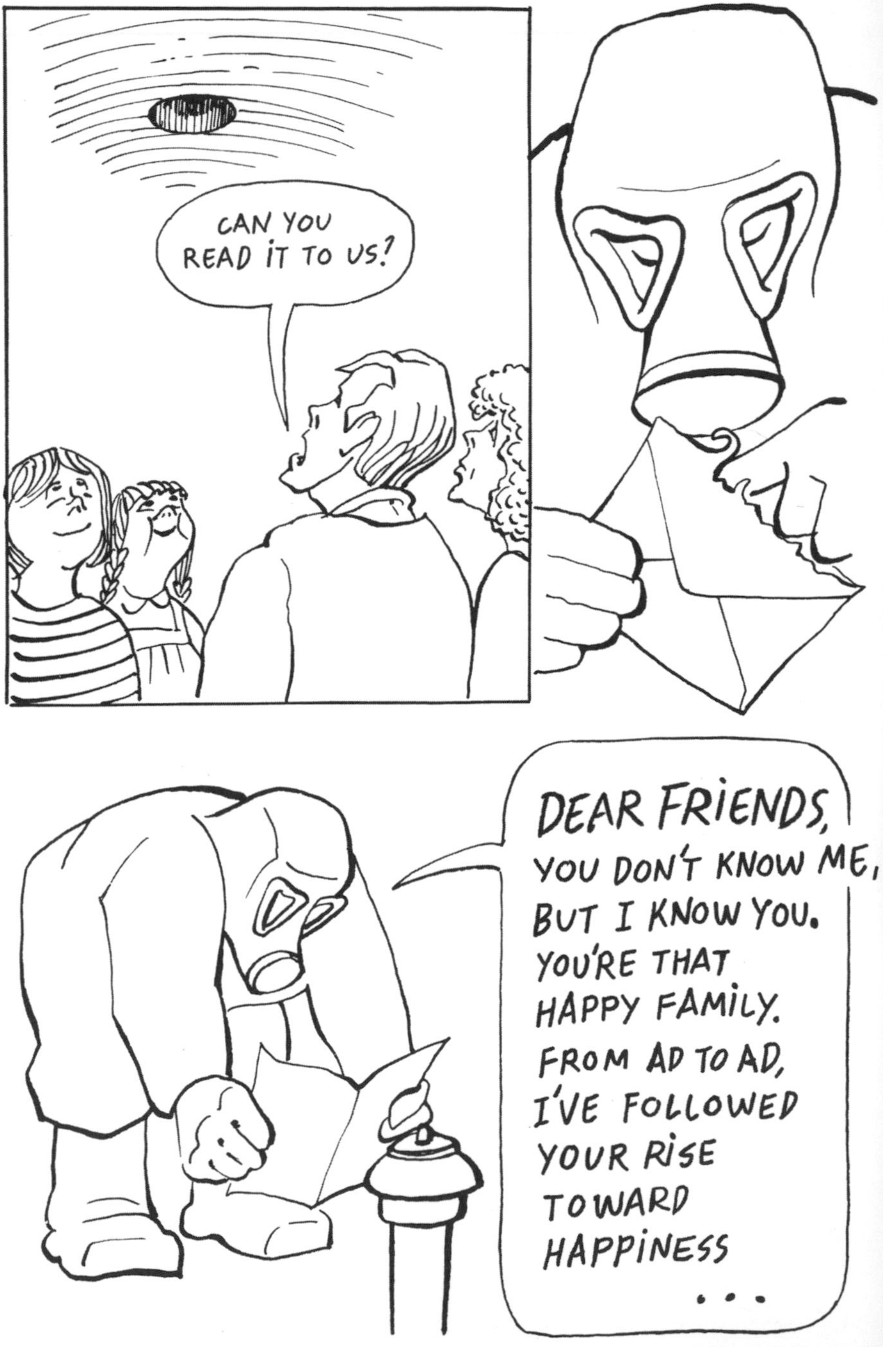
CAN YOU READ IT TO US?
DEAR FRIENDS, YOU DON'T KNOW ME, BUT I KNOW YOU. YOU'RE THAT HAPPY FAMILY. FROM AD TO AD, I'VE FOLLOWED YOUR RISE TOWARD HAPPINESS . . .

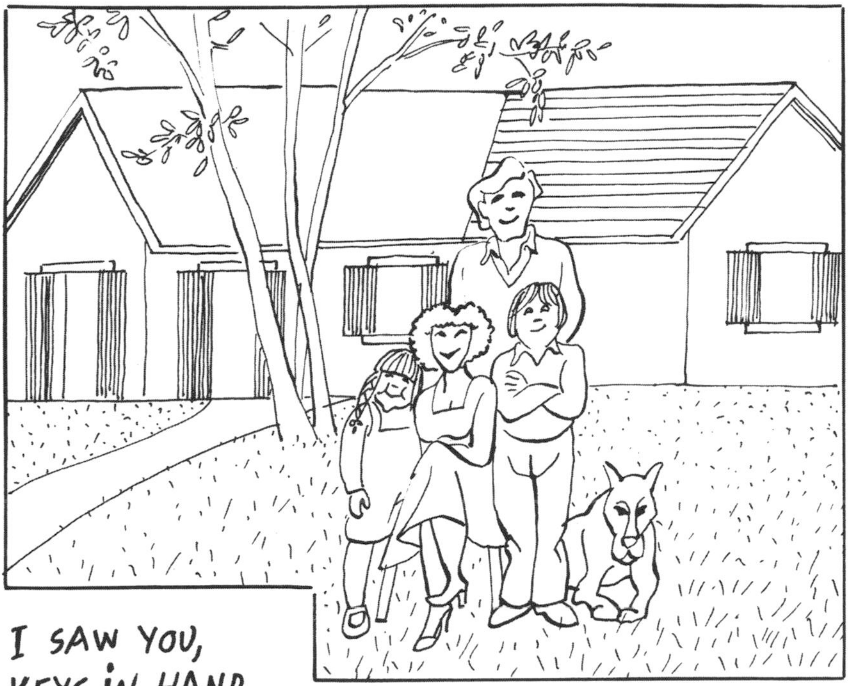

I SAW YOU,
KEYS IN HAND,
BUY THE HOUSE
OF YOUR DREAMS.

I SAW YOU
YIELD TO THE LURE
OF AN APARTMENT
BY THE SHORE.

I SAW YOU
MAKE A DEPOSIT
ON A SPLIT-LEVEL
AT
THE FOOT
OF THE SLOPES...

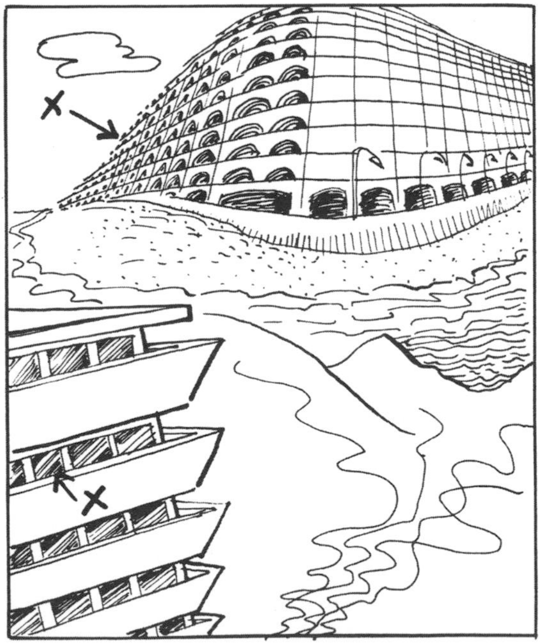

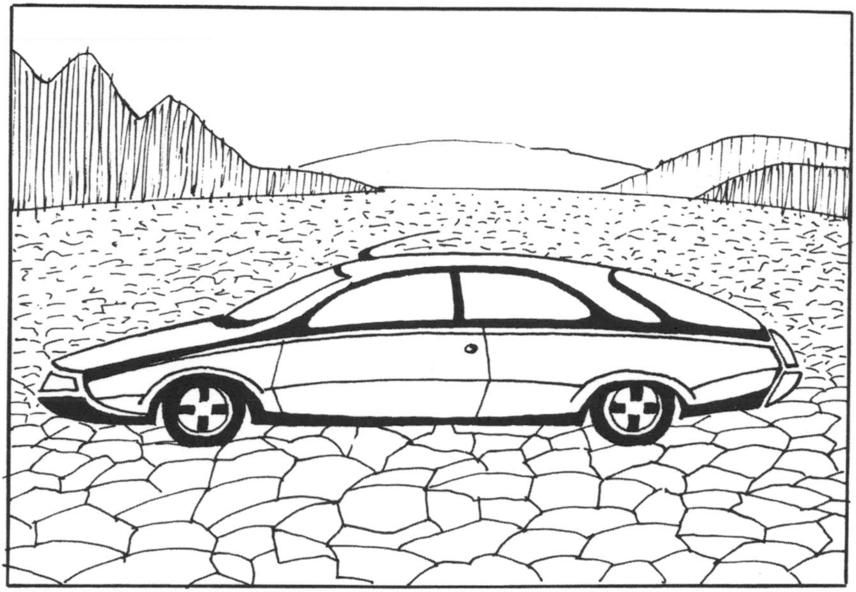

YOU'VE NEVER LET ME DOWN. WITH UNERRING TASTE, YOU SELECTED FROM AMONG TWENTY SEDUCTIVE MODELS THE ONLY LUXURY SEDAN CAPABLE OF CONQUERING THE DESOLATE WASTES BETWEEN YOUR PRIMARY RESIDENCE AND YOUR SECONDARY OASES.

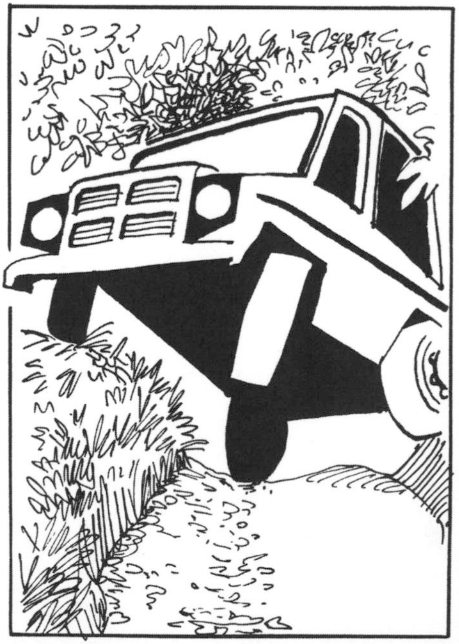

SAME GOES FOR YOUR SUPERIOR CHOICE OF ALL-TERRAIN VEHICLE FOR INTREPID TREKS INTO THE UNTAMED WILDS AROUND YOUR COUNTRY HOUSE.

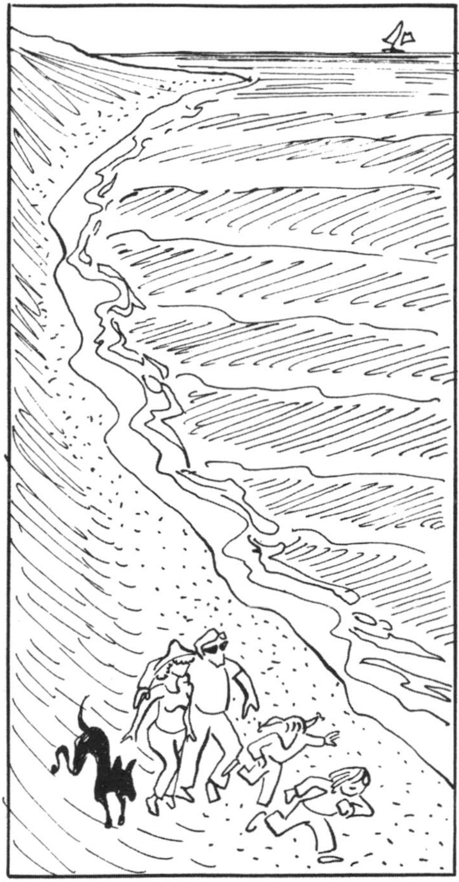

IN THE HUMAN PROLIFERATION OF THE 80s, YOU WERE ALWAYS TO BE SEEN ON YOUR OWN, JUST YOU FOUR AND THE DOG.

THE PERFECT FAMILY.

ALONE ON ENDLESS LAWNS, ALONE ON PRIVATE ROADS, ALONE ON INFINITE BEACHES,

ALONE ON SKI-LIFTS SOARING TOWARD THE SILENT PEAKS.

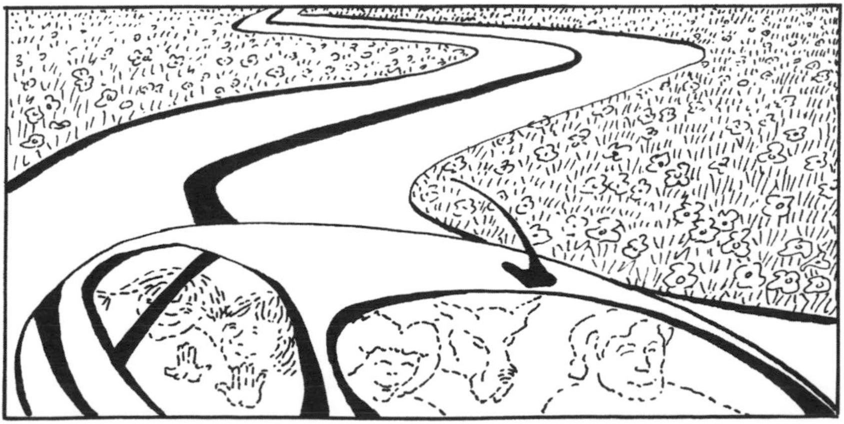

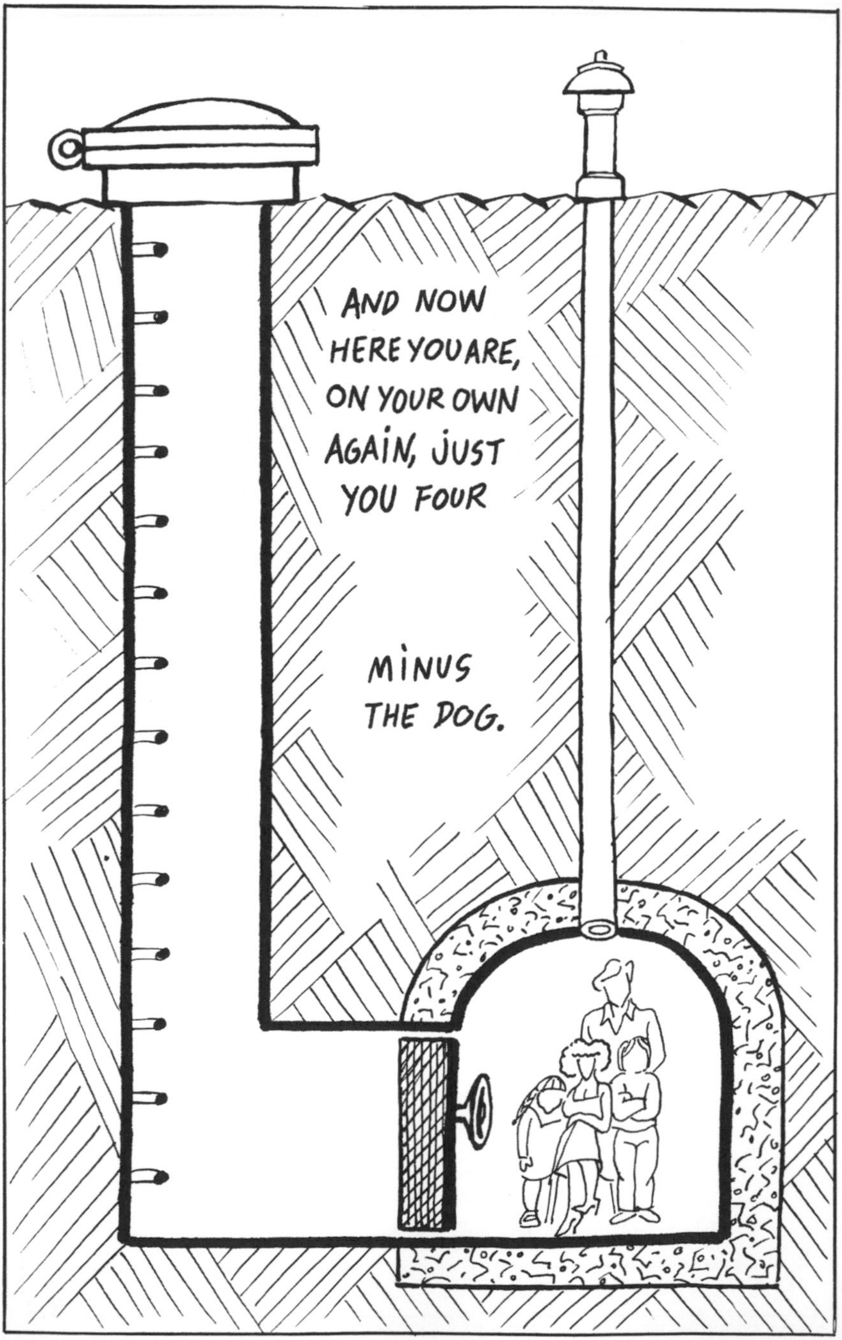
AND NOW HERE YOU ARE, ON YOUR OWN AGAIN, JUST YOU FOUR
MINUS THE DOG.

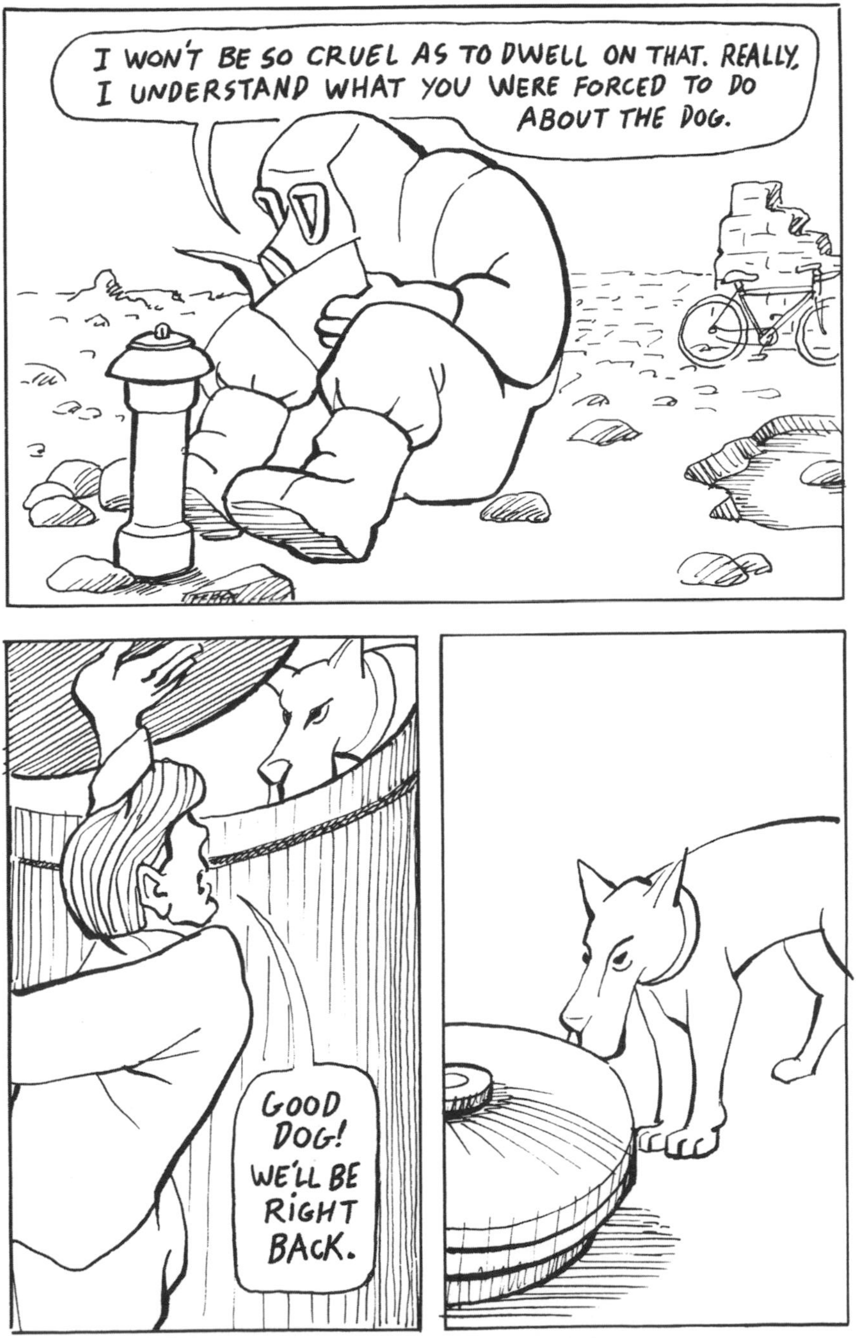
I WON'T BE SO CRUEL AS TO DWELL ON THAT. REALLY, I UNDERSTAND WHAT YOU WERE FORCED TO DO ABOUT THE DOG.
GOOD DOG! WE'LL BE RIGHT BACK.

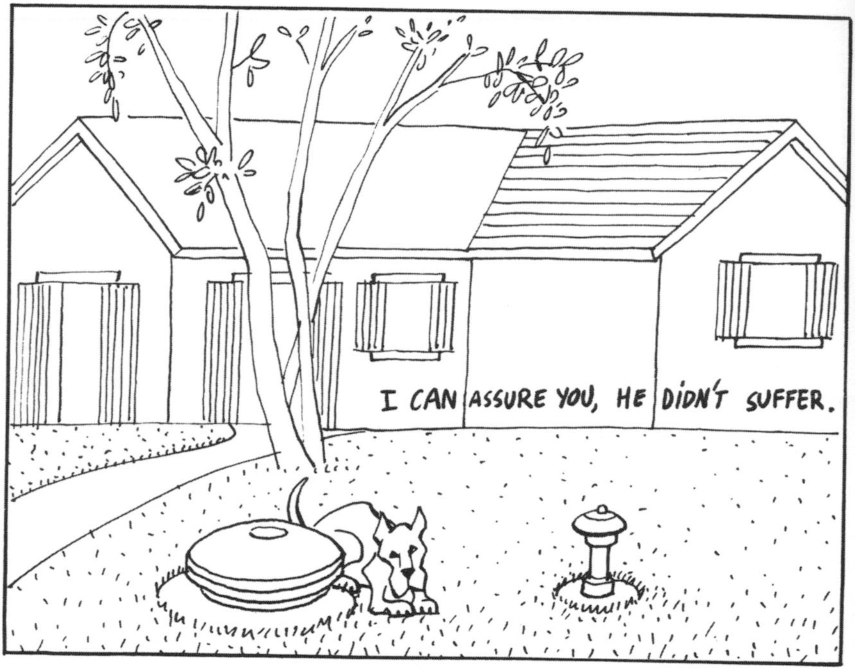
I CAN ASSURE YOU, HE DIDN'T SUFFER.

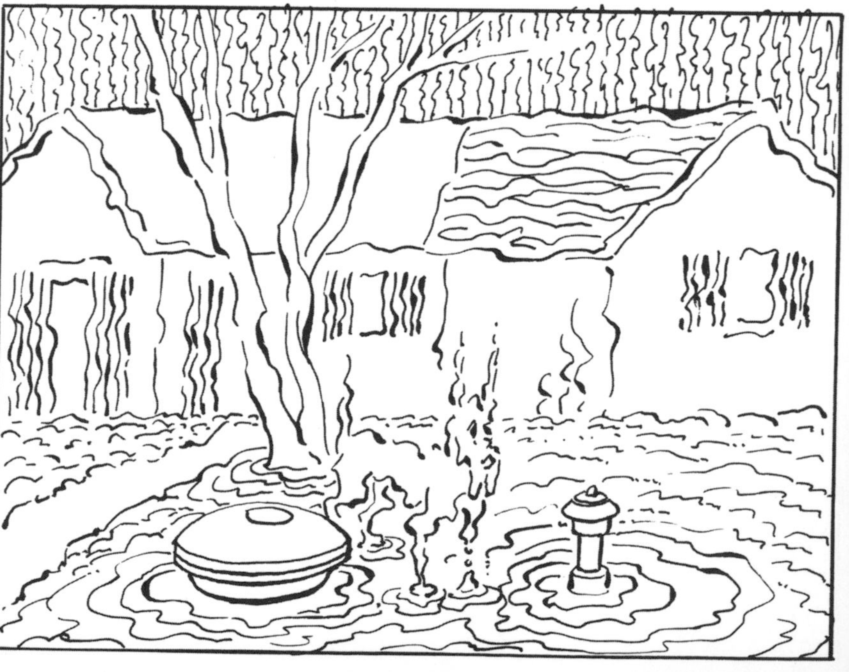

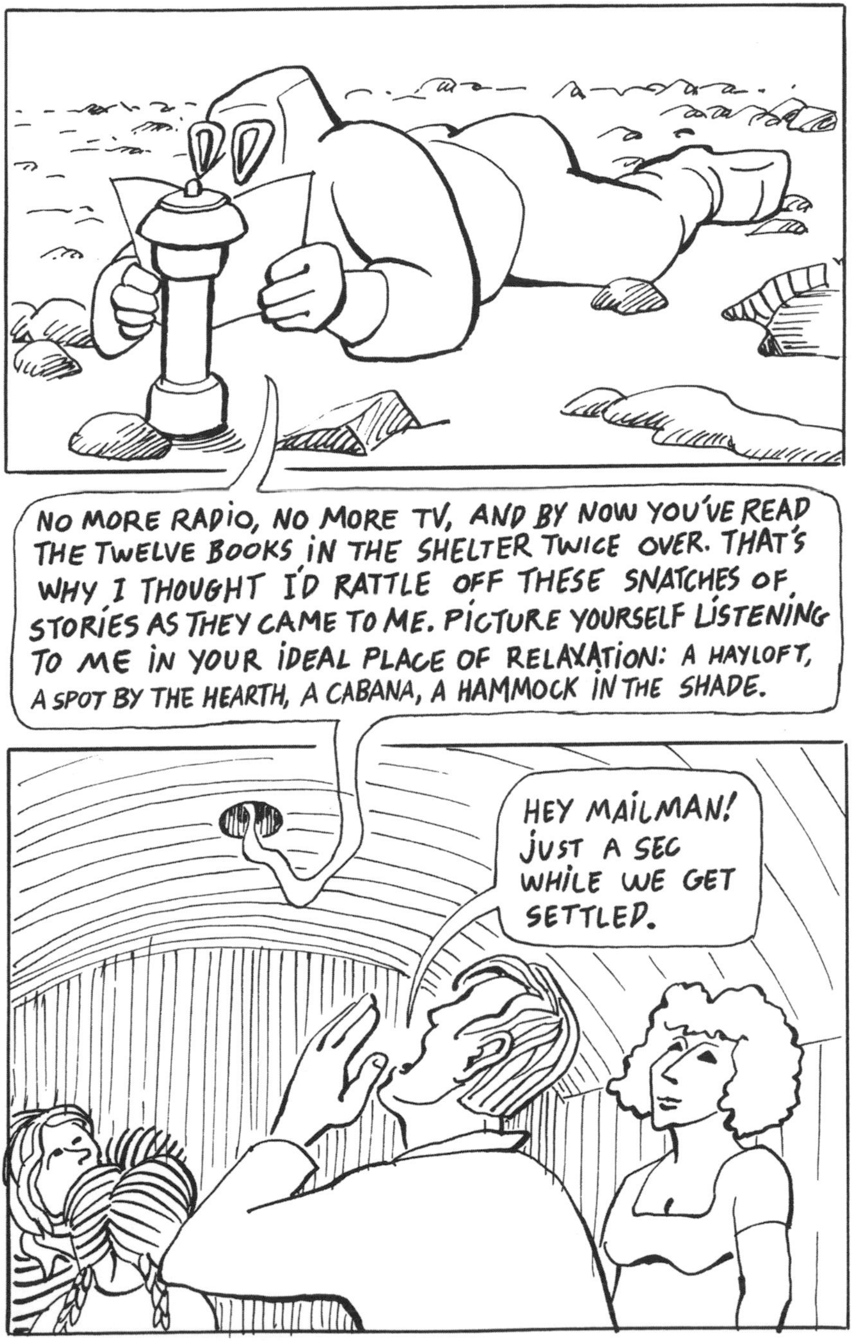
NO MORE RADIO, NO MORE TV, AND BY NOW YOU'VE READ THE TWELVE BOOKS IN THE SHELTER TWICE OVER. THAT'S WHY I THOUGHT I'D RATTLE OFF THESE SNATCHES OF STORIES AS THEY CAME TO ME. PICTURE YOURSELF LISTENING TO ME IN YOUR IDEAL PLACE OF RELAXATION: A HAYLOFT, A SPOT BY THE HEARTH, A CABANA, A HAMMOCK IN THE SHADE.
HEY MAILMAN! JUST A SEC WHILE WE GET SETTLED.

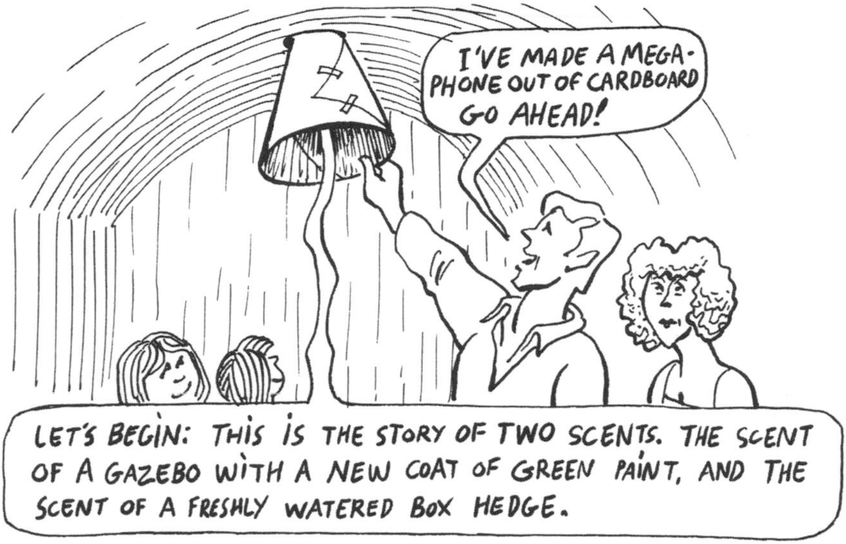
I'VE MADE A MEGA-PHONE OUT OF CARDBOARD GO AHEAD!
LET'S BEGIN: THIS IS THE STORY OF TWO SCENTS. THE SCENT OF A GAZEBO WITH A NEW COAT OF GREEN PAINT, AND THE SCENT OF A FRESHLY WATERED BOX HEDGE.

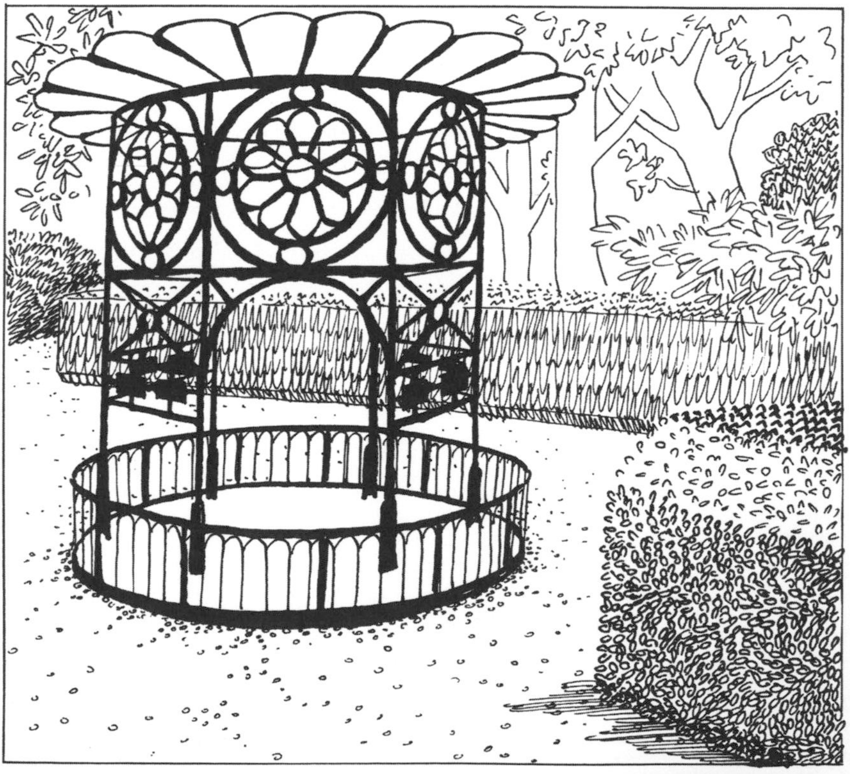

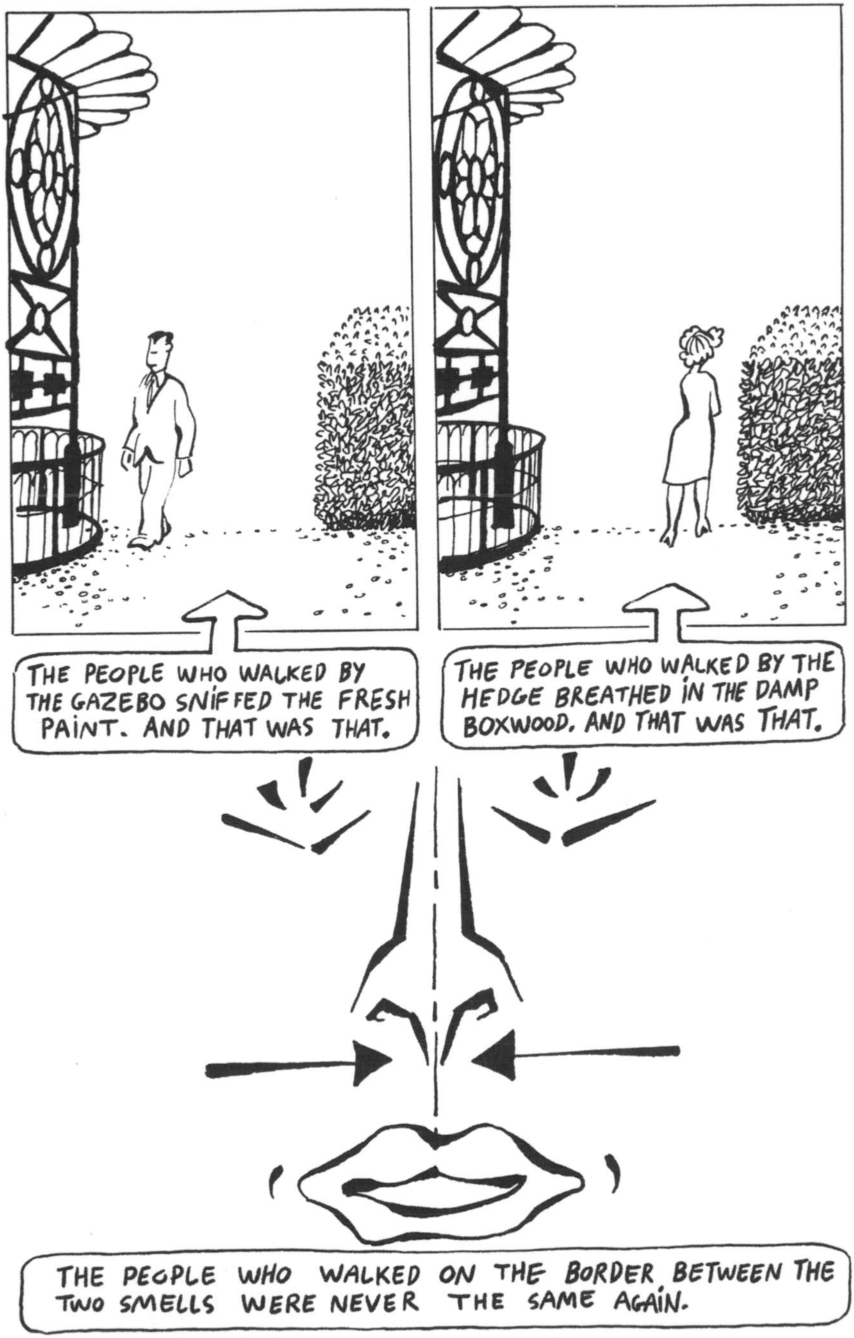
THE PEOPLE WHO WALKED BY THE GAZEBO SNIFFED THE FRESH PAINT. AND THAT WAS THAT.
THE PEOPLE WHO WALKED BY THE HEDGE BREATHED IN THE DAMP BOXWOOD. AND THAT WAS THAT.
THE PEOPLE WHO WALKED ON THE BORDER BETWEEN THE TWO SMELLS WERE NEVER THE SAME AGAIN.

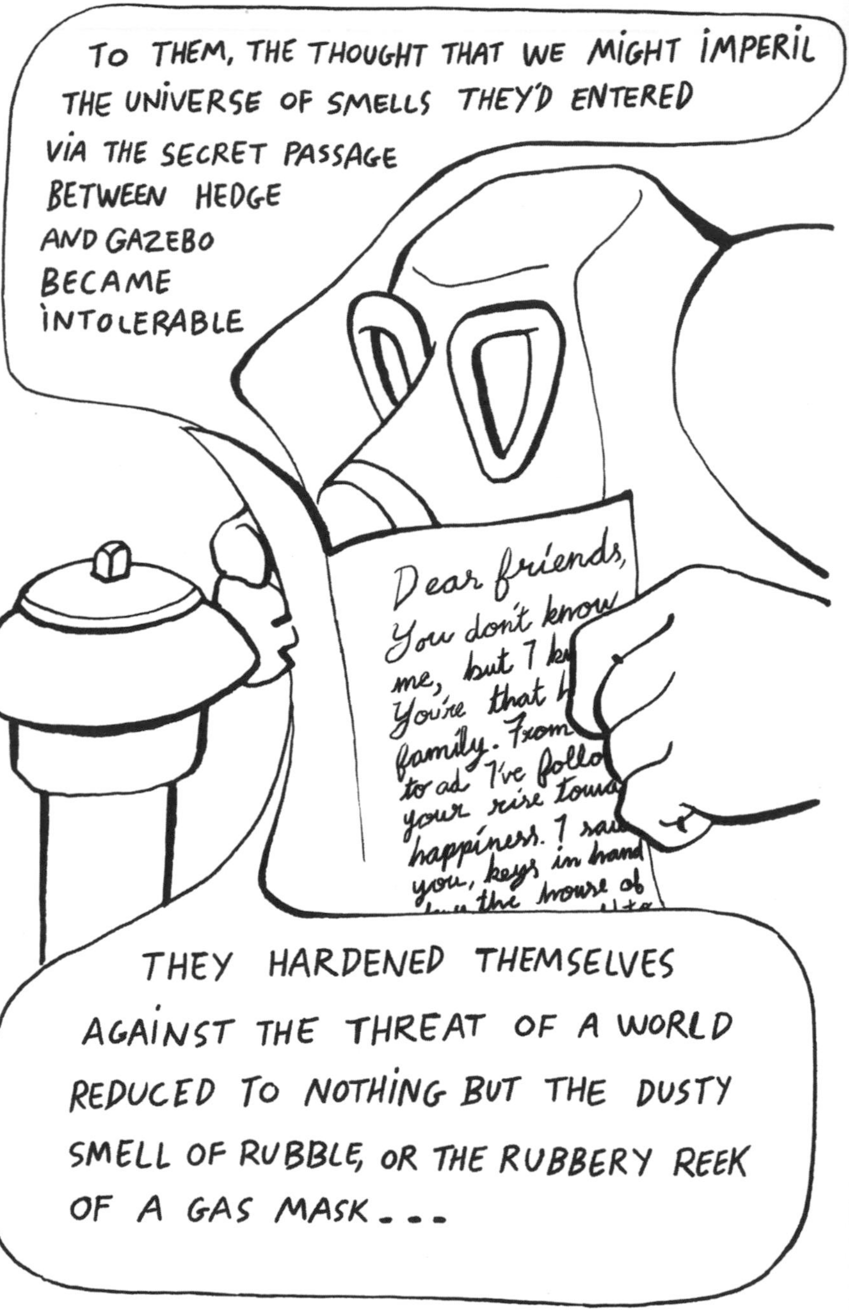
TO THEM, THE THOUGHT THAT WE MIGHT IMPERIL THE UNIVERSE OF SMELLS THEY'D ENTERED VIA THE SECRET PASSAGE BETWEEN HEDGE AND GAZEBO BECAME INTOLERABLE
Dear friends,
You don't know
me, but I
You're that
family. From
to ad I've
your rise
happiness. I
you, keys in hand
the house of
THEY HARDENED THEMSELVES AGAINST THE THREAT OF A WORLD REDUCED TO NOTHING BUT THE DUSTY SMELL OF RUBBLE, OR THE RUBBERY REEK OF A GAS MASK...

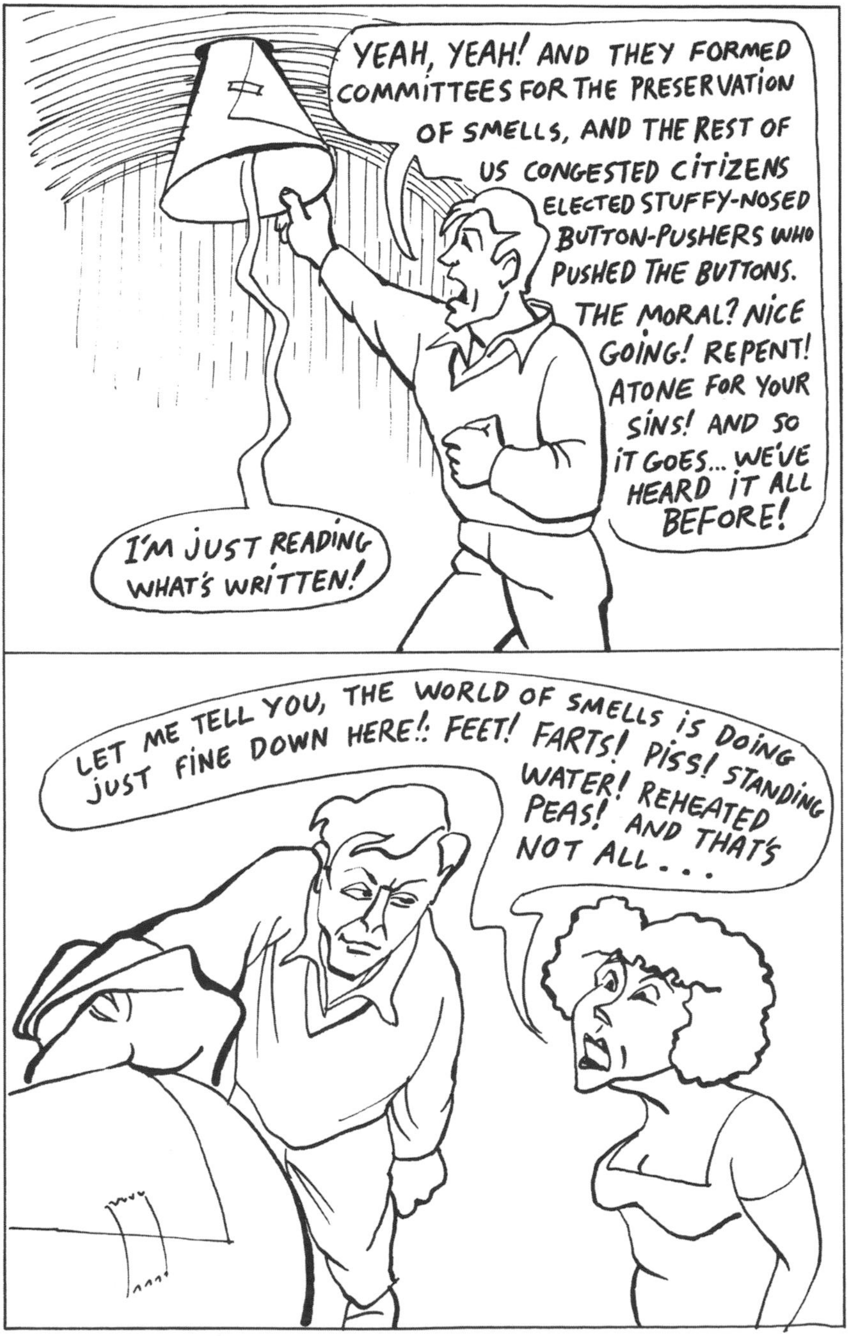
YEAH, YEAH! AND THEY FORMED COMMITTEES FOR THE PRESERVATION OF SMELLS, AND THE REST OF US CONGESTED CITIZENS ELECTED STUFFY-NOSED BUTTON-PUSHERS WHO PUSHED THE BUTTONS. THE MORAL? NICE GOING! REPENT! ATONE FOR YOUR SINS! AND SO IT GOES... WE'VE HEARD IT ALL BEFORE!
I'M JUST READING WHAT'S WRITTEN!
LET ME TELL YOU, THE WORLD OF SMELLS IS DOING JUST FINE DOWN HERE!: FEET! FARTS! PISS! STANDING WATER! REHEATED PEAS! AND THAT'S NOT ALL . . .

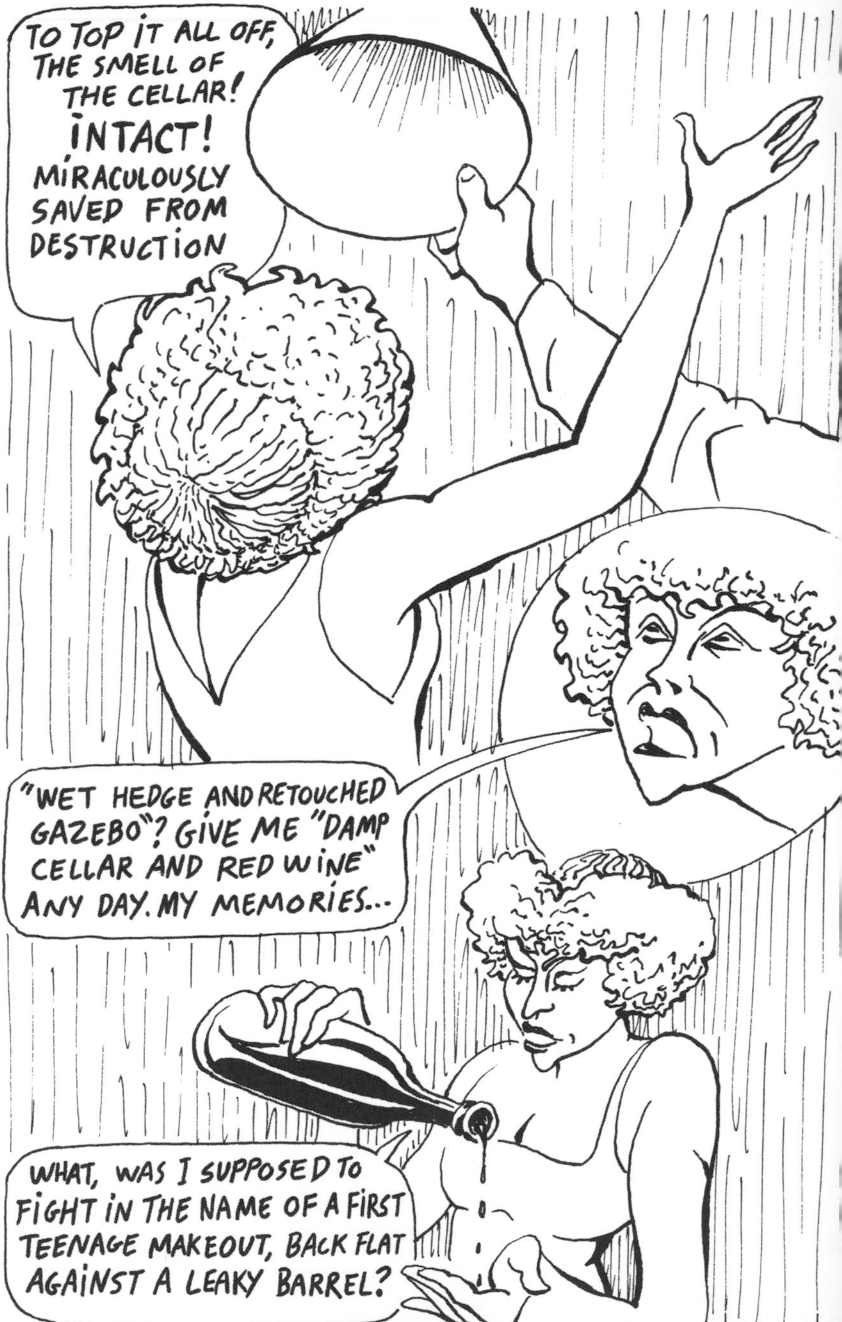
TO TOP IT ALL OFF, THE SMELL OF THE CELLAR! INTACT! MIRACULOUSLY SAVED FROM DESTRUCTION
"WET HEDGE AND RETOUCHED GAZEBO"? GIVE ME "DAMP CELLAR AND RED WINE" ANY DAY. MY MEMORIES...
WHAT, WAS I SUPPOSED TO FIGHT IN THE NAME OF A FIRST TEENAGE MAKEOUT, BACK FLAT AGAINST A LEAKY BARREL?

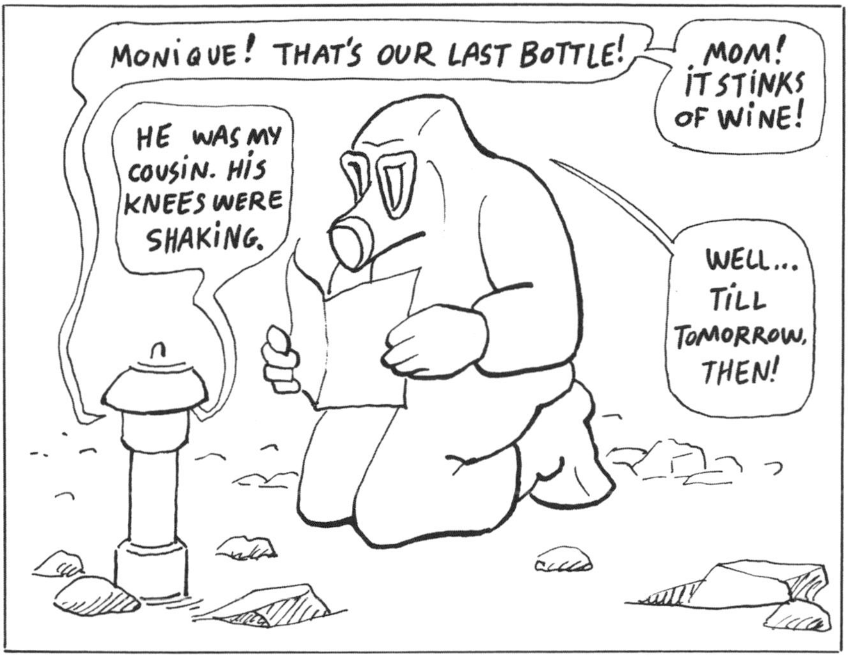
MONIQUE! THAT'S OUR LAST BOTTLE!
MOM! IT STINKS OF WINE!
HE WAS MY COUSIN. HIS KNEES WERE SHAKING.
WELL... TILL TOMORROW, THEN!

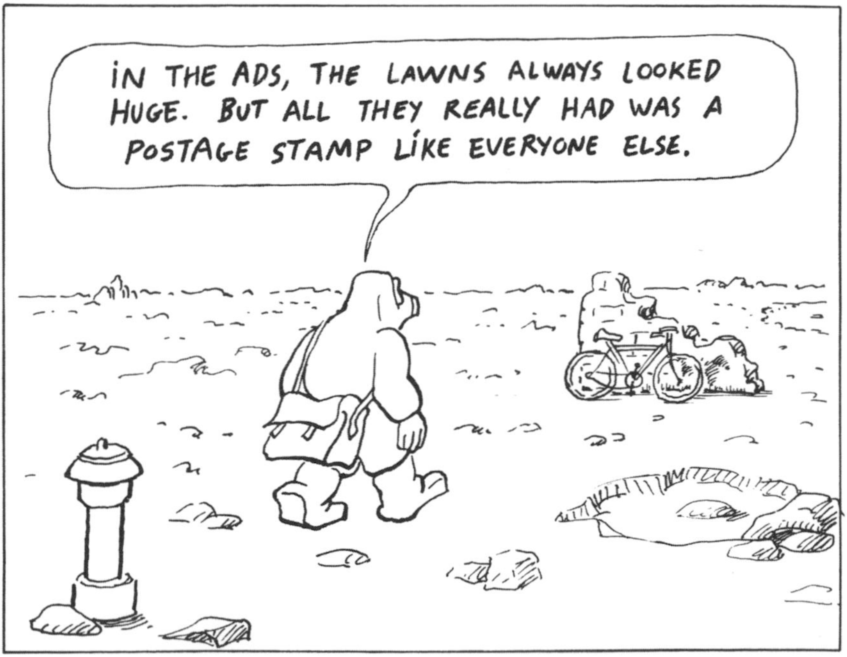
IN THE ADS, THE LAWNS ALWAYS LOOKED HUGE. BUT ALL THEY REALLY HAD WAS A POSTAGE STAMP LIKE EVERYONE ELSE.

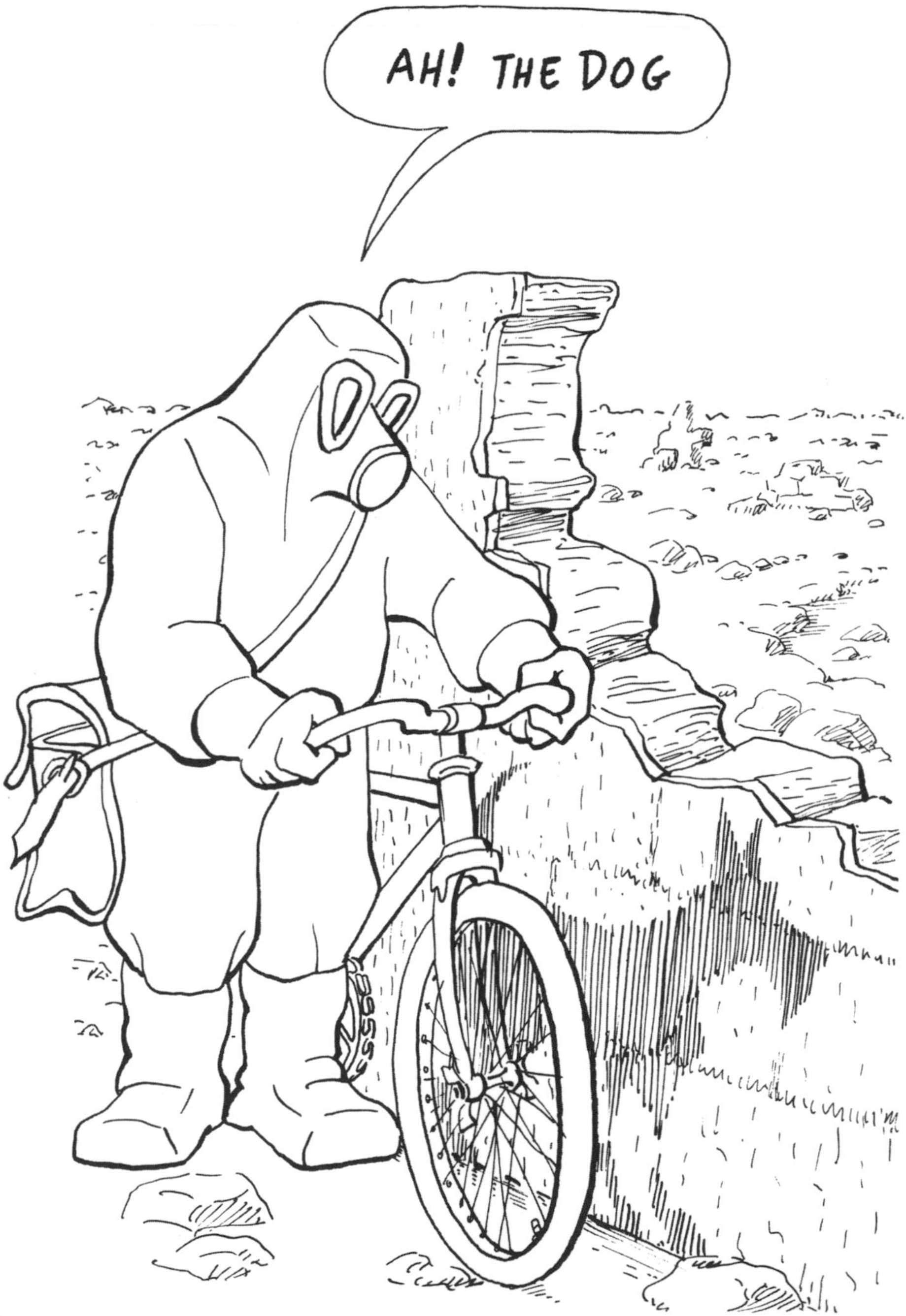
AH! THE DOG

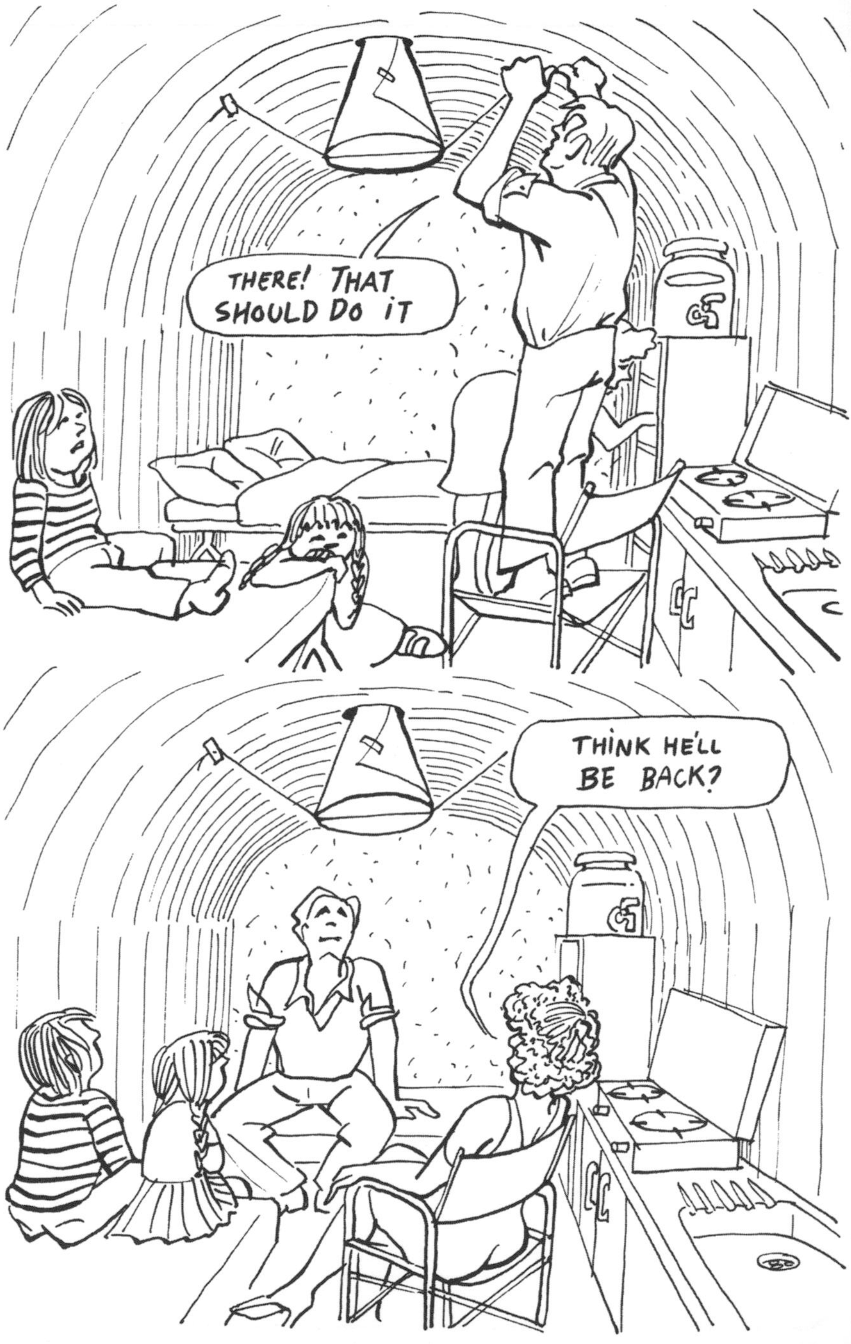
THERE! THAT SHOULD DO IT
THINK HE'LL BE BACK?

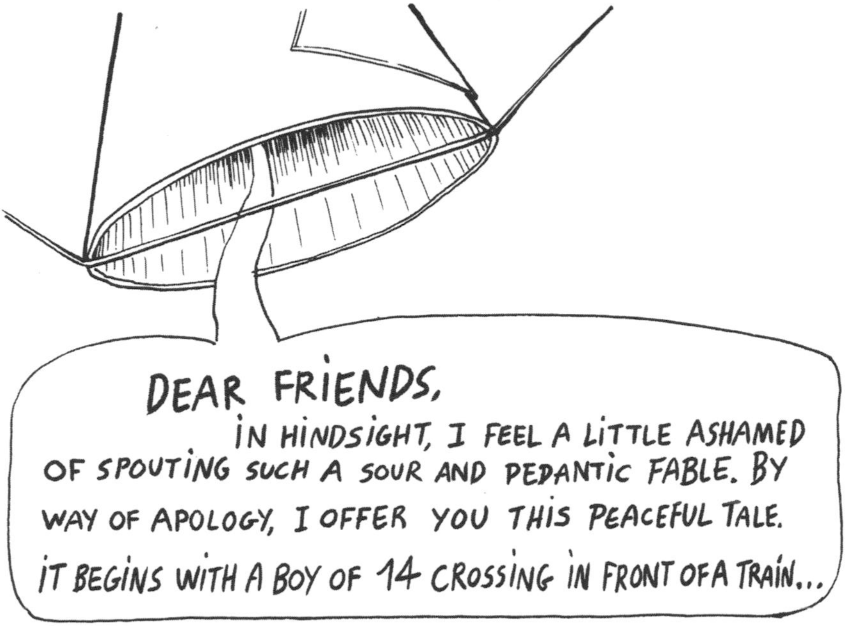
DEAR FRIENDS,
IN HINDSIGHT, I FEEL A LITTLE ASHAMED OF SPOUTING SUCH A SOUR AND PEDANTIC FABLE. BY WAY OF APOLOGY, I OFFER YOU THIS PEACEFUL TALE.
IT BEGINS WITH A BOY OF 14 CROSSING IN FRONT OF A TRAIN...

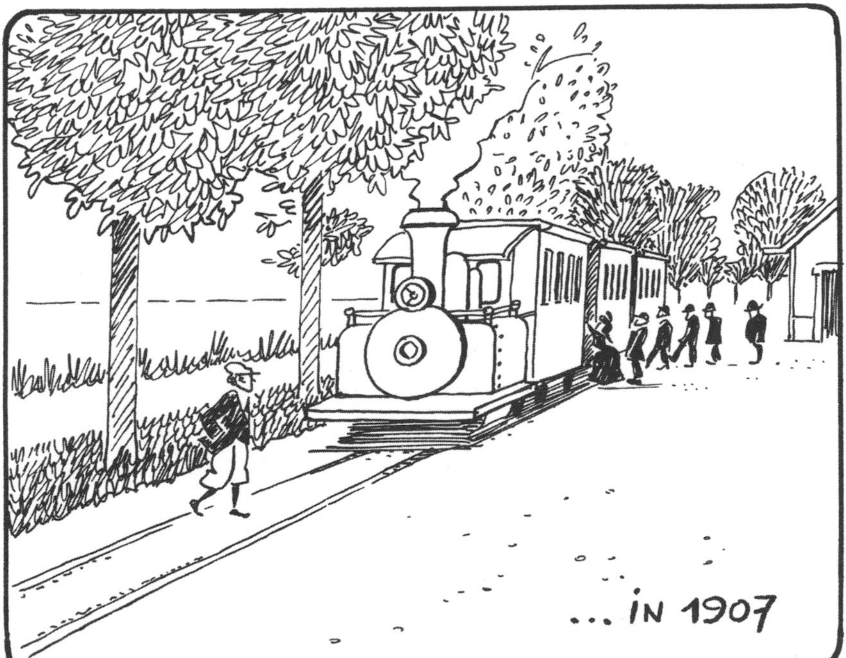
...IN 1907

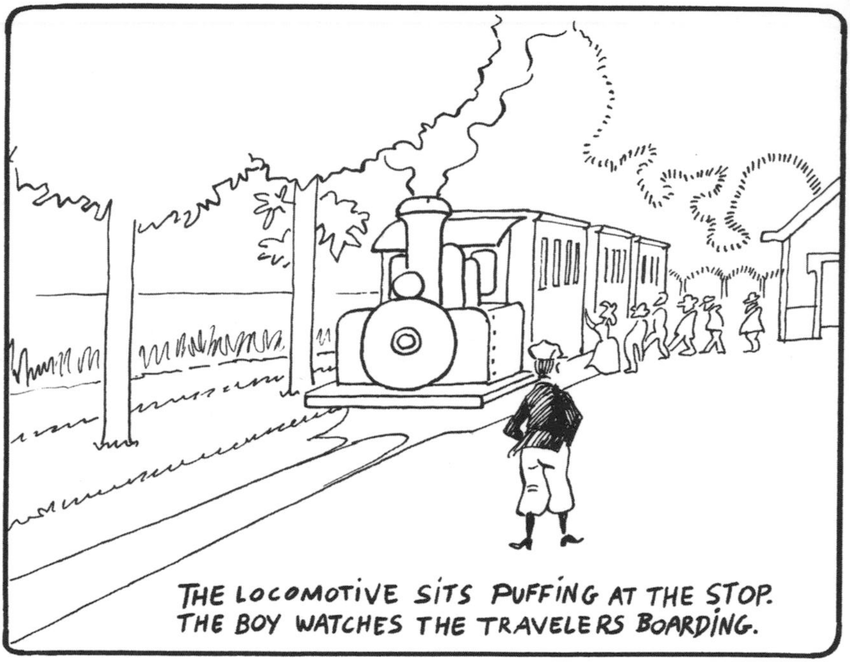
THE LOCOMOTIVE SITS PUFFING AT THE STOP.
THE BOY WATCHES THE TRAVELERS BOARDING.

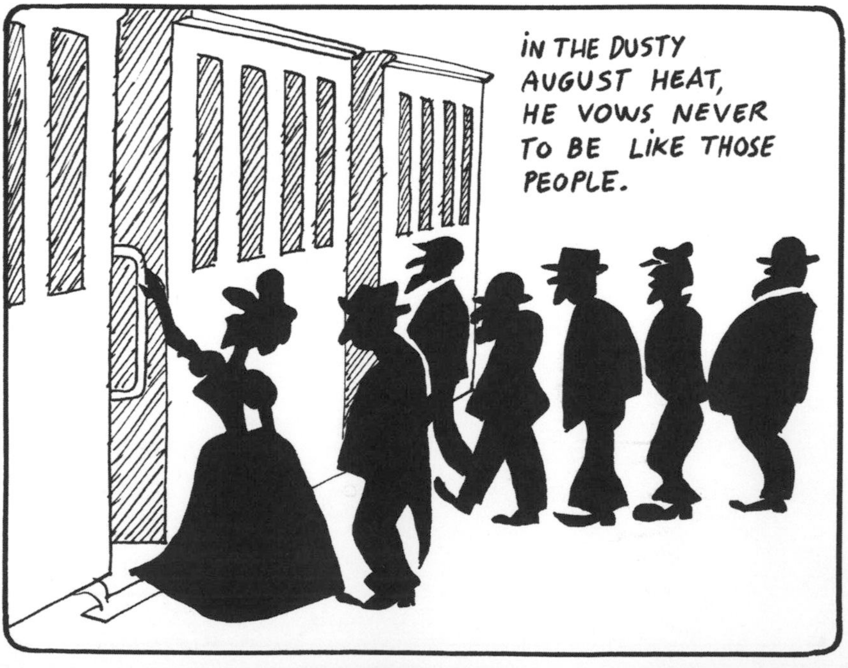
IN THE DUSTY AUGUST HEAT, HE VOWS NEVER TO BE LIKE THOSE PEOPLE.

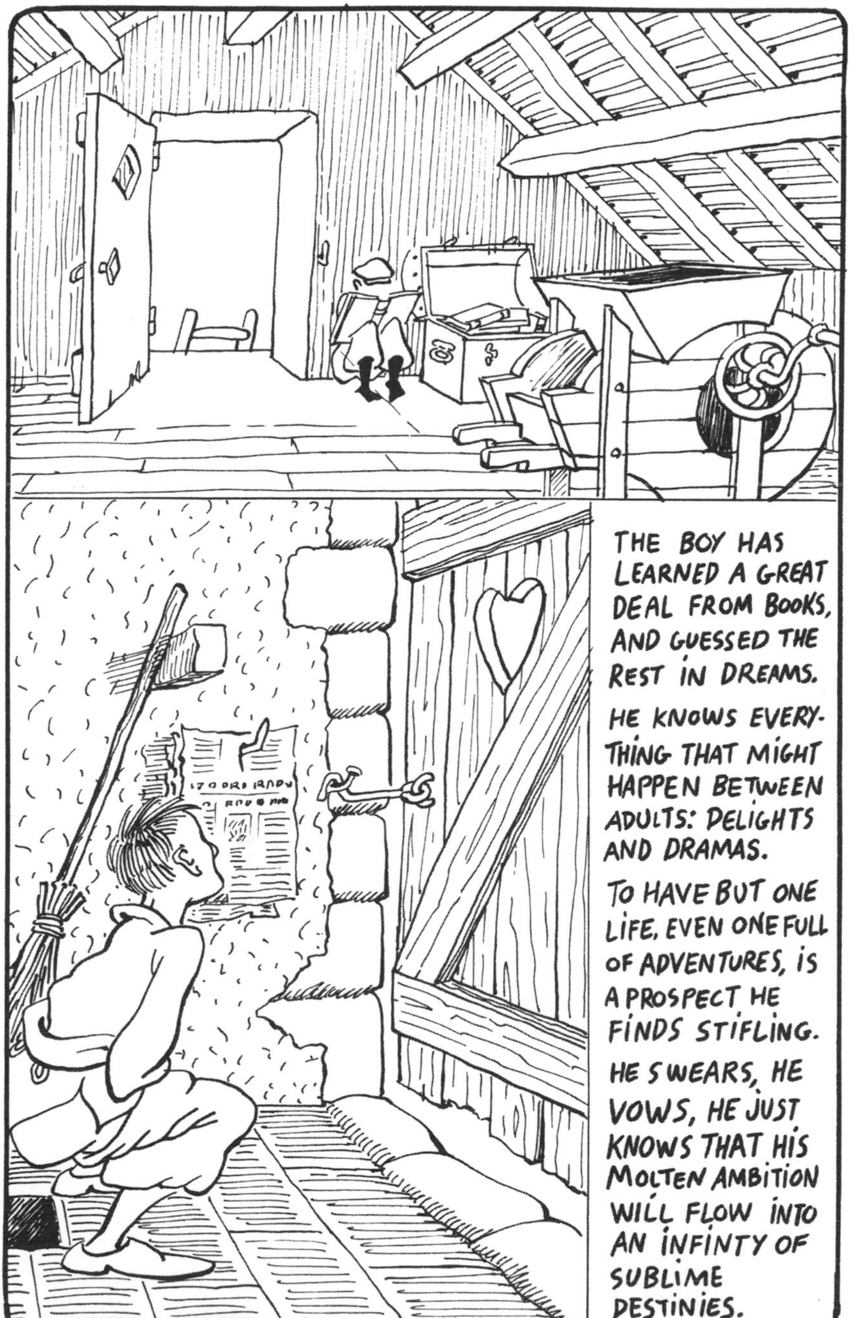
THE BOY HAS LEARNED A GREAT DEAL FROM BOOKS, AND GUESSED THE REST IN DREAMS.
HE KNOWS EVERYTHING THAT MIGHT HAPPEN BETWEEN ADULTS: DELIGHTS AND DRAMAS.
TO HAVE BUT ONE LIFE, EVEN ONE FULL OF ADVENTURES, IS A PROSPECT HE FINDS STIFLING.
HE SWEARS, HE VOWS, HE JUST KNOWS THAT HIS MOLTEN AMBITION WILL FLOW INTO AN INFINTY OF SUBLIME DESTINIES.

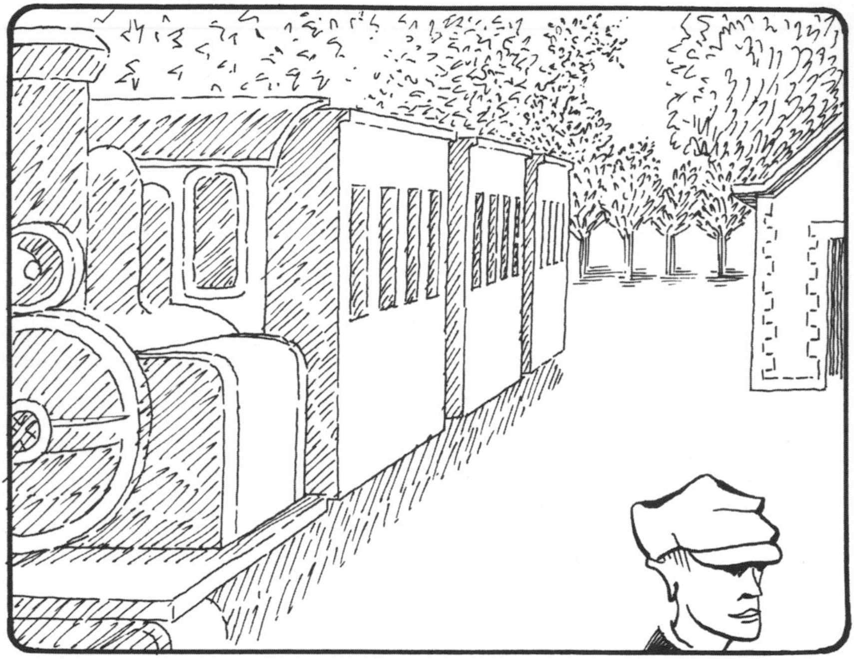

FOR STARTERS, HE WILL BECOME A PAINTER OF THE MYSTERIOUS INSIDES OF STONES, THE INTERIORS OF FLOWERS, OF SAP AND OF SHADOW, OF WOMEN'S SECRET HOLLOWS.

THEN? WELL, HE'LL SEE.

SEVEN YEARS LATER, HE WILL GO TO WAR FOR FOUR LONG YEARS.

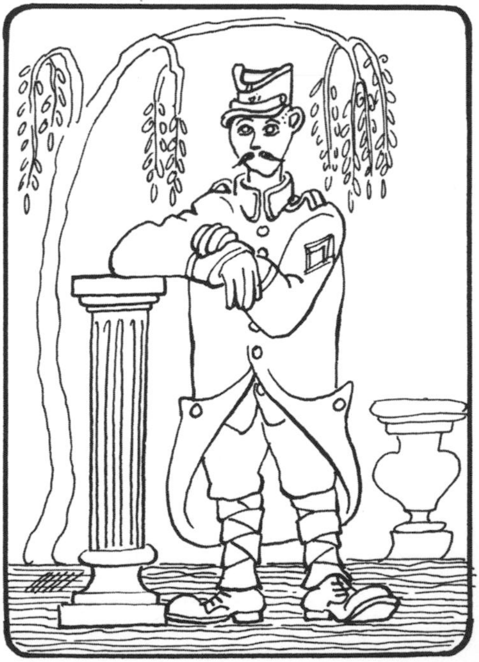

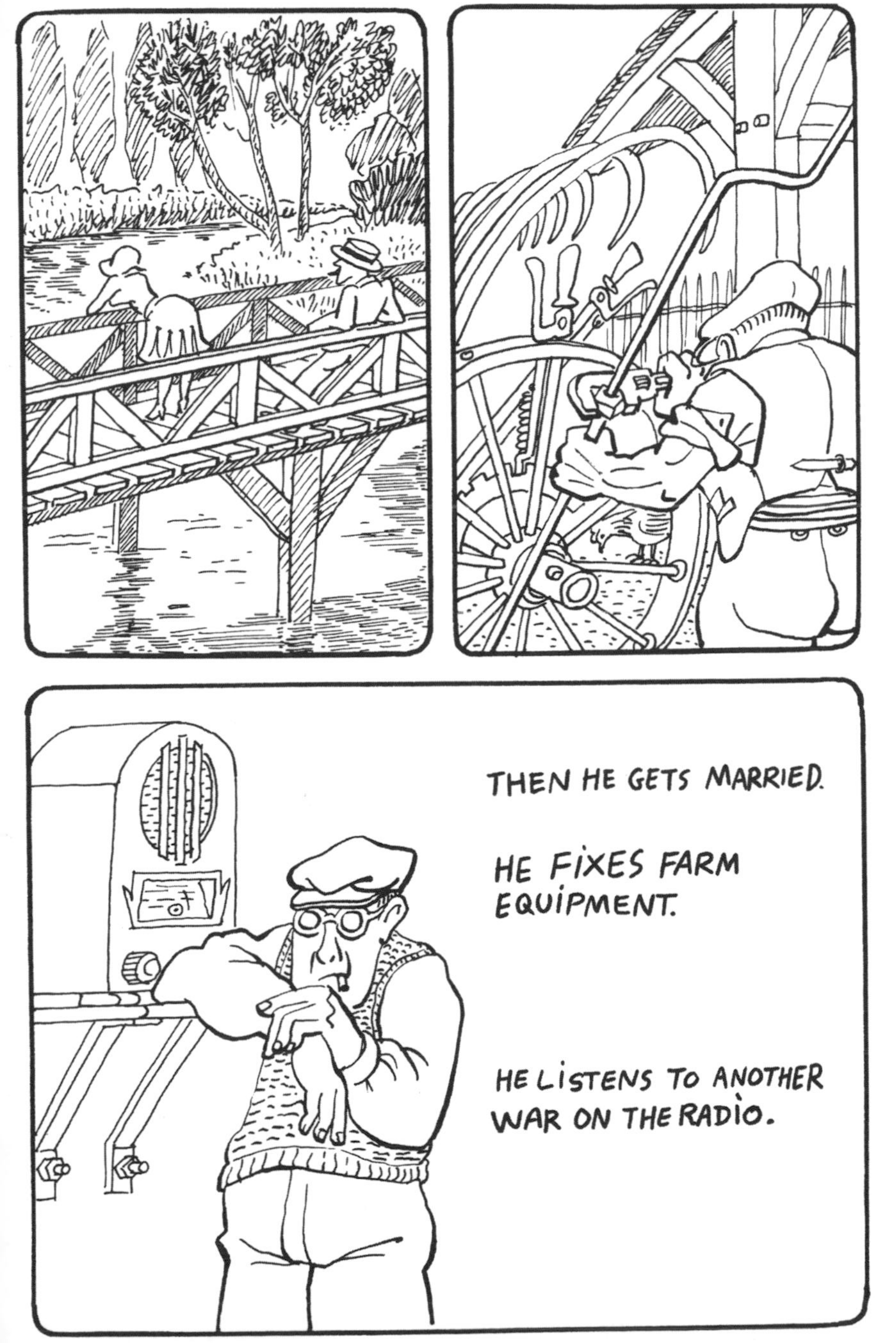
THEN HE GETS MARRIED.
HE FIXES FARM EQUIPMENT.
HE LISTENS TO ANOTHER WAR ON THE RADIO.

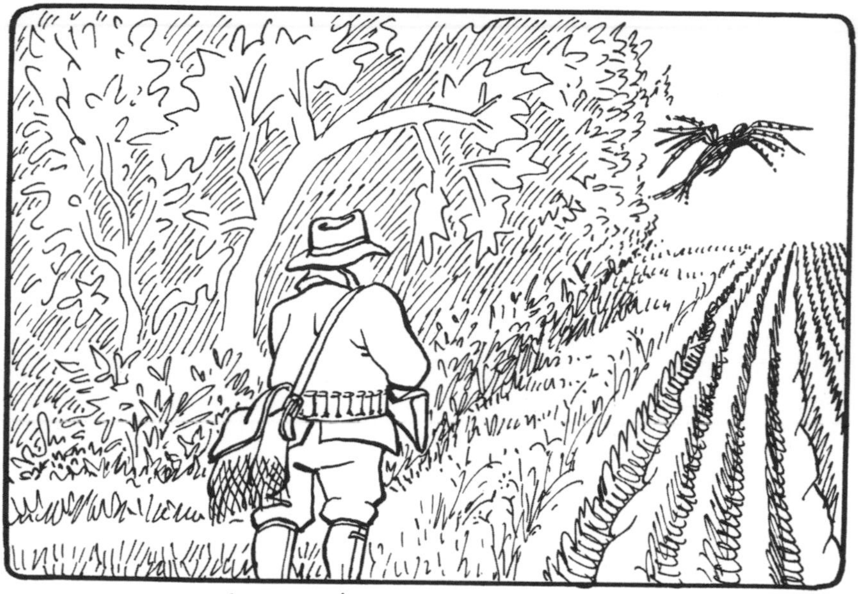

ONE DAY, OUT HUNTING, HE WILL RECALL THAT DAY IN FRONT OF THE TRAIN.
HE WILL STOP HUNTING.

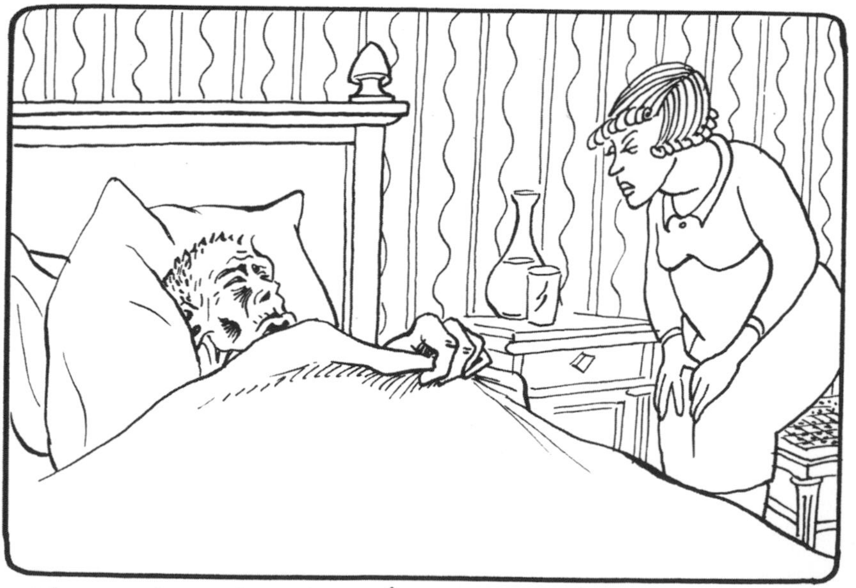

HE'LL RECALL THAT DAY AGAIN ONE LAST TIME.
HE'LL LET OUT A MOAN.
HE'LL BE GIVEN A SIP OF WATER.

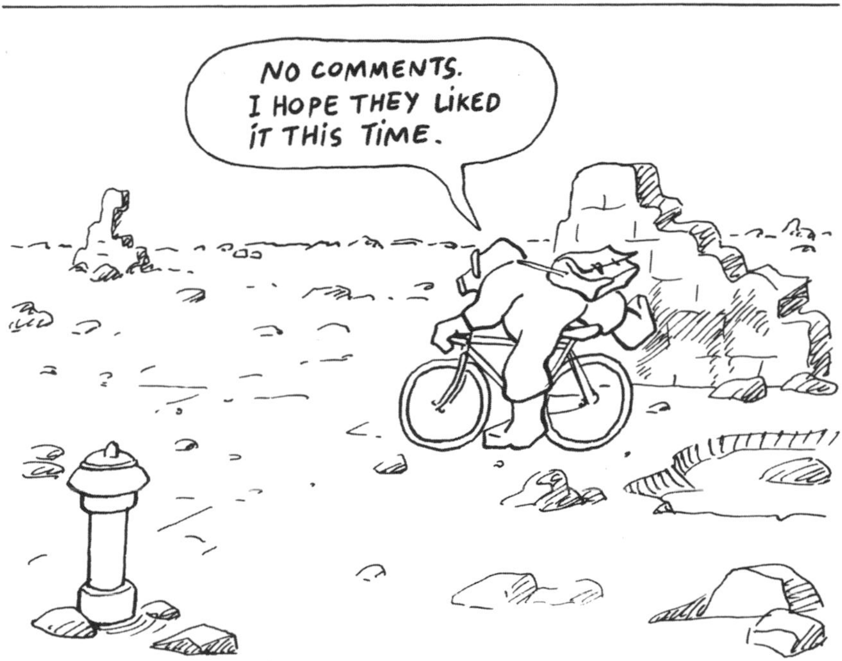
NO COMMENTS. I HOPE THEY LIKED IT THIS TIME.

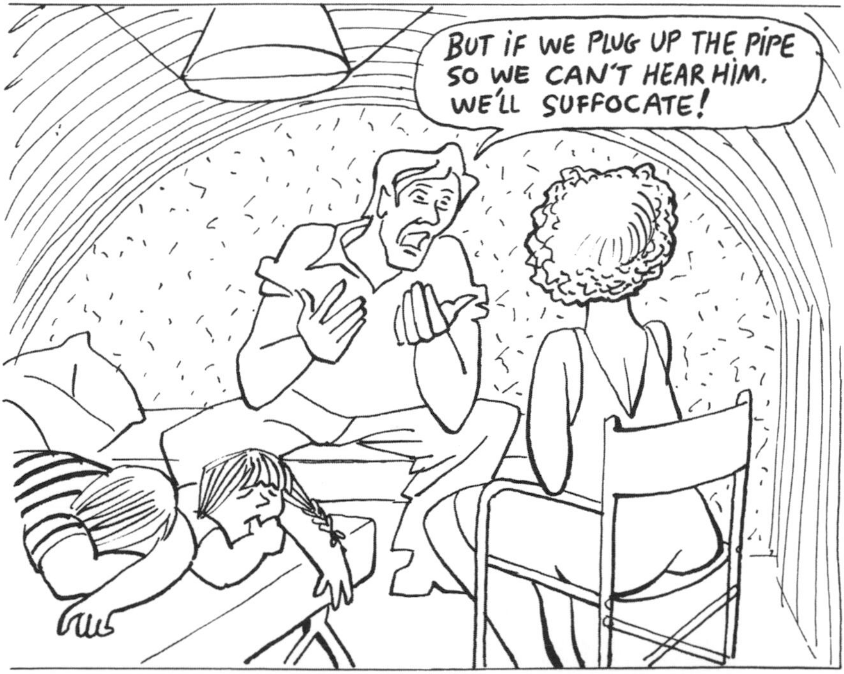
BUT IF WE PLUG UP THE PIPE SO WE CAN'T HEAR HIM, WE'LL SUFFOCATE!

WHERE ARE WE?

EVERYTHING STILL LIVING IS NOW UNDERGROUND.

A MAILMAN RIDES ACROSS THE SURFACE THROUGH ASHES BOTH ANIMAL AND VEGETABLE, AMONG THE SHATTERED SUPERSTRUCTURES OF CIVILIZATION.

HE ZIGZAGS TO AVOID THE PIECES THAT ARE TOO BIG.

HE BRINGS A LETTER TO A FAMILY LANGUISHING BENEATH THE SITE OF THEIR ANNIHILATED LAWN.

NO MORE MAILBOX.

THE MAILMAN CAN ONLY COMMUNICATE WITH THEM BY SPEAKING ALOUD THROUGH THEIR BOMB SHELTER'S VENTILATION SHAFT.

HE OPENS THE LETTER AND READS IT TO THEM.

IT'S A LONG LETTER.

A VERY LONG LETTER, IN INSTALLMENTS.

IT TELLS OF THE GREEN AND HUMID DAYS BEFORE EVERYTHING BURNED TO A CRISP.

THE PICTURES THAT ILLUSTRATE THE LETTER HERE SERVE TO SHOW THE POSTMAN IN HIS GLOOMY LANDSCAPE AND THE ADDRESSEES IN THEIR DISMAL SHELTER.

THEY ALSO SHOW THE IMAGES THAT THE STORIES FROM THE LETTER'S AUTHOR INSPIRE IN THE POSTMAN AND HIS CAPTIVE AUDIENCE.

FOR ALL THESE REASONS, PICTURES ARE USEFUL.

MOVING ON

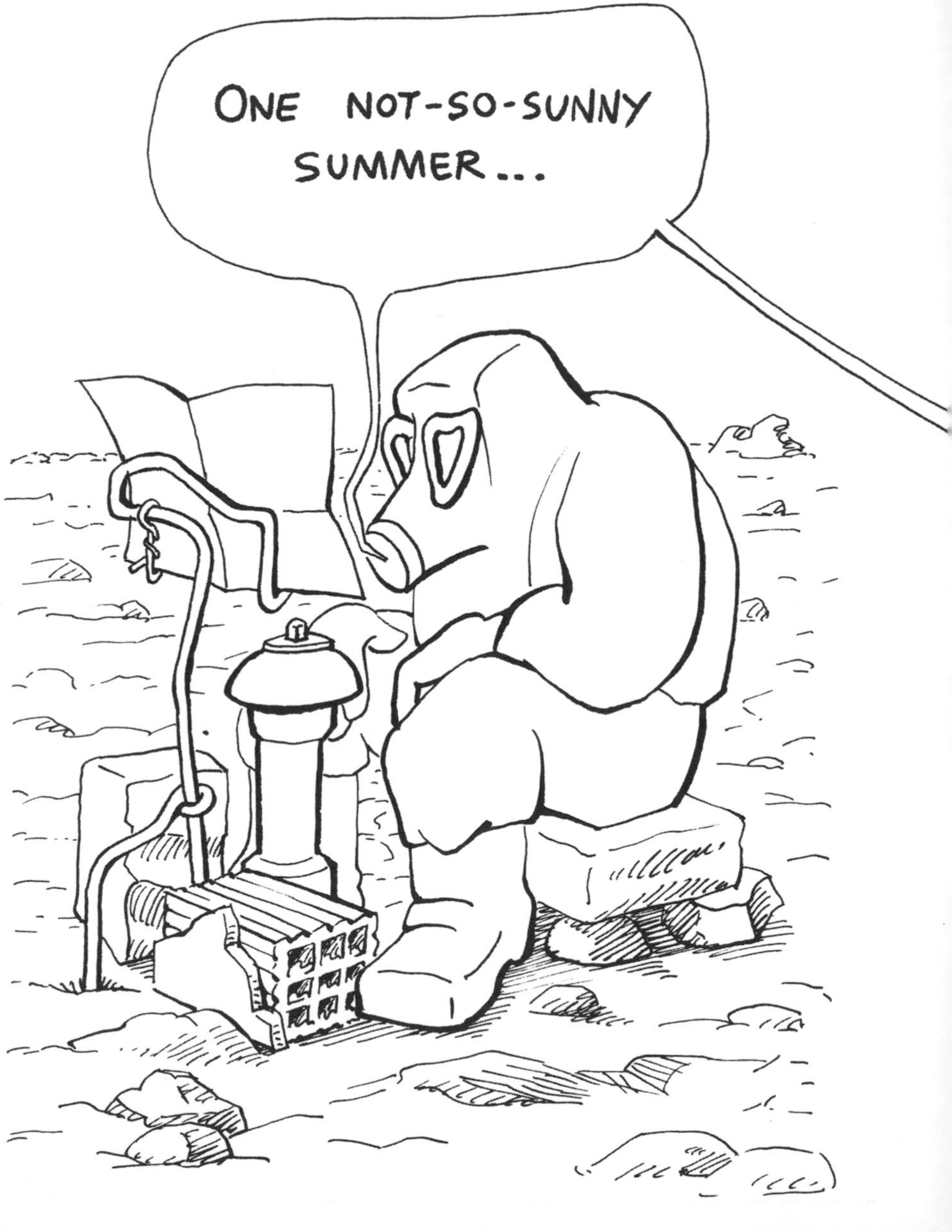
ONE NOT-SO-SUNNY SUMMER...

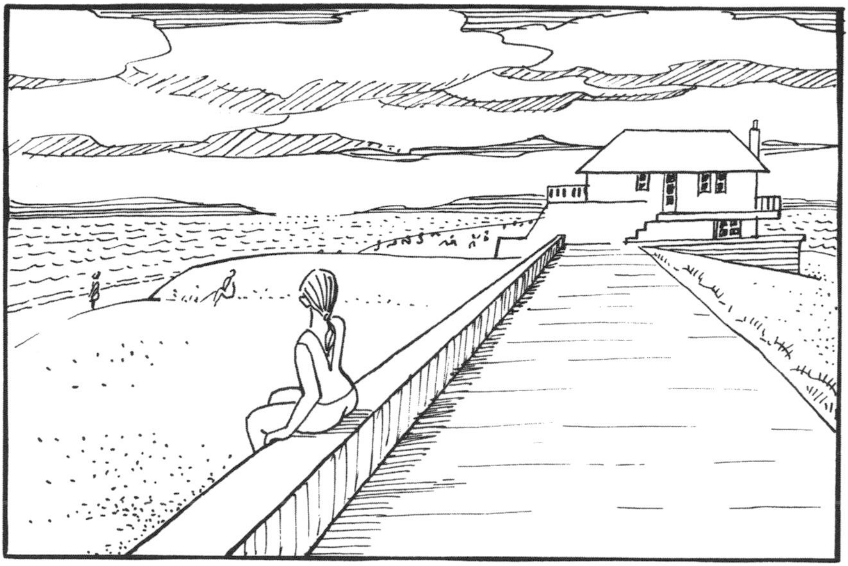

...A HOUSE AT THE END OF A ROAD, FACING THE SEA. THERE'S BEEN A CRIME THERE. THE UNCLE OF THREE YOUNG WOMEN WAS MURDERED. A DETECTIVE CONDUCTS HIS INVESTIGATION WITH A CERTAIN STIFFNESS. THE REASONS FOR THIS ARE MANY. THE INTIMIDATING PRESENCE OF THE YOUNG WOMEN, THE DREARY ORDINARINESS OF THE HOUSE.

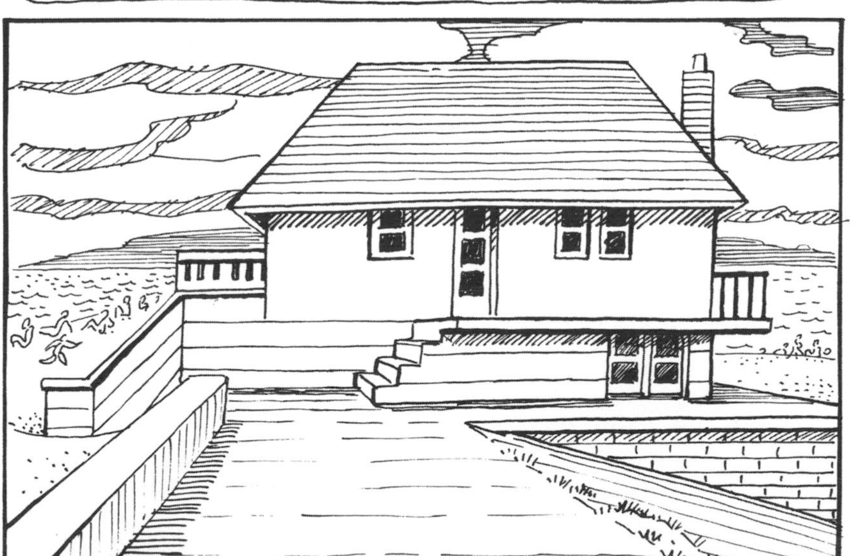

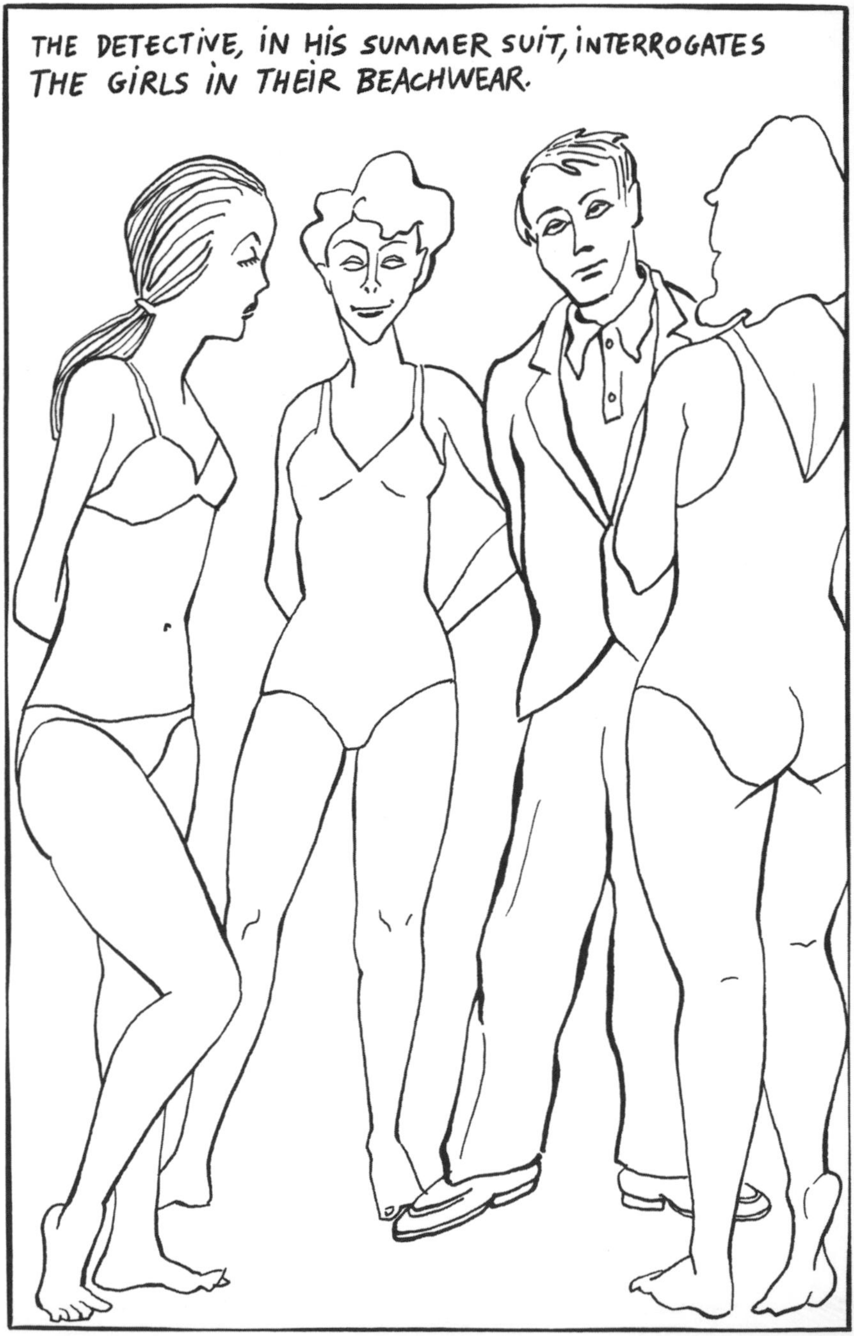
THE DETECTIVE, IN HIS SUMMER SUIT, INTERROGATES THE GIRLS IN THEIR BEACHWEAR.

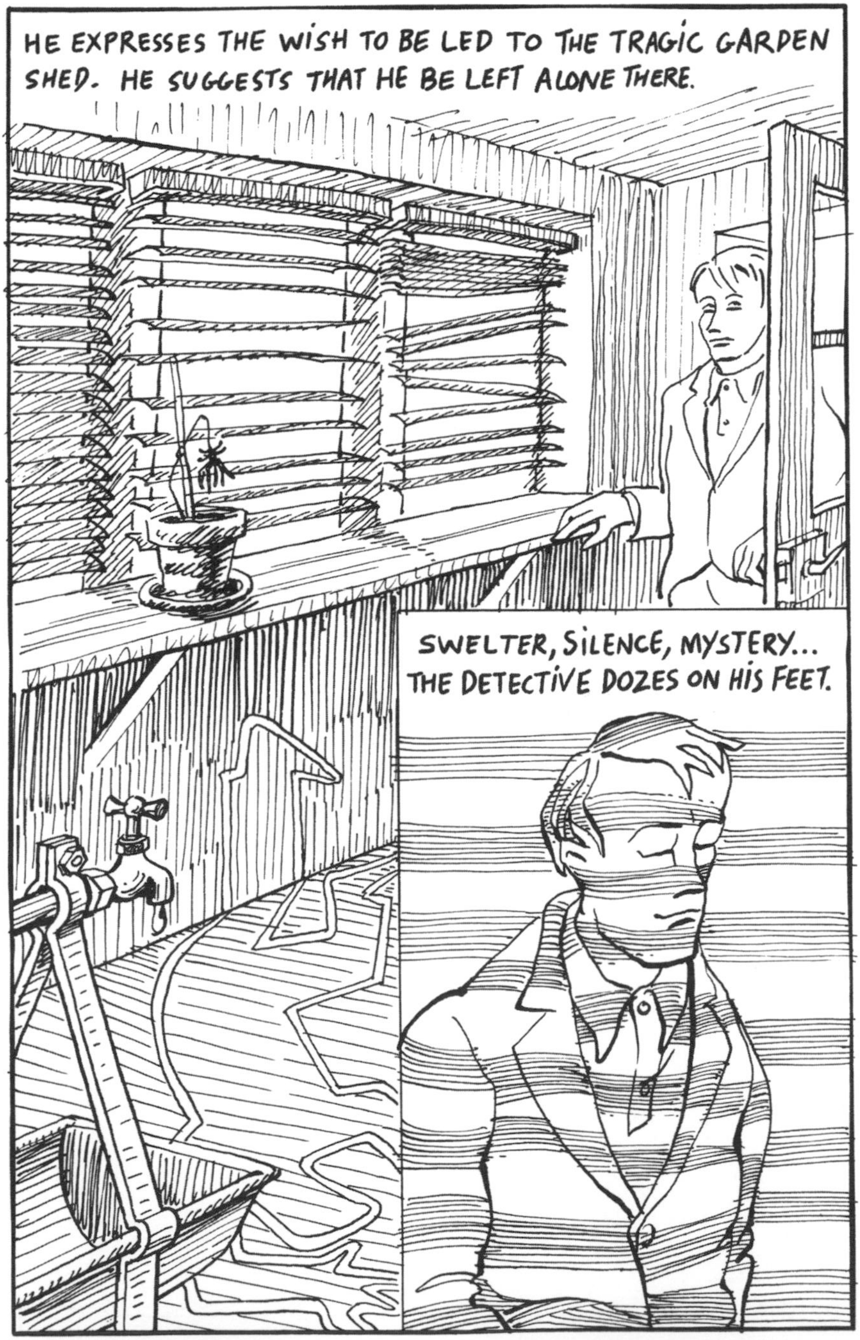
HE EXPRESSES THE WISH TO BE LED TO THE TRAGIC GARDEN SHED. HE SUGGESTS THAT HE BE LEFT ALONE THERE.
SWELTER, SILENCE, MYSTERY... THE DETECTIVE DOZES ON HIS FEET.

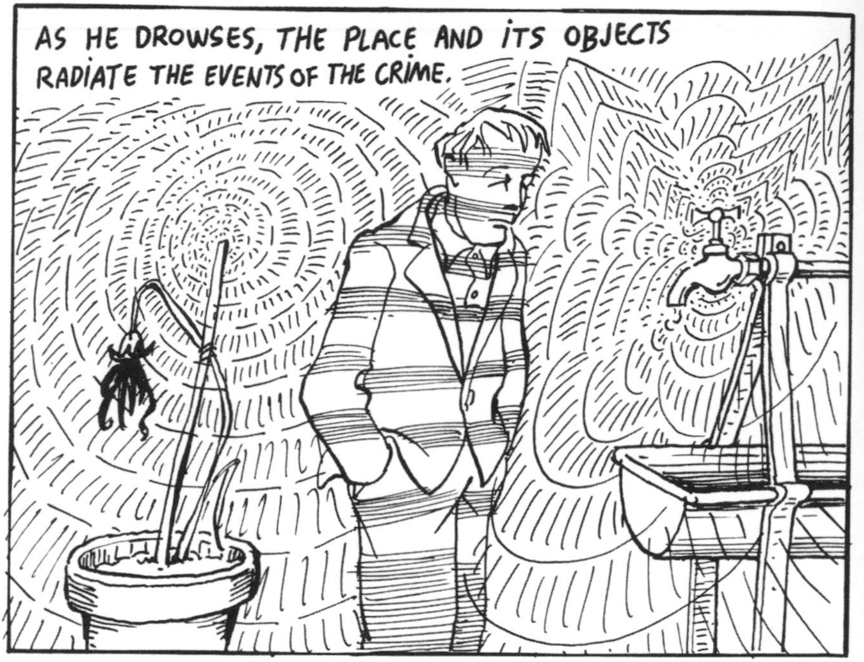
AS HE DROWSES, THE PLACE AND ITS OBJECTS RADIATE THE EVENTS OF THE CRIME.

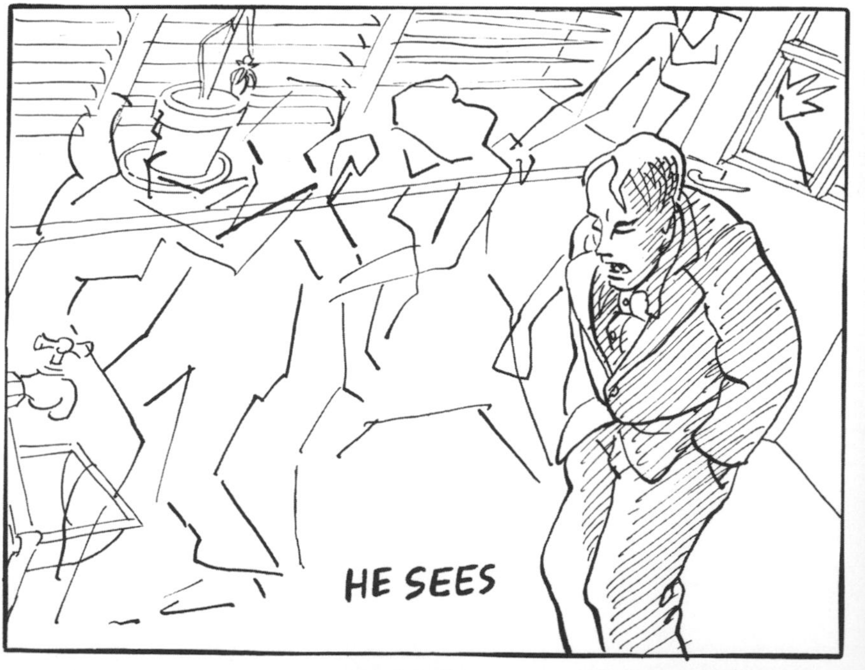
HE SEES

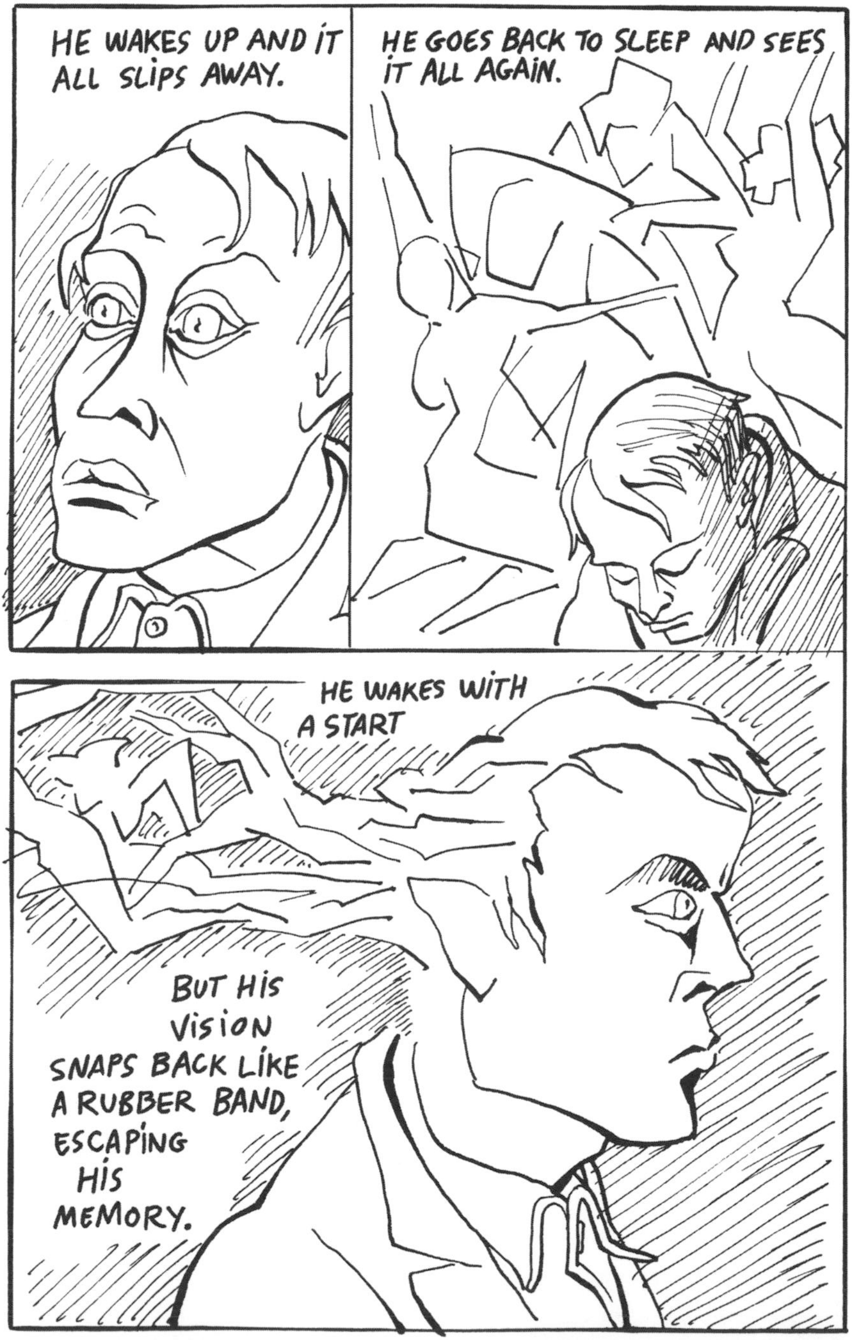
HE WAKES UP AND IT ALL SLIPS AWAY.
HE GOES BACK TO SLEEP AND SEES IT ALL AGAIN.
HE WAKES WITH A START
BUT HIS VISION SNAPS BACK LIKE A RUBBER BAND, ESCAPING HIS MEMORY.

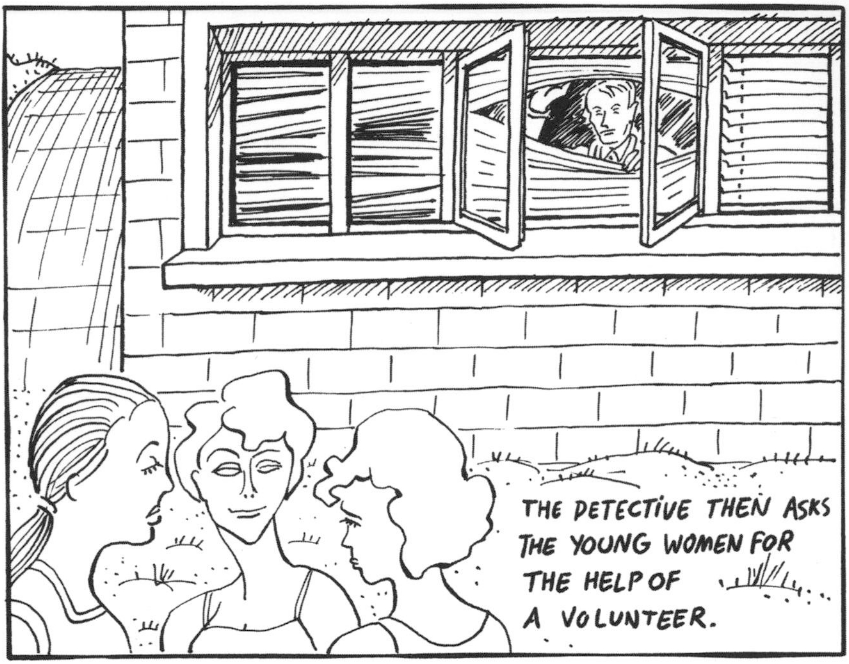
THE DETECTIVE THEN ASKS THE YOUNG WOMEN FOR THE HELP OF A VOLUNTEER.

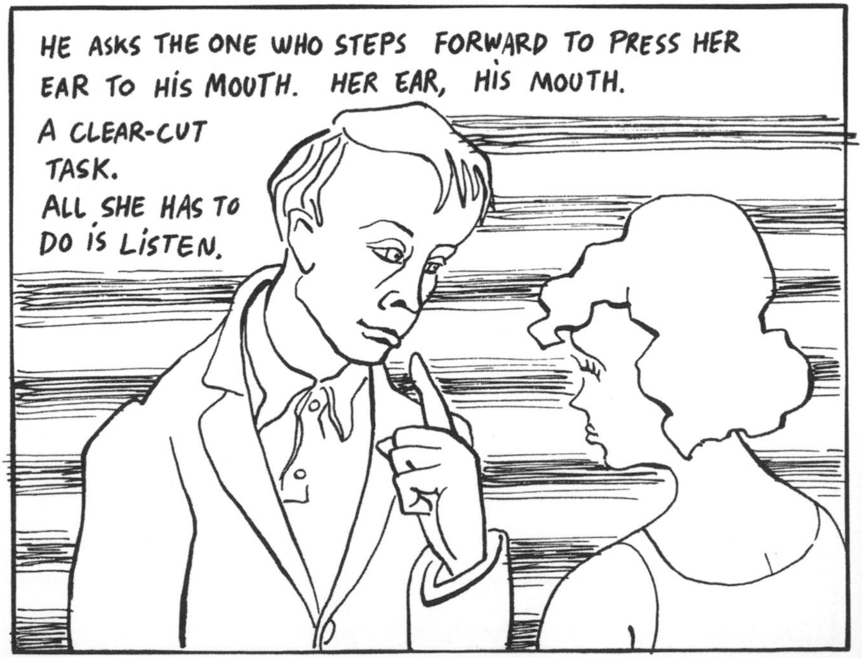
HE ASKS THE ONE WHO STEPS FORWARD TO PRESS HER EAR TO HIS MOUTH. HER EAR, HIS MOUTH.
A CLEAR-CUT TASK.
ALL SHE HAS TO DO IS LISTEN.

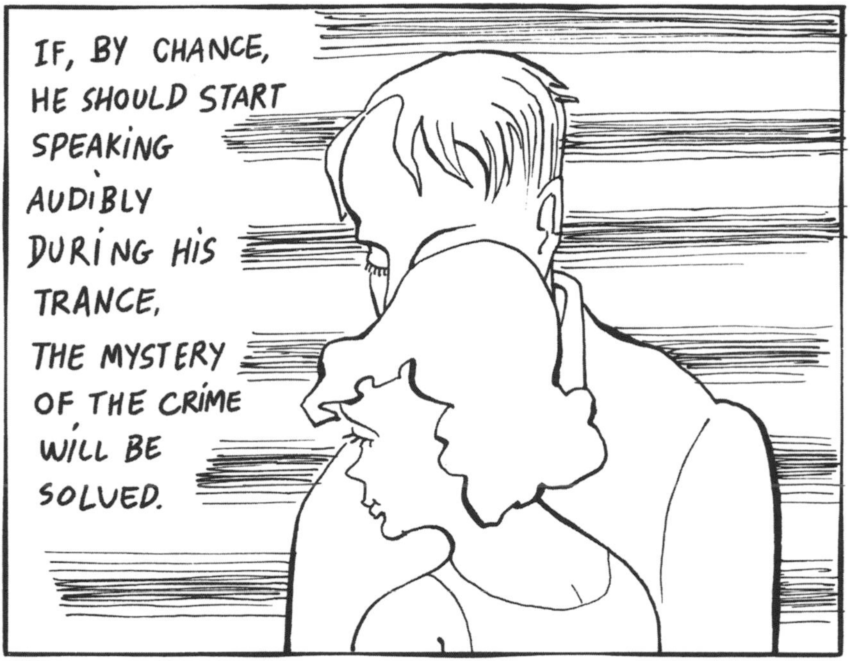
IF, BY CHANCE, HE SHOULD START SPEAKING AUDIBLY DURING HIS TRANCE, THE MYSTERY OF THE CRIME WILL BE SOLVED.

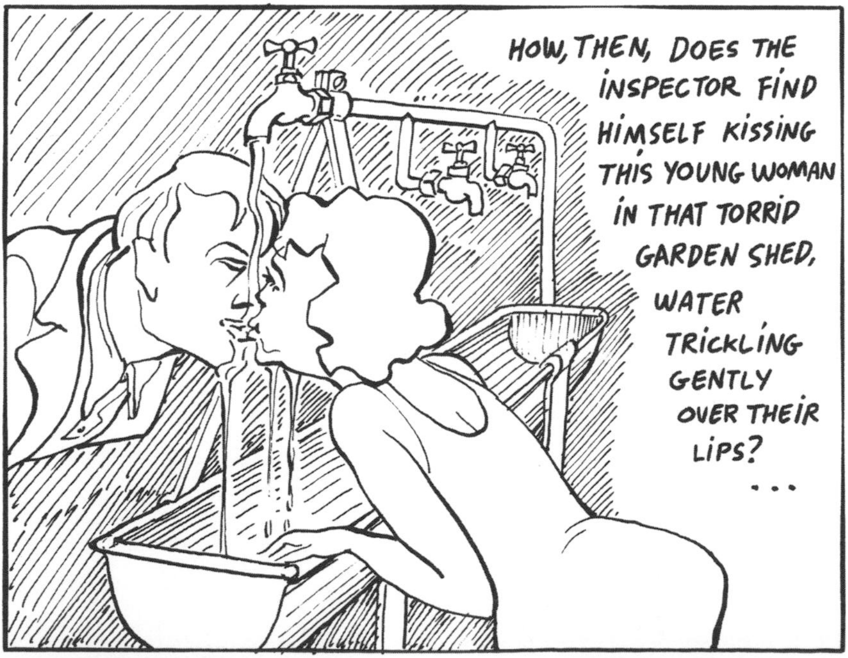
HOW, THEN, DOES THE INSPECTOR FIND HIMSELF KISSING THIS YOUNG WOMAN IN THAT TORRID GARDEN SHED, WATER TRICKLING GENTLY OVER THEIR LIPS?
. . .

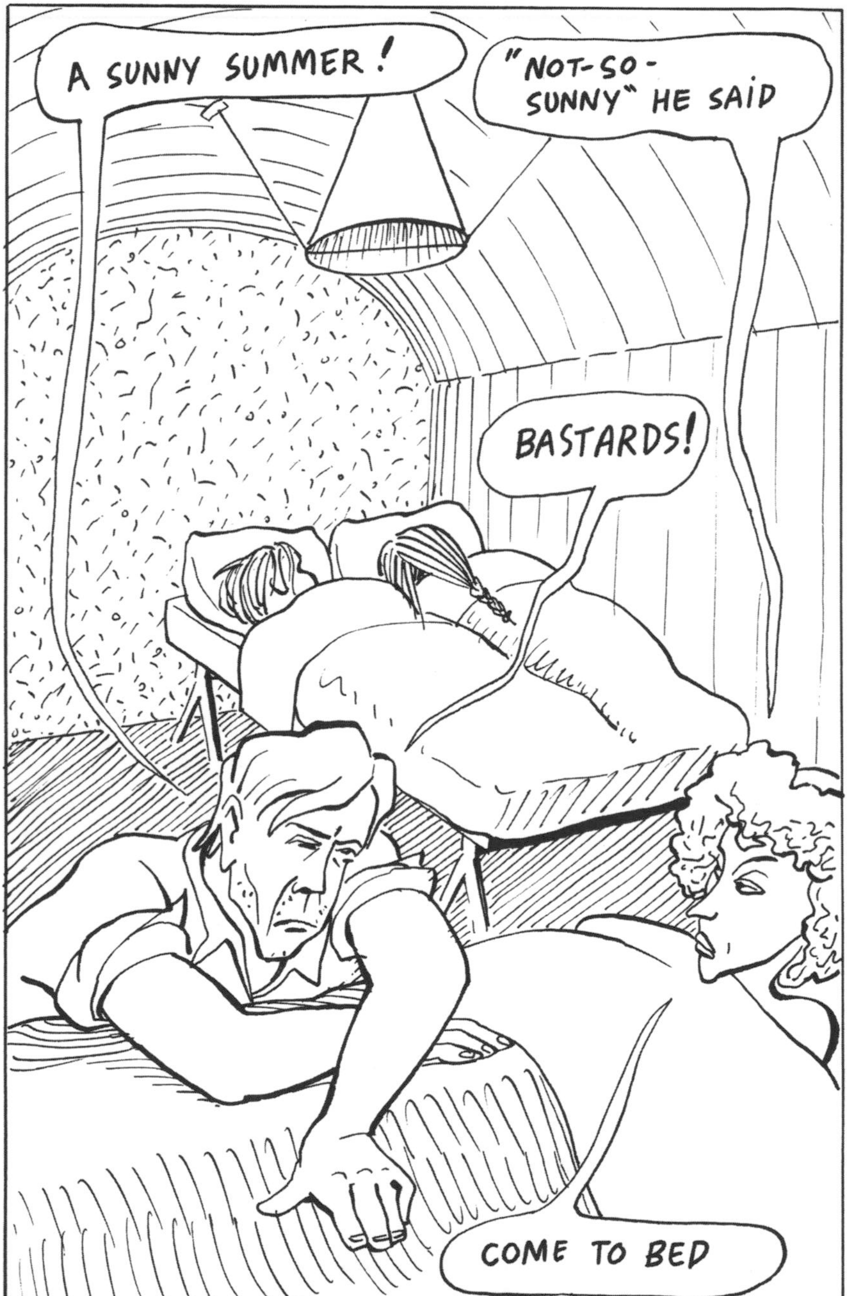
A SUNNY SUMMER!
"NOT-SO-SUNNY" HE SAID
BASTARDS!
COME TO BED

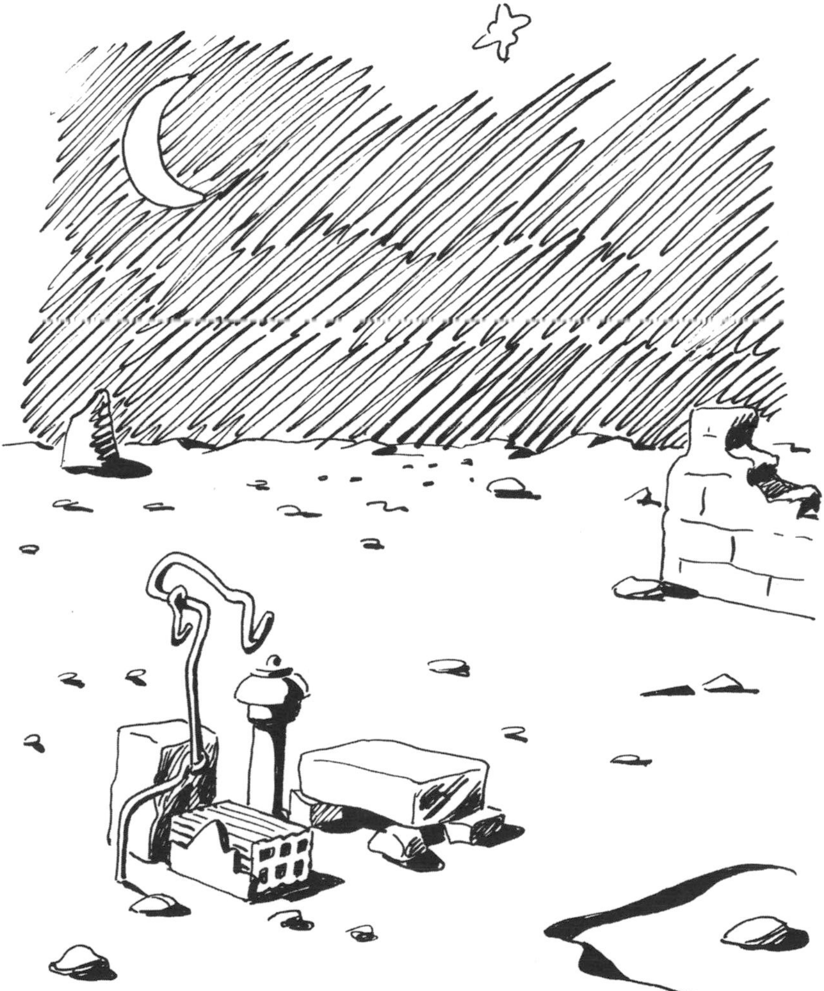

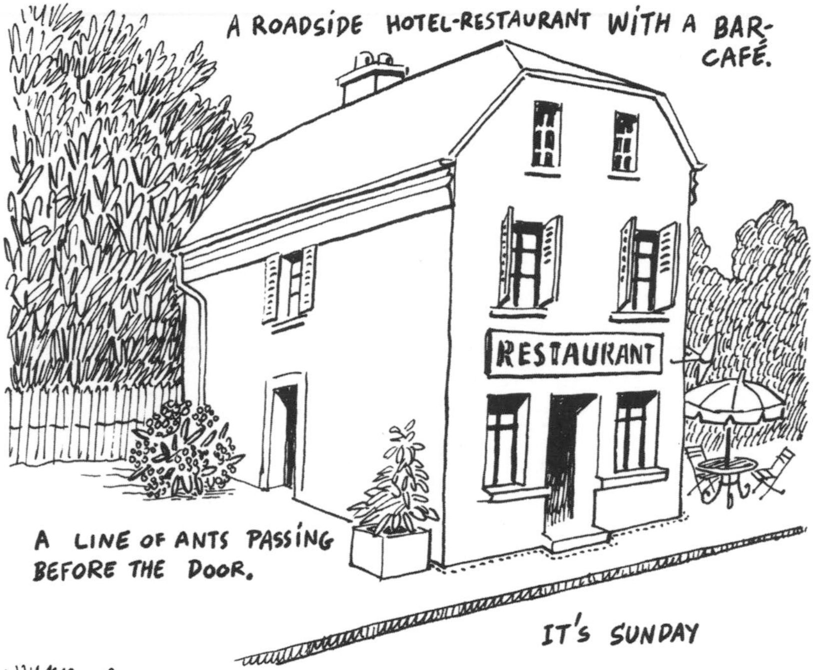
A ROADSIDE HOTEL-RESTAURANT WITH A BAR-CAFÉ.
RESTAURANT
A LINE OF ANTS PASSING BEFORE THE DOOR.

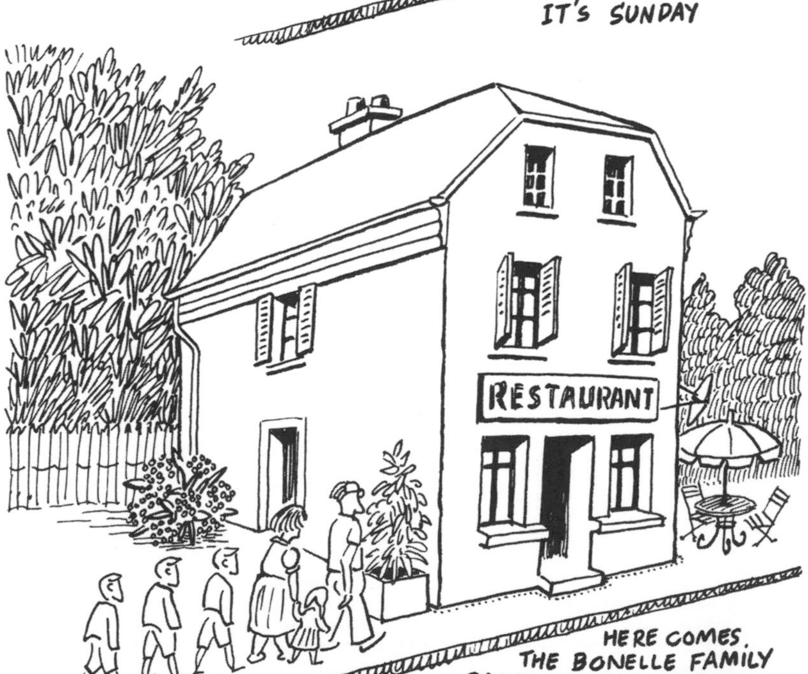
IT'S SUNDAY
RESTAURANT
HERE COMES THE BONELLE FAMILY BACK FROM A WALK

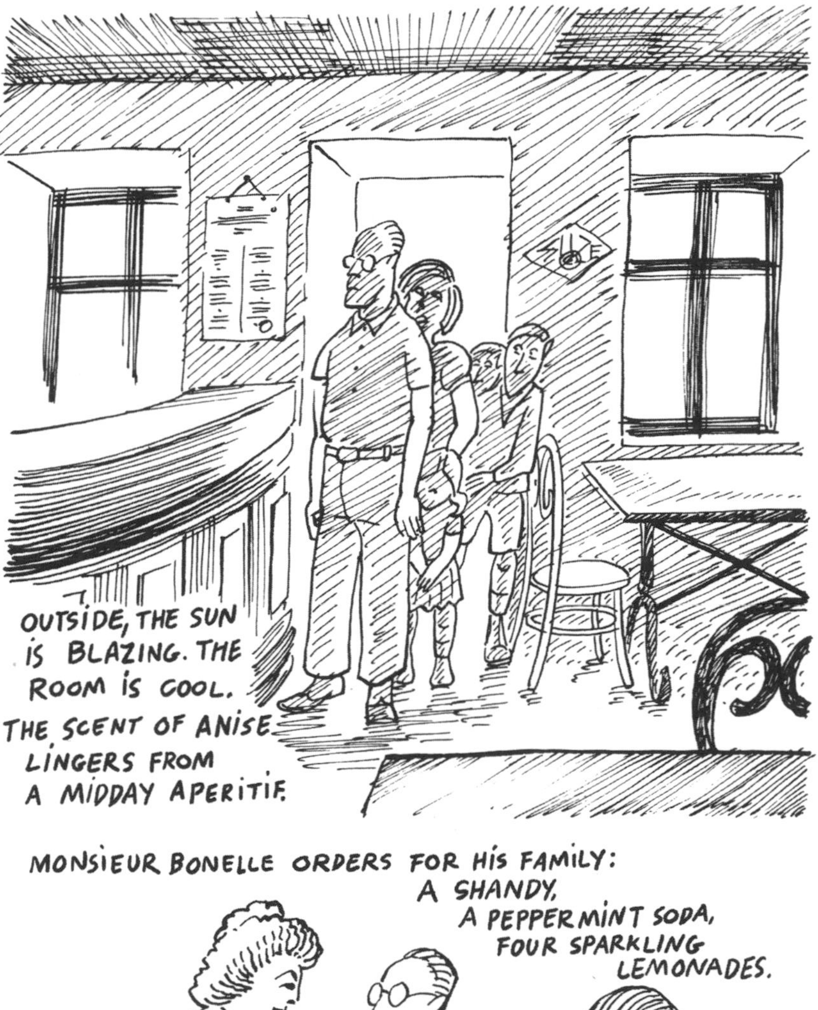
OUTSIDE, THE SUN IS BLAZING. THE ROOM IS COOL.
THE SCENT OF ANISE LINGERS FROM A MIDDAY APERITIF.

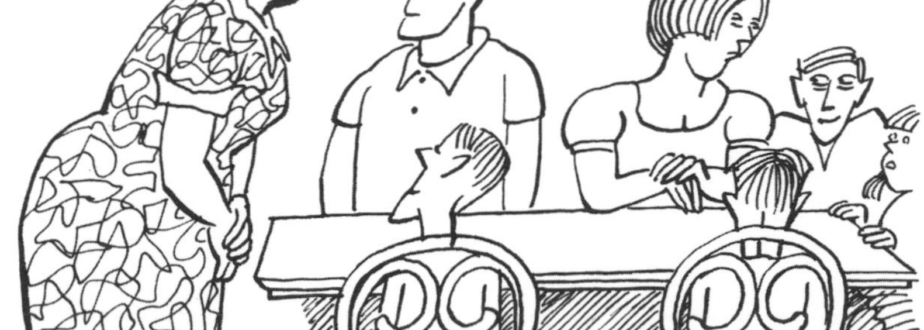
MONSIEUR BONELLE ORDERS FOR HIS FAMILY:
A SHANDY,
A PEPPERMINT SODA,
FOUR SPARKLING LEMONADES.

NEXT TO THE BONELLES' TABLE, A MAN WITH A MANDOLIN SMILES AT MARIE-VÉRONIQUE, WHO STARES AT THE INSTRUMENT.

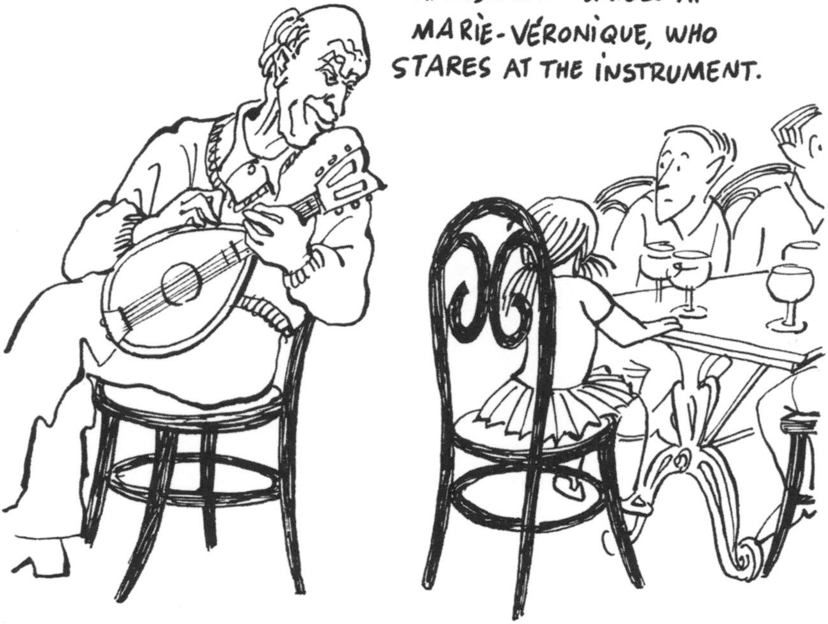

SO THE OLD MAN BEGINS TO PLUCK OUT A LITTLE TUNE FOR THE CHILD

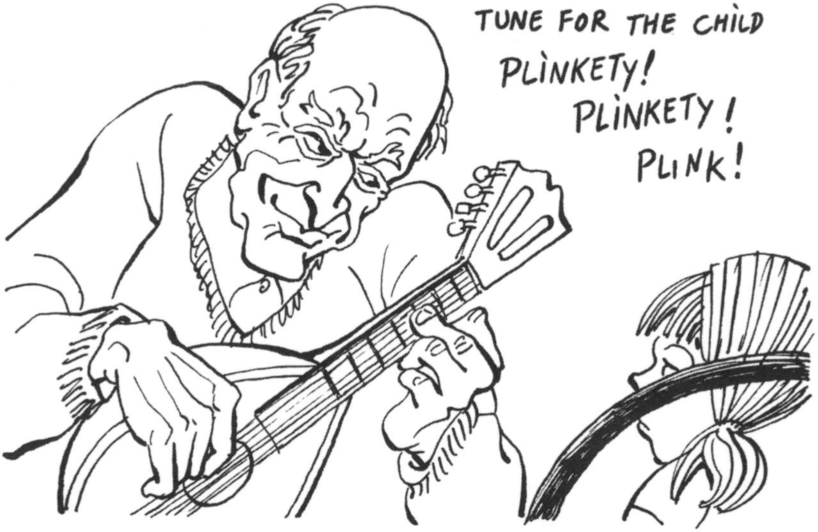
PLINKETY!
PLINKETY!
PLINK!

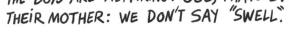

THE PARENTS THANK HIM WARMLY.
THE BOYS ARE ADMIRING: GEE, THAT'S SWELL!
THEIR MOTHER: WE DON'T SAY "SWELL."

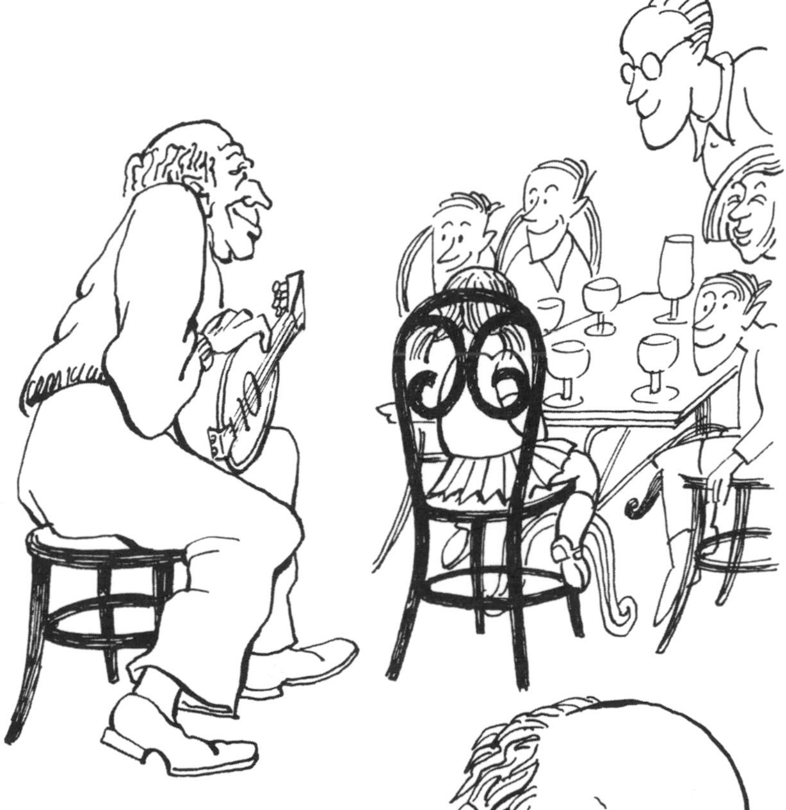

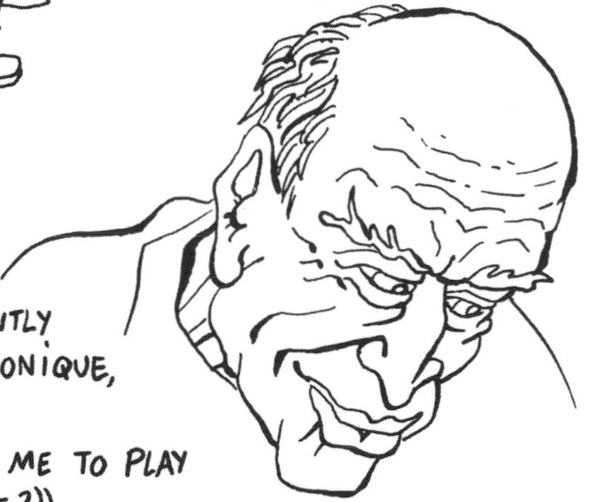

THE OLD MAN GENTLY
ASKS MARIE-VÉRONIQUE,
WHO IS SILENT,
"WOULD YOU LIKE ME TO PLAY
SOMETHING ELSE?"

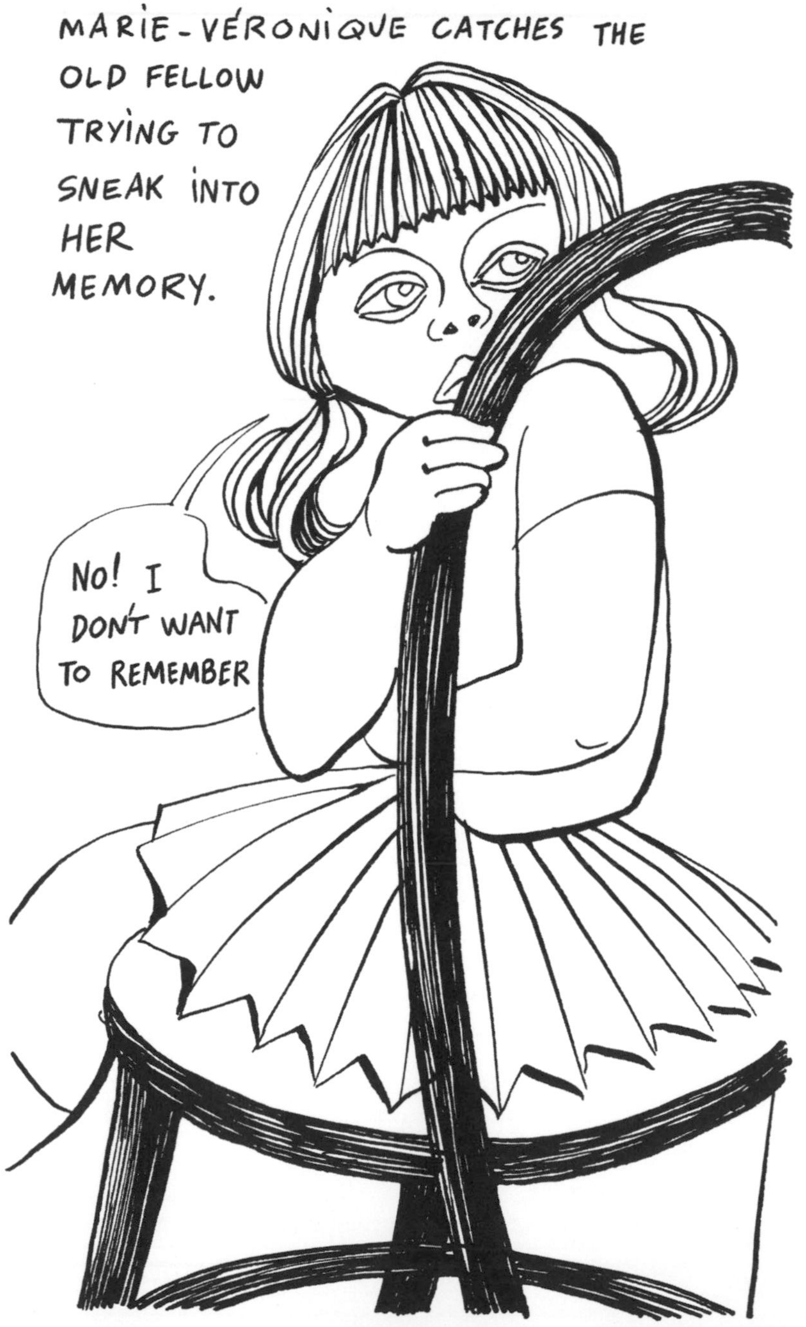
MARIE-VÉRONIQUE CATCHES THE OLD FELLOW TRYING TO SNEAK INTO HER MEMORY.
NO! I DON'T WANT TO REMEMBER

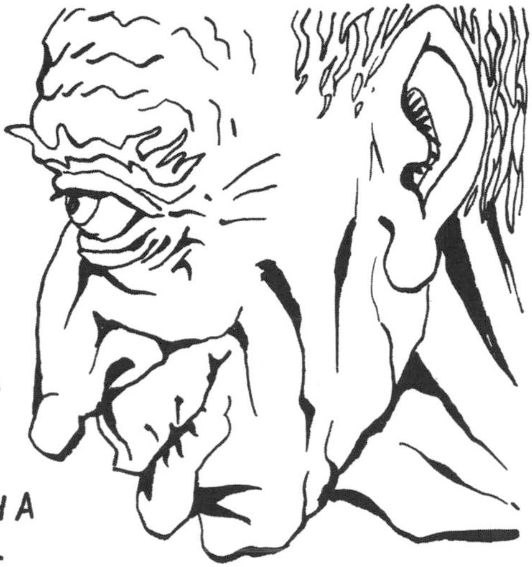

IN A FLASH,
MARIE-VÉRONIQUE
SEES HERSELF BECOME A
MADAME.
BESIDE HER, ONE OF
HER BROTHERS, NOW A
MONSIEUR.

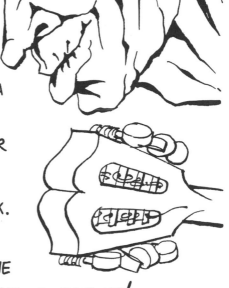

HE SAYS TO HER, WITH A
SMILE THAT INVOKES
THE PAST: REMEMBER
THAT OLD MUSICIAN?
IT WAS AFTER A WALK.
WHAT A HOT SUMMER!
AND PAPA, BOY COULD HE
EVER WALK! SO WE HAD TO KEEP UP!
... SPARKLING LEMONADES. "DRINK SLOWLY, YOU'RE
DRENCHED IN SWEAT." ... A MANDOLIN, RIGHT?
WASN'T IT? HE PLAYED FOR YOU, AND THEN HE
ASKED IF YOU WANTED HIM TO PLAY
ANYTHING ELSE. DO YOU REMEMBER?

AND MARIE-VÉRONIQUE, A LITTLE GIRL ONCE MORE, SAID
AT THE TOP OF HER VOICE, "NO! I DON'T WANT TO REMEMBER!"

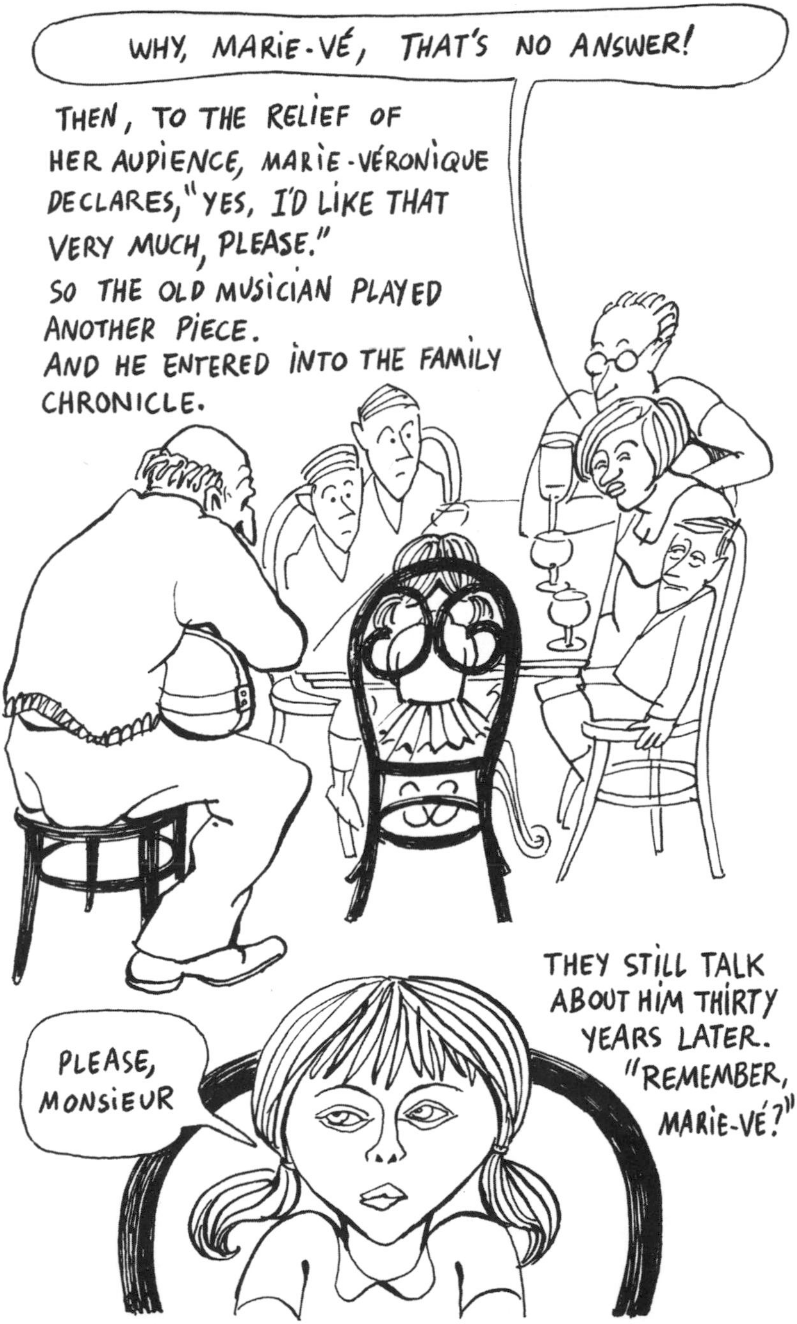
WHY, MARIE-VÉ, THAT'S NO ANSWER!
THEN, TO THE RELIEF OF HER AUDIENCE, MARIE-VÉRONIQUE DECLARES, "YES, I'D LIKE THAT VERY MUCH, PLEASE."
SO THE OLD MUSICIAN PLAYED ANOTHER PIECE.
AND HE ENTERED INTO THE FAMILY CHRONICLE.
PLEASE, MONSIEUR
THEY STILL TALK ABOUT HIM THIRTY YEARS LATER. "REMEMBER, MARIE-VÉ?"

WHILE THE OLD MUSICIAN WAS PLAYING THAT SUNDAY AFTERNOON, MARIE-VÉRONIQUE WAS THINKING: "I SEE EVERY ROOT OF EVERY TREE UNDERGROUND. I SEE EVERY DROP OF WATER IN EVERY CLOUD. I SEE THE ROOTS OF PEOPLE'S THOUGHTS. AND THE CLOUDS OF THEIR THOUGHTS. I SEE THEIR LIVES. THEIR WHOLE LIVES. FROM BEGINNING TO END. BEIGE.

I SEE PEOPLE'S DESIRE FOR SWEET LITTLE MEMORIES, ALL STICKY. FOR SUCKING ON LATER, WHEN DUSTY.

MY HEART ACHES."

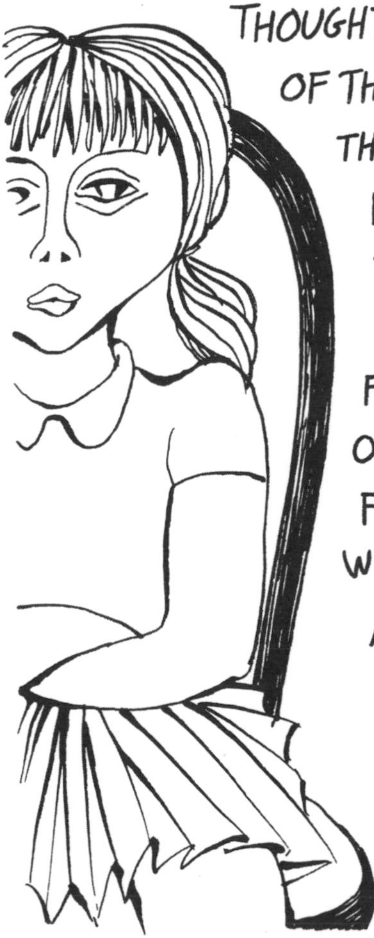

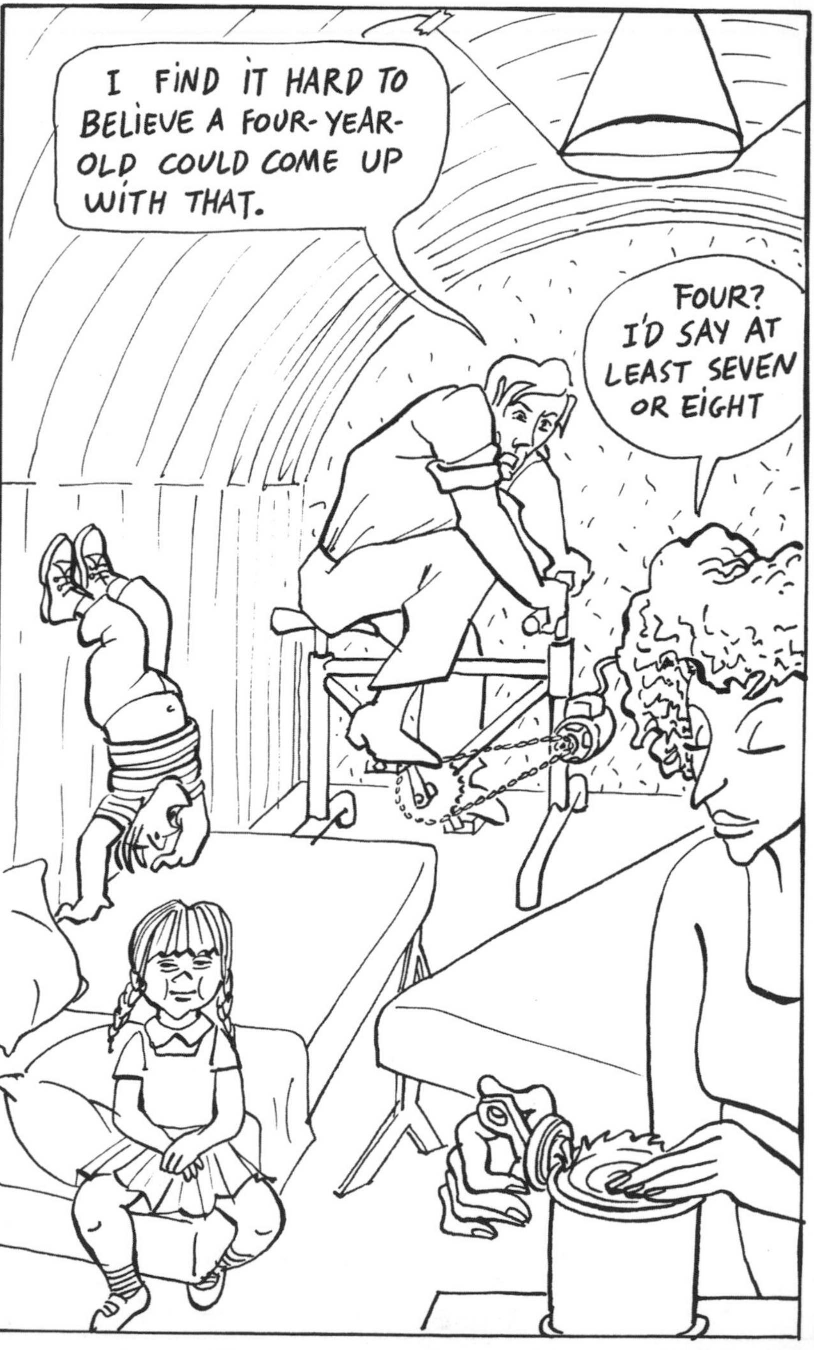
I FIND IT HARD TO BELIEVE A FOUR-YEAR-OLD COULD COME UP WITH THAT.
FOUR? I'D SAY AT LEAST SEVEN OR EIGHT

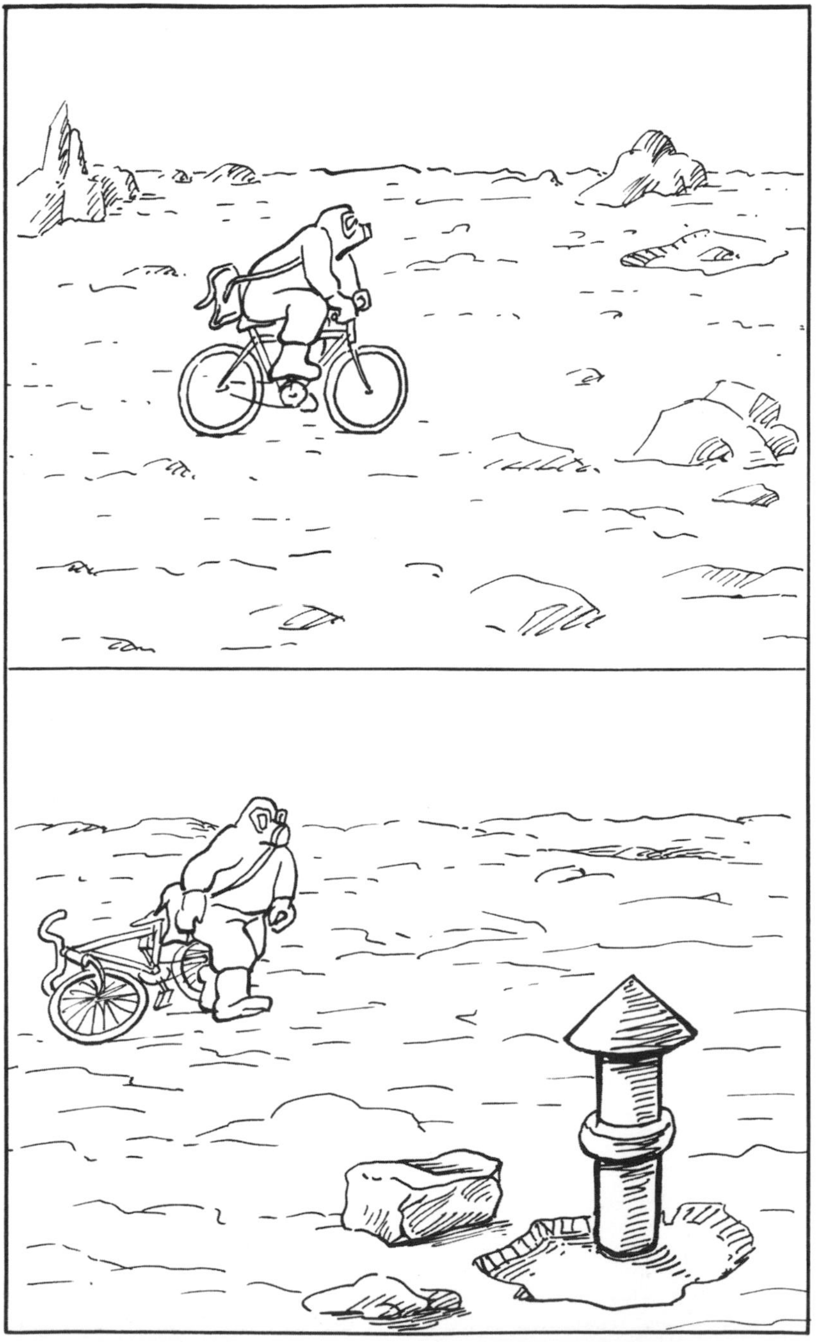

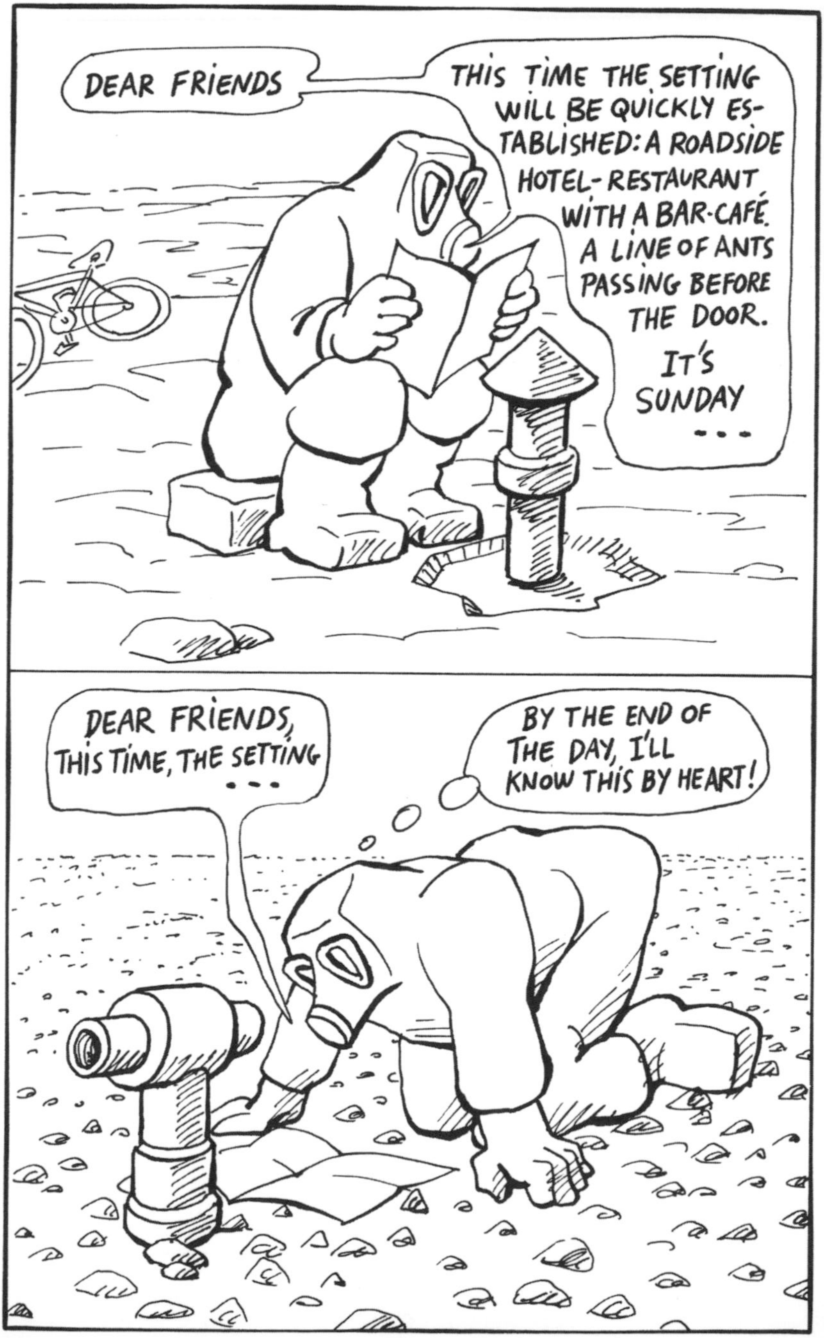
DEAR FRIENDS
THIS TIME THE SETTING WILL BE QUICKLY ESTABLISHED: A ROADSIDE HOTEL-RESTAURANT WITH A BAR-CAFÉ. A LINE OF ANTS PASSING BEFORE THE DOOR.
IT'S SUNDAY ...
DEAR FRIENDS, THIS TIME, THE SETTING ...
BY THE END OF THE DAY, I'LL KNOW THIS BY HEART!

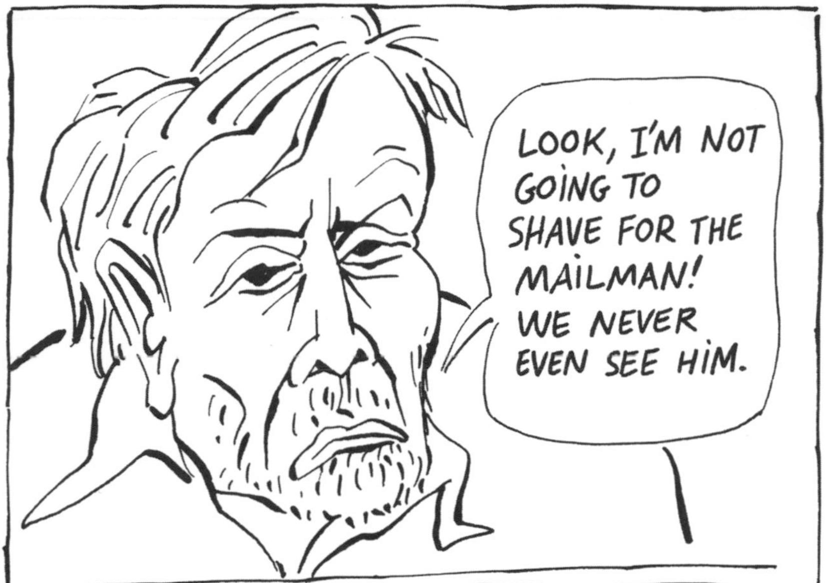
LOOK, I'M NOT GOING TO SHAVE FOR THE MAILMAN! WE NEVER EVEN SEE HIM.

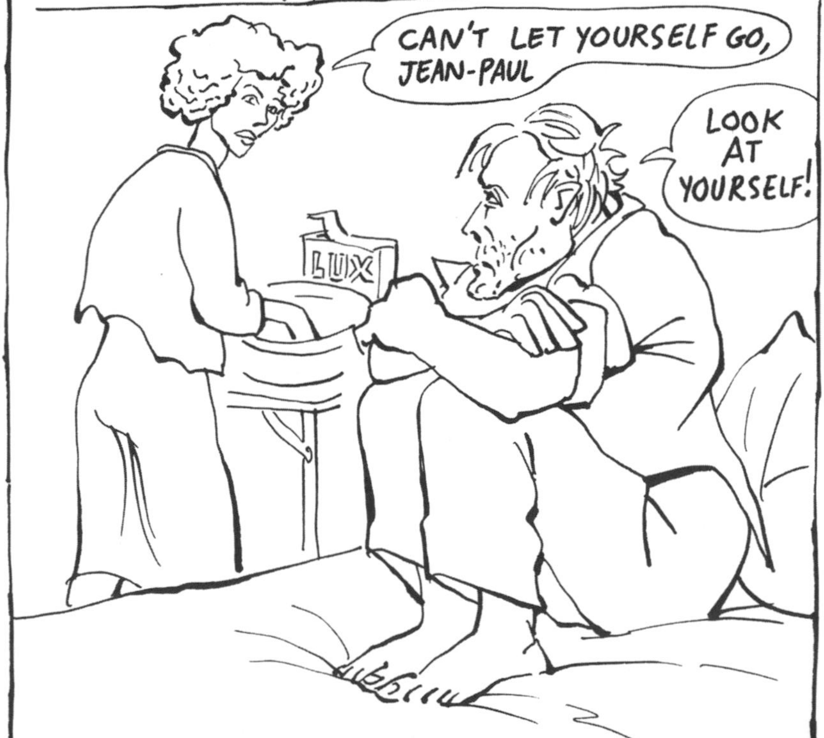
CAN'T LET YOURSELF GO, JEAN-PAUL
LOOK AT YOURSELF!
LUX

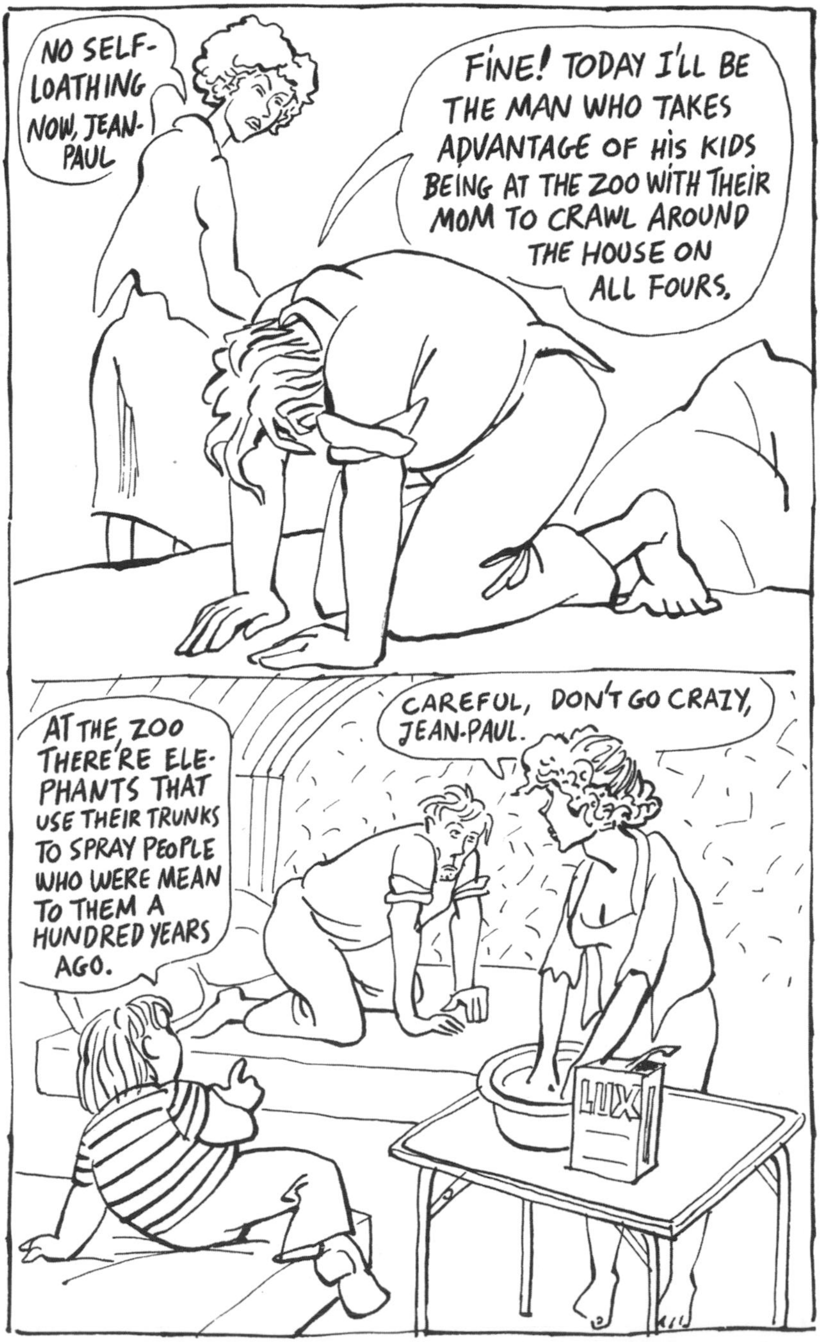
NO SELF-LOATHING NOW, JEAN-PAUL
FINE! TODAY I'LL BE THE MAN WHO TAKES ADVANTAGE OF HIS KIDS BEING AT THE ZOO WITH THEIR MOM TO CRAWL AROUND THE HOUSE ON ALL FOURS.
AT THE ZOO THERE'RE ELEPHANTS THAT USE THEIR TRUNKS TO SPRAY PEOPLE WHO WERE MEAN TO THEM A HUNDRED YEARS AGO.
CAREFUL, DON'T GO CRAZY, JEAN-PAUL.
LUX

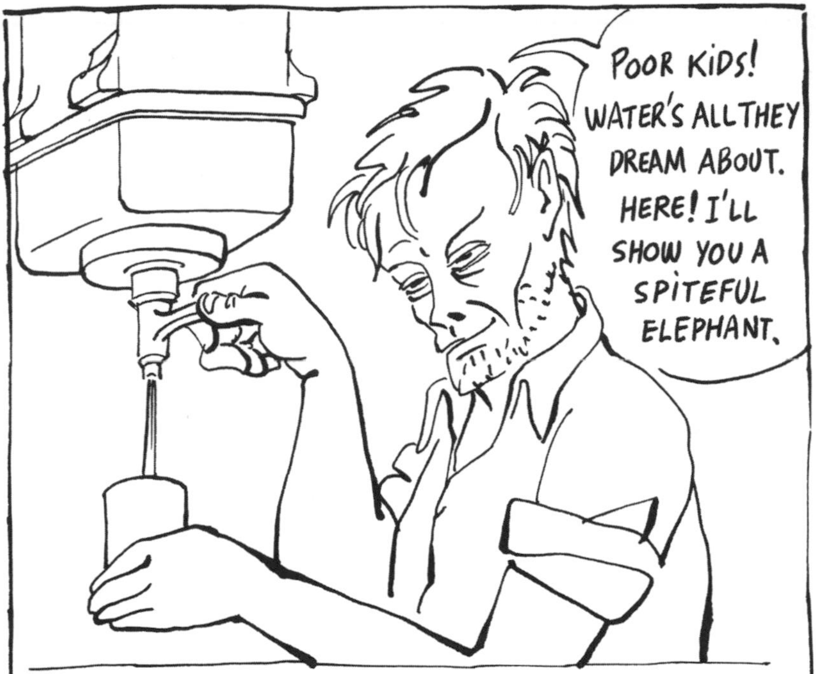
POOR KIDS! WATER'S ALLTHEY DREAM ABOUT. HERE! I'LL SHOW YOU A SPITEFUL ELEPHANT.

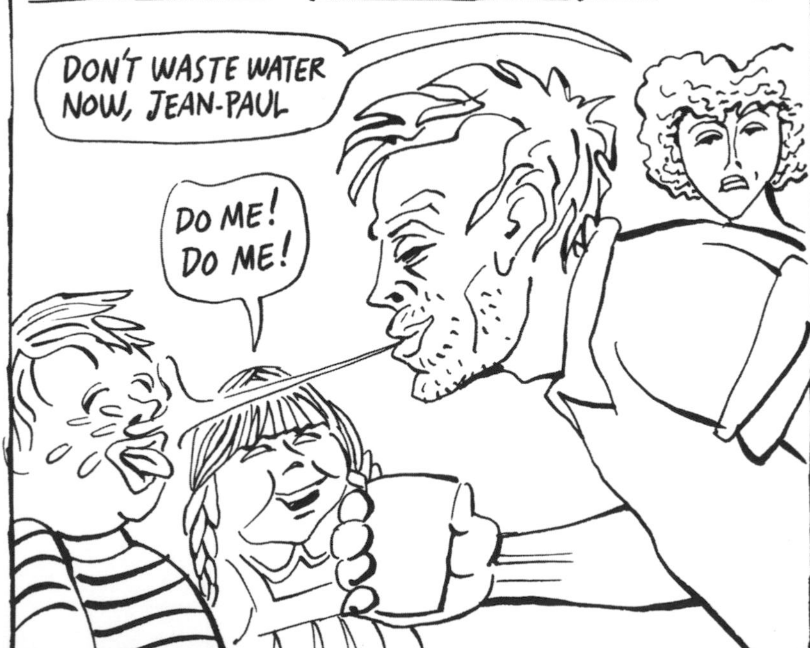
DON'T WASTE WATER NOW, JEAN-PAUL
DO ME! DO ME!

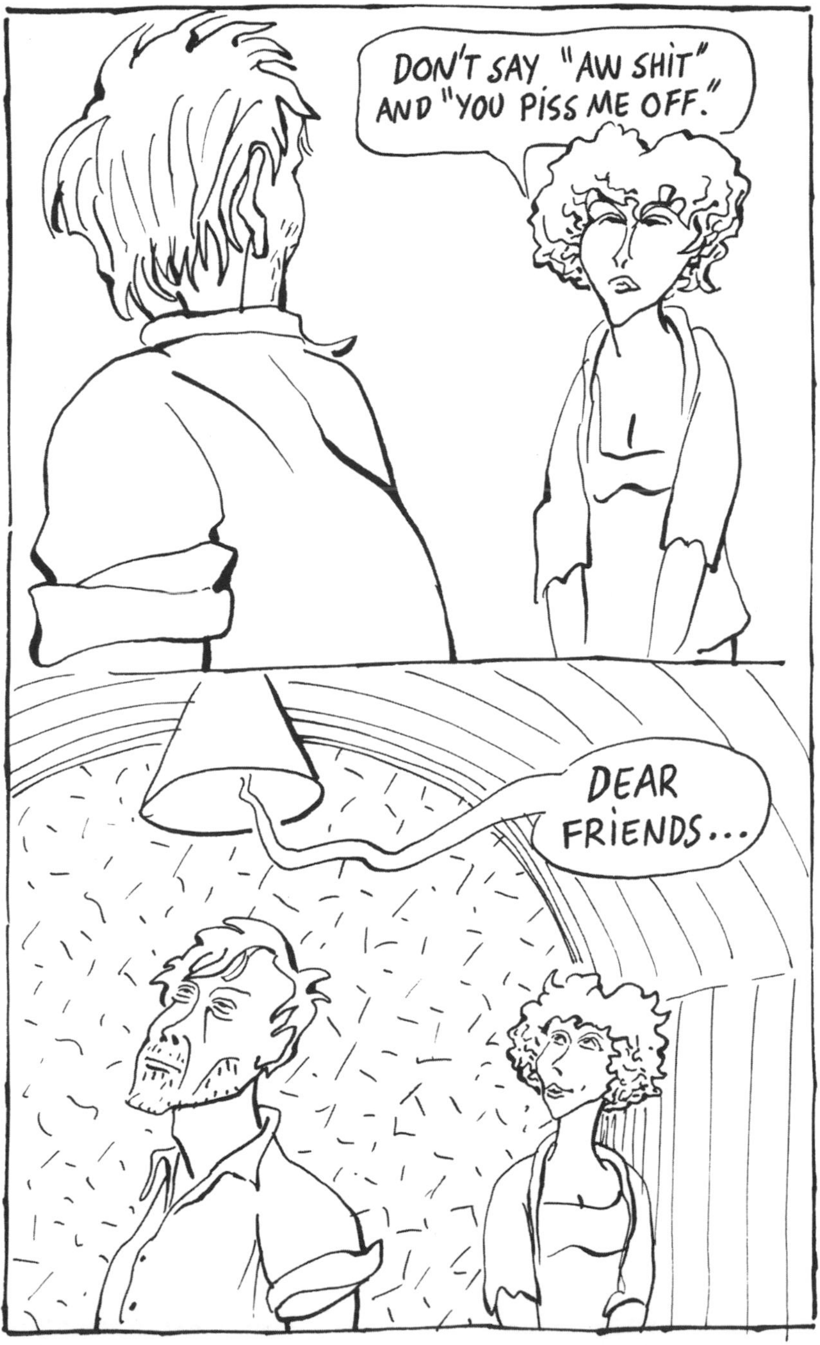
DON'T SAY "AW SHIT" AND "YOU PISS ME OFF."
DEAR FRIENDS...

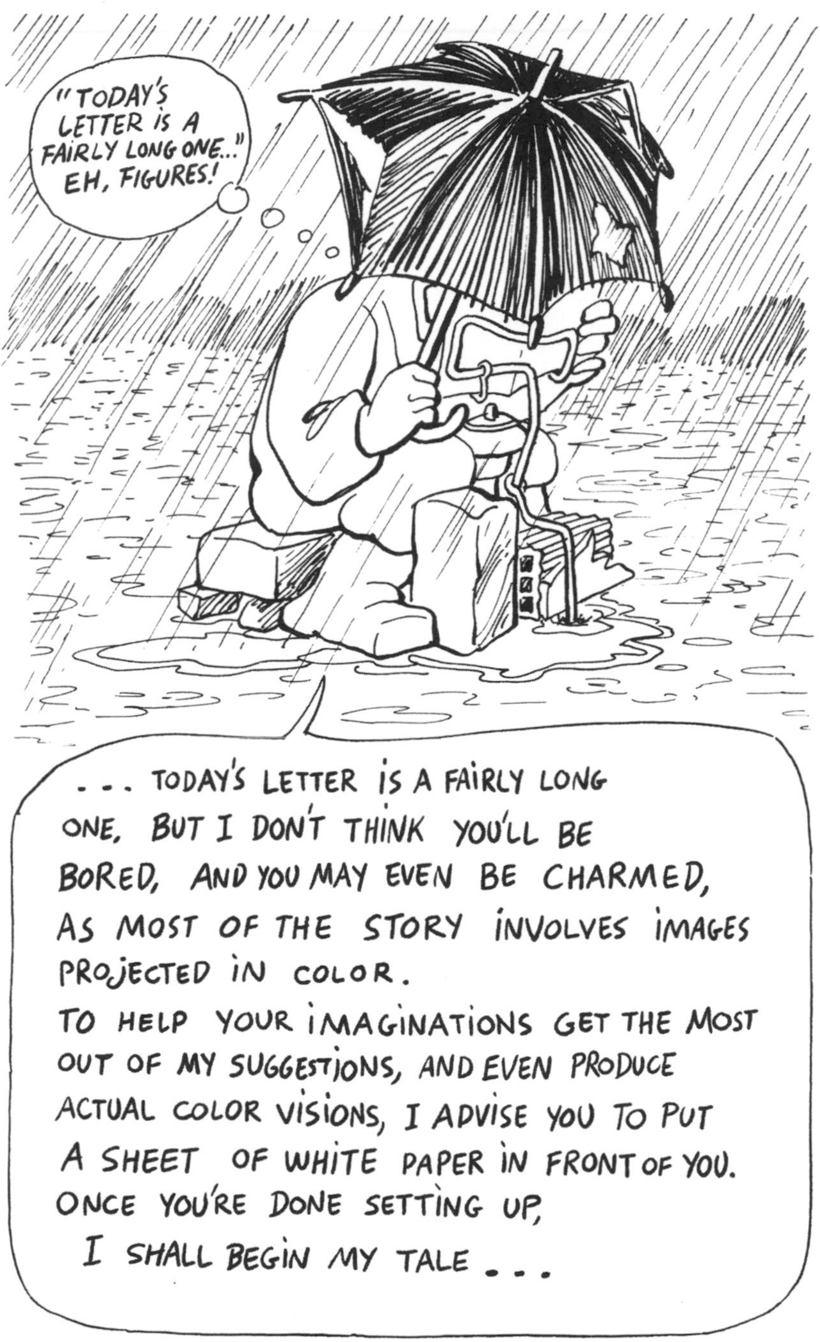
"TODAY'S LETTER IS A FAIRLY LONG ONE..." EH, FIGURES!
... TODAY'S LETTER IS A FAIRLY LONG ONE, BUT I DON'T THINK YOU'LL BE BORED, AND YOU MAY EVEN BE CHARMED, AS MOST OF THE STORY INVOLVES IMAGES PROJECTED IN COLOR.
TO HELP YOUR IMAGINATIONS GET THE MOST OUT OF MY SUGGESTIONS, AND EVEN PRODUCE ACTUAL COLOR VISIONS, I ADVISE YOU TO PUT A SHEET OF WHITE PAPER IN FRONT OF YOU.
ONCE YOU'RE DONE SETTING UP,
I SHALL BEGIN MY TALE ...

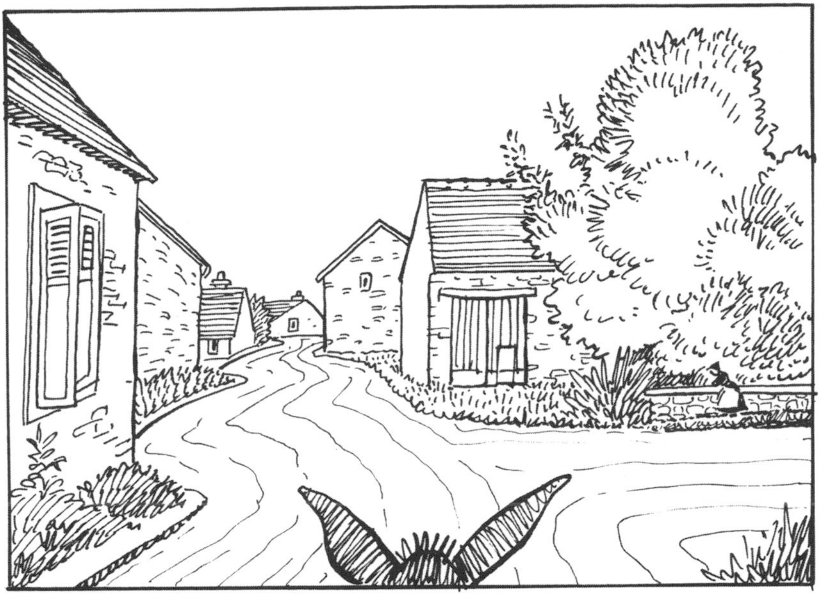

EIGHTY-SOME YEARS AGO, OR THEREABOUTS, JOSEPH BACHDROPP, HIS DONKEY, HIS DONKEY-DRAWN CART, AND ALL HIS PARAPHERNALIA MADE THEIR ENTRANCE INTO A VILLAGE WHOSE NAME I HAVE FORGOTTEN.

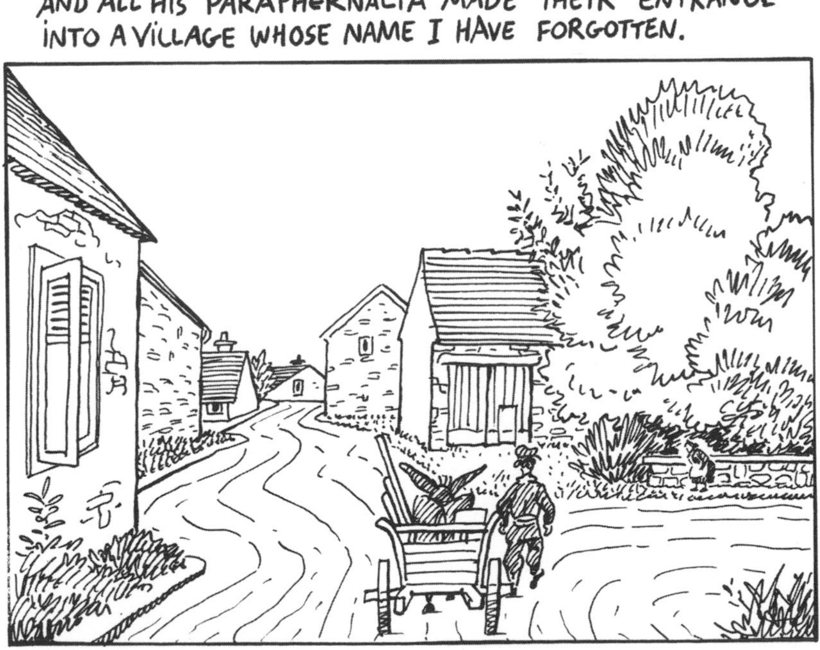

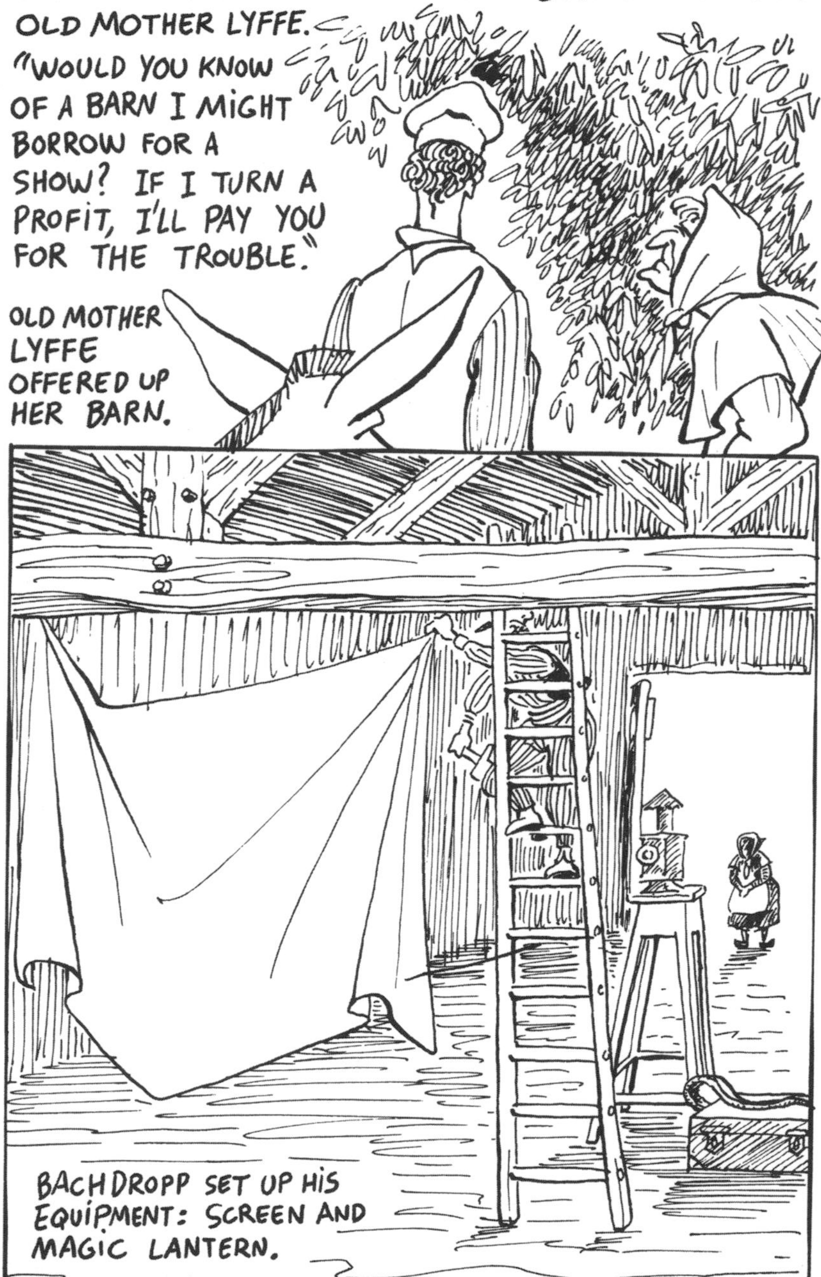
THE FIRST PERSON TO RUN ACROSS BACHDROPP WAS OLD MOTHER LYFFE.
"WOULD YOU KNOW OF A BARN I MIGHT BORROW FOR A SHOW? IF I TURN A PROFIT, I'LL PAY YOU FOR THE TROUBLE."
OLD MOTHER LYFFE OFFERED UP HER BARN.
BACHDROPP SET UP HIS EQUIPMENT: SCREEN AND MAGIC LANTERN.

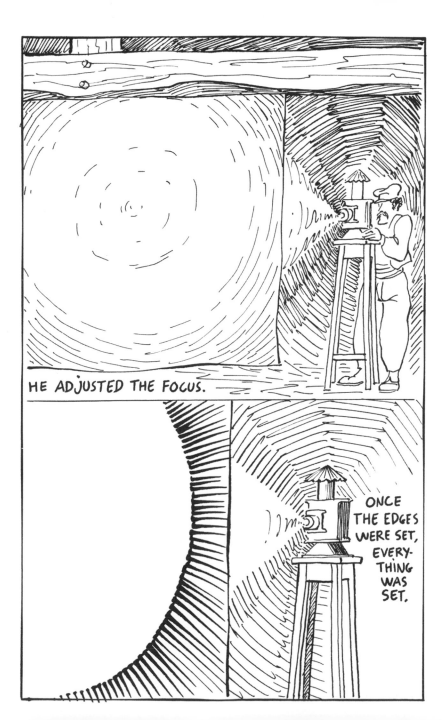

HE ADJUSTED THE FOCUS.

ONCE THE EDGES WERE SET, EVERYTHING WAS SET.

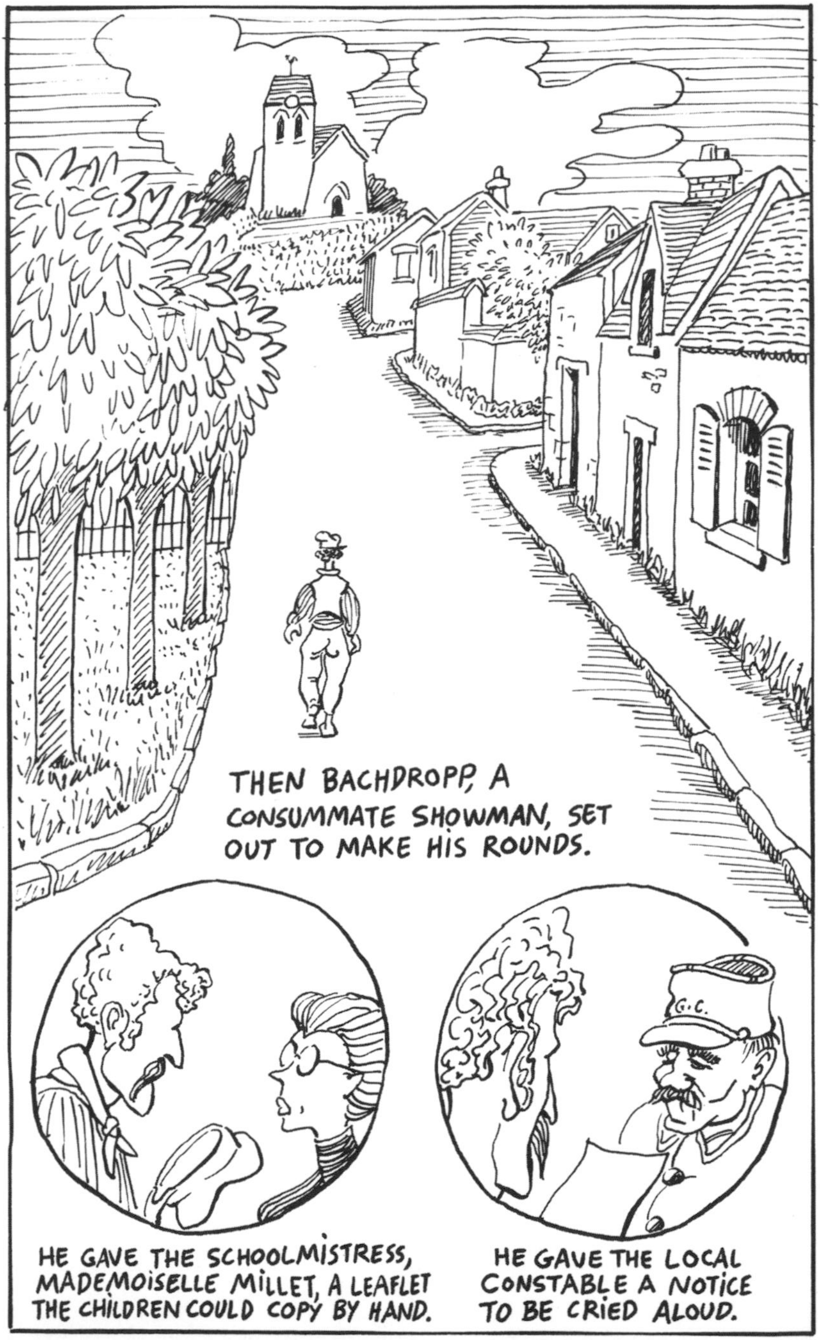
THEN BACHDROPP, A CONSUMMATE SHOWMAN, SET OUT TO MAKE HIS ROUNDS.
G.C.
HE GAVE THE SCHOOLMISTRESS, MADEMOISELLE MILLET, A LEAFLET THE CHILDREN COULD COPY BY HAND.
HE GAVE THE LOCAL CONSTABLE A NOTICE TO BE CRIED ALOUD.

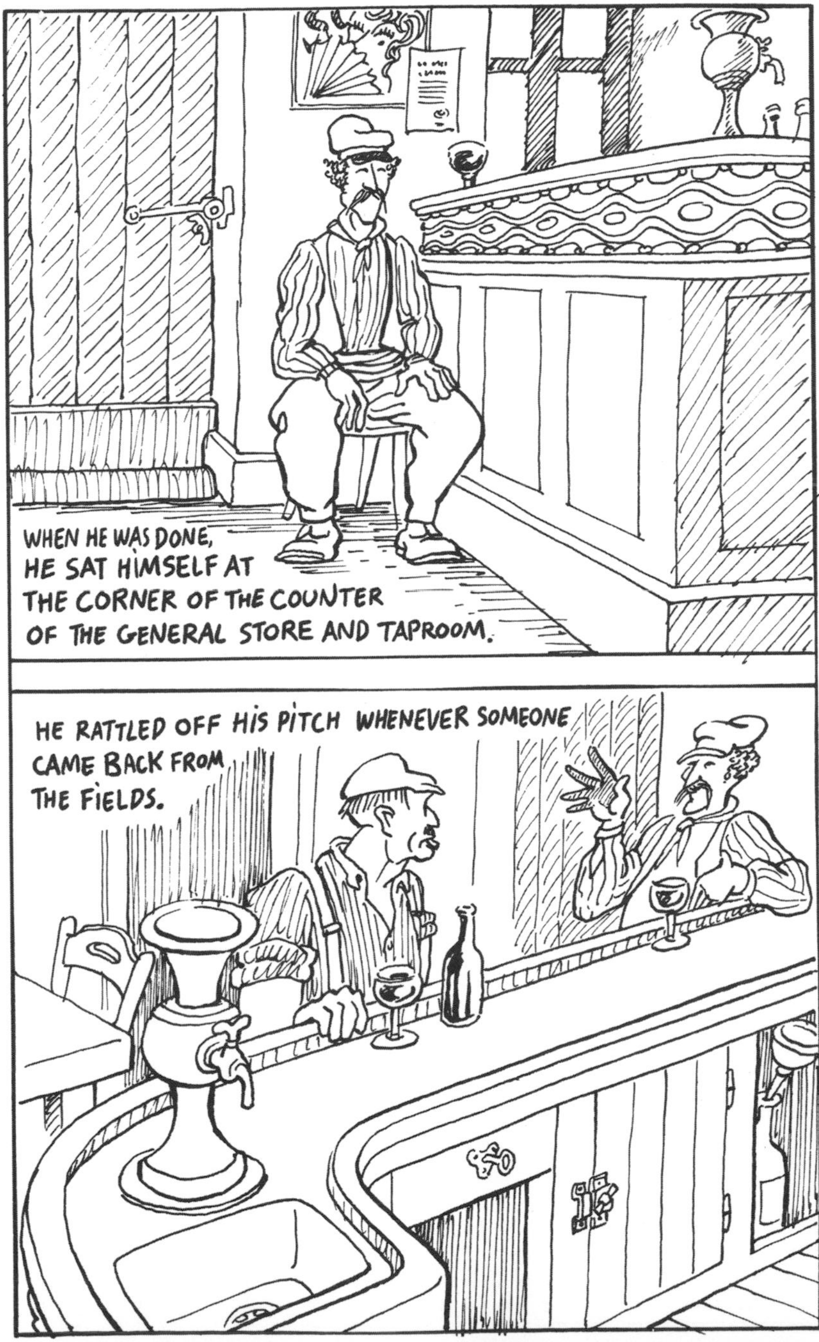
WHEN HE WAS DONE,
HE SAT HIMSELF AT
THE CORNER OF THE COUNTER
OF THE GENERAL STORE AND TAPROOM.
HE RATTLED OFF HIS PITCH WHENEVER SOMEONE
CAME BACK FROM
THE FIELDS.

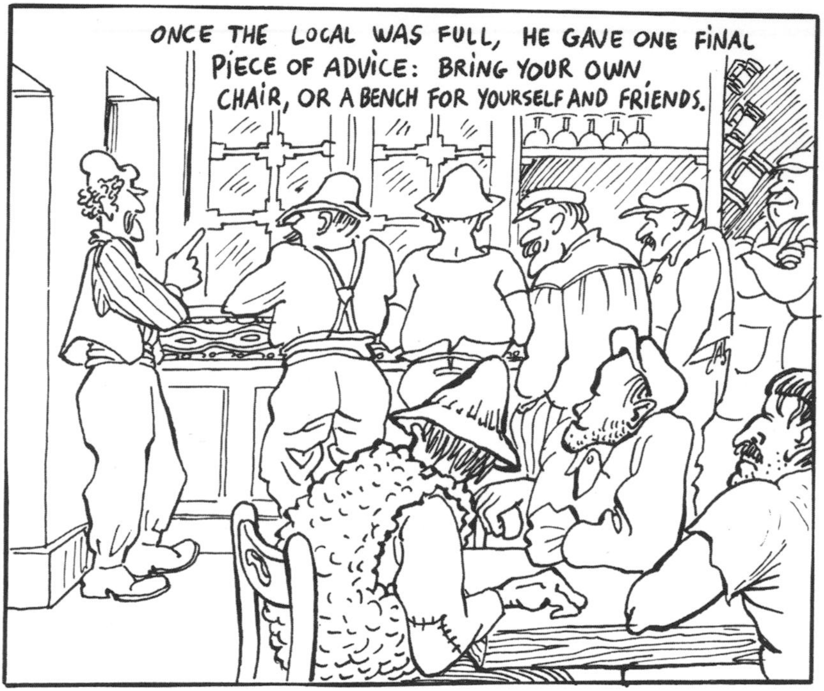
ONCE THE LOCAL WAS FULL, HE GAVE ONE FINAL PIECE OF ADVICE: BRING YOUR OWN CHAIR, OR A BENCH FOR YOURSELF AND FRIENDS.

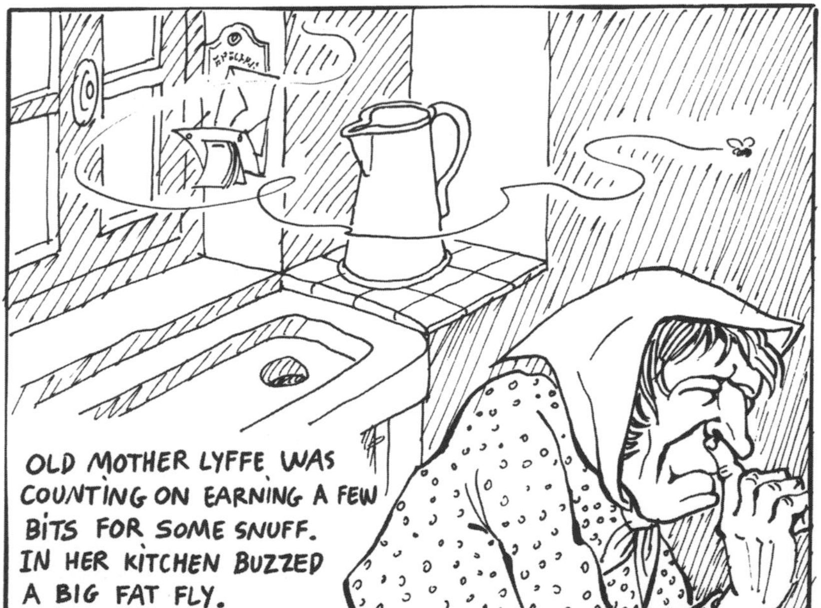
OLD MOTHER LYFFE WAS COUNTING ON EARNING A FEW BITS FOR SOME SNUFF. IN HER KITCHEN BUZZED A BIG FAT FLY.

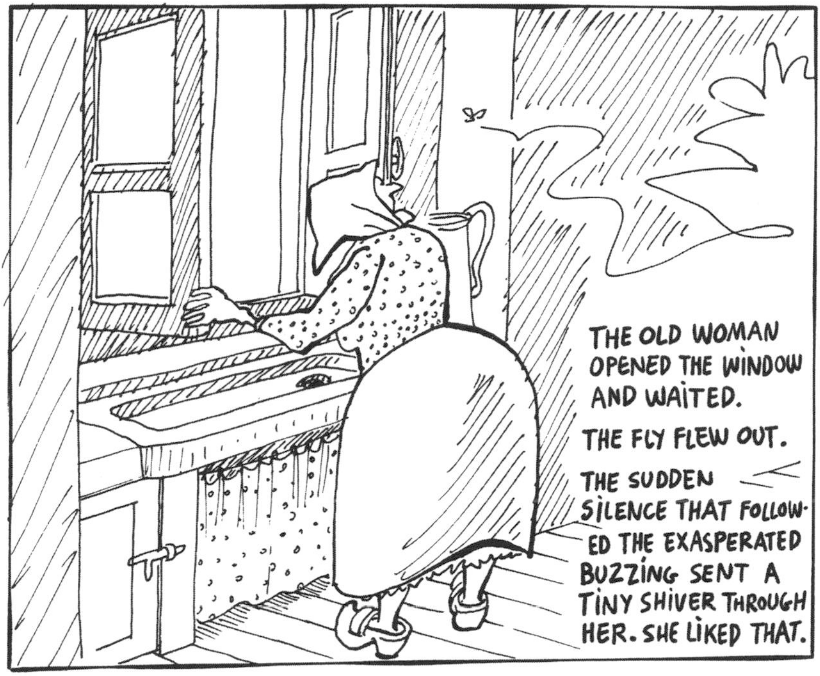
THE OLD WOMAN OPENED THE WINDOW AND WAITED.
THE FLY FLEW OUT.
THE SUDDEN SILENCE THAT FOLLOWED THE EXASPERATED BUZZING SENT A TINY SHIVER THROUGH HER. SHE LIKED THAT.

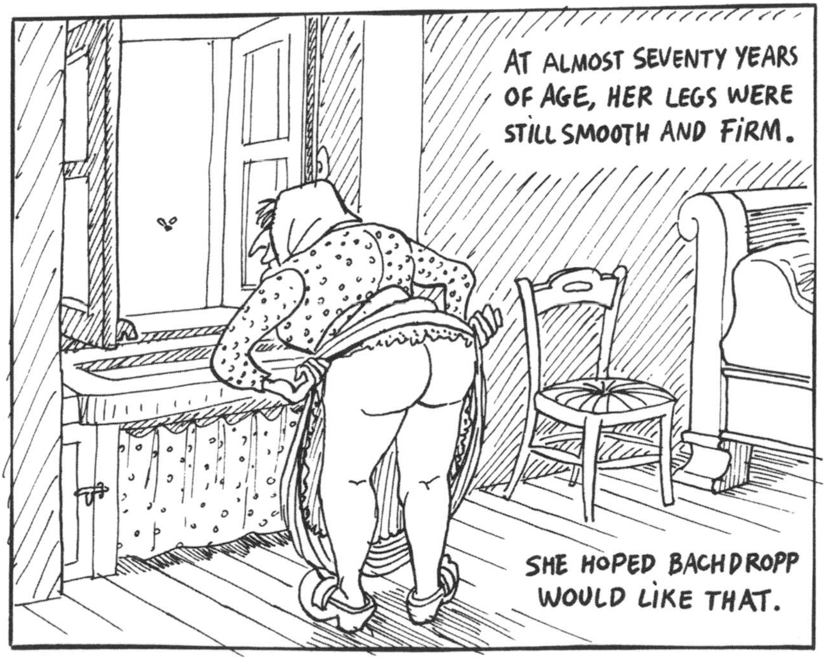
AT ALMOST SEVENTY YEARS OF AGE, HER LEGS WERE STILL SMOOTH AND FIRM.
SHE HOPED BACHDROPP WOULD LIKE THAT.

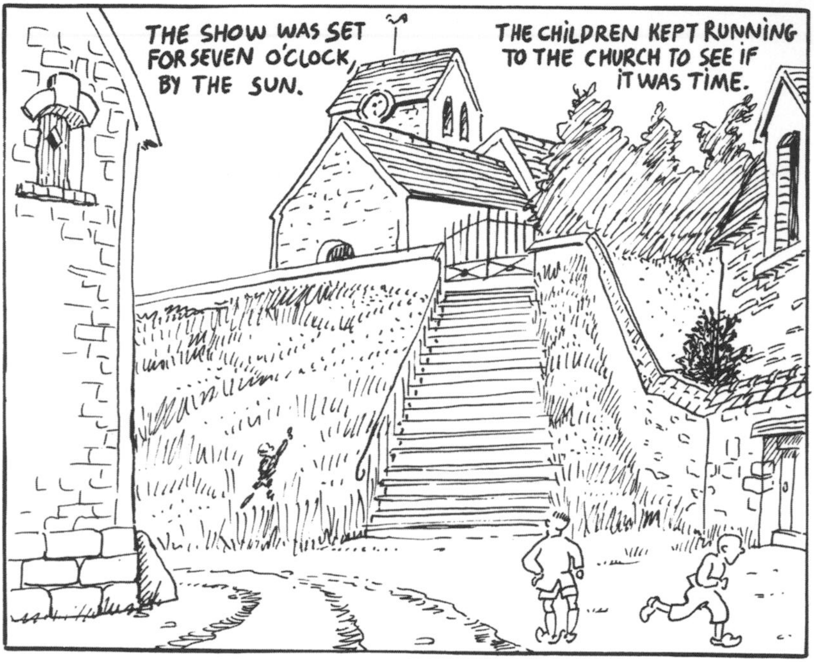
THE SHOW WAS SET FOR SEVEN O'CLOCK, BY THE SUN.
THE CHILDREN KEPT RUNNING TO THE CHURCH TO SEE IF IT WAS TIME.

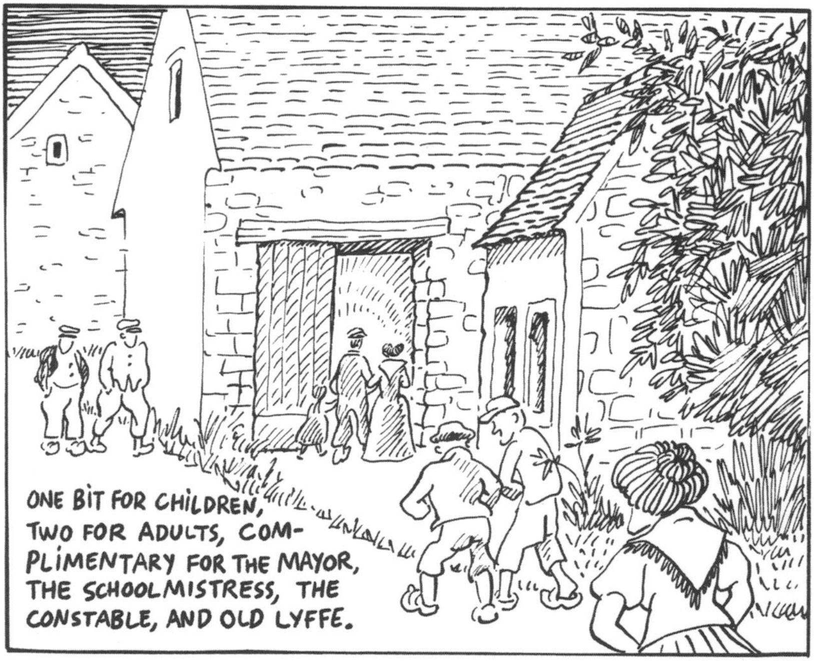
ONE BIT FOR CHILDREN, TWO FOR ADULTS, COMPLIMENTARY FOR THE MAYOR, THE SCHOOLMISTRESS, THE CONSTABLE, AND OLD LYFFE.

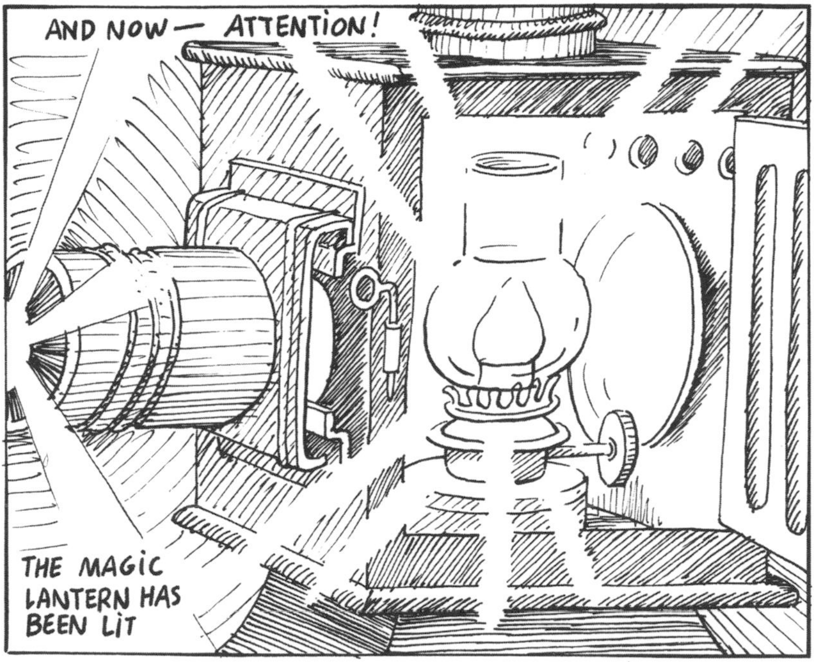
AND NOW— ATTENTION!
THE MAGIC LANTERN HAS BEEN LIT

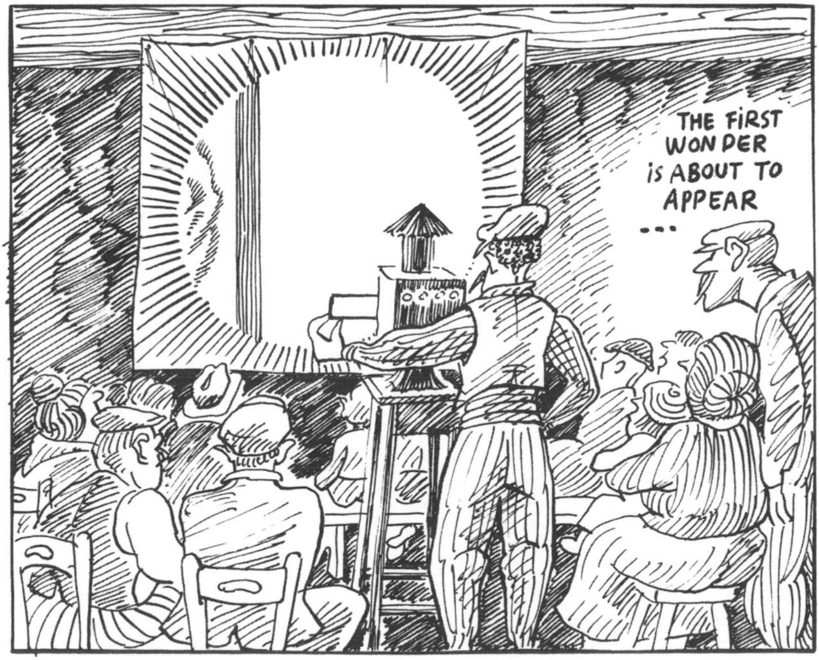
THE FIRST WONDER is ABOUT TO APPEAR ...

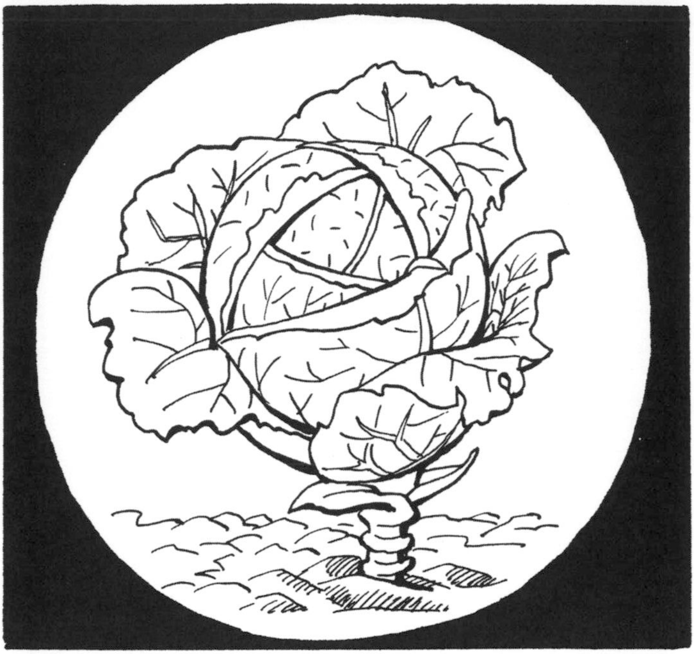

A CABBAGE! ALL GREEN ON A BACKDROP OF BLUE SKY AND BROWN EARTH.

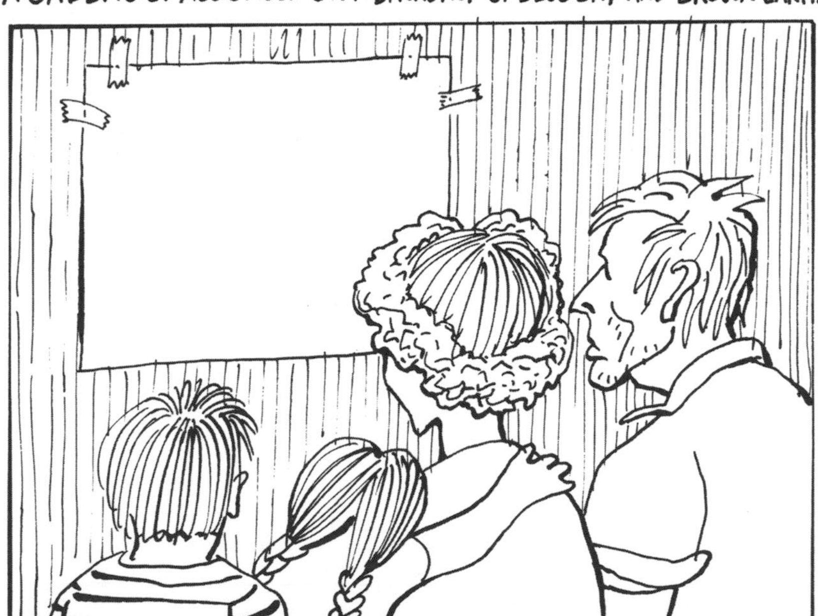

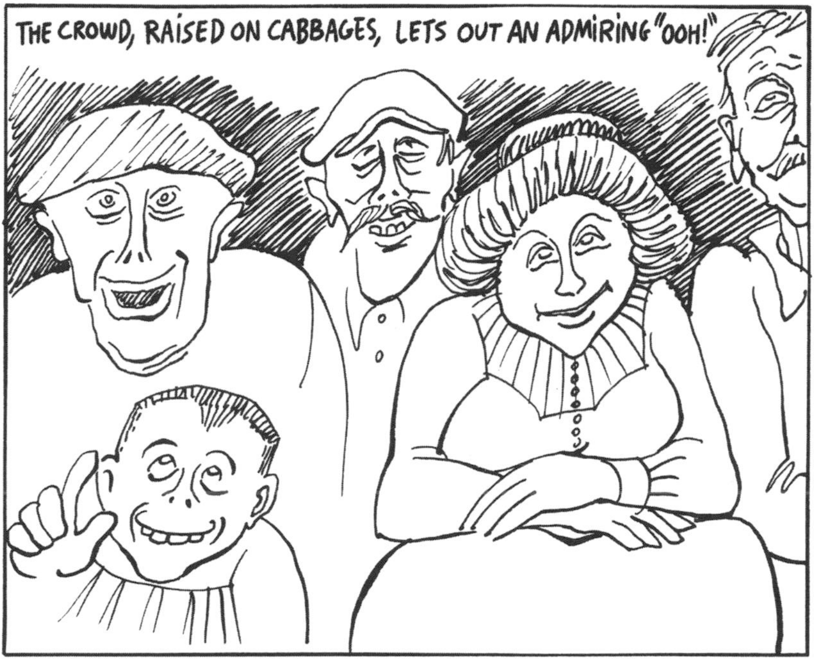
THE CROWD, RAISED ON CABBAGES, LETS OUT AN ADMIRING "OOH!"

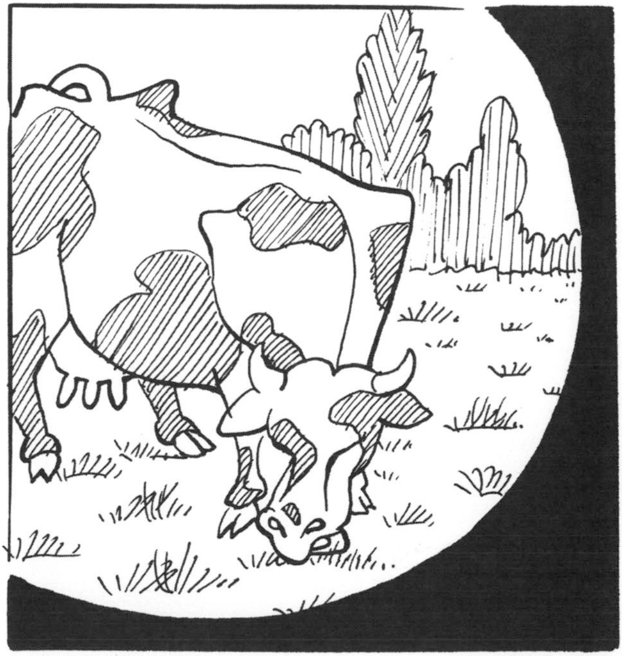

A COW!

"WHY, IT'S OUR BABETTE!" PELLERIN'S DAUGHTER-IN-LAW EXCLAIMS.

AUDIENCE MEMBERS CORKSCREW IN THEIR SEATS AND GO "MOO!"

AFTER THAT COMES:

- A CAVALRYMAN ON HORSEBACK.
- A SHIP IN A STORM.
- A CLUMP OF PEONIES.
- A PEACOCK.
- FIERCE ANIMALS: LION, TIGER, BOA.

AND JUST WHEN THEY THINK THEY'VE SEEN IT ALL, THERE'S MORE:

"SPOT PLAYING A TRICK ON BUTCHER BIGWURST."

"THE ADVENTURES OF CIRAGE, THE LITTLE BLACK BOY."

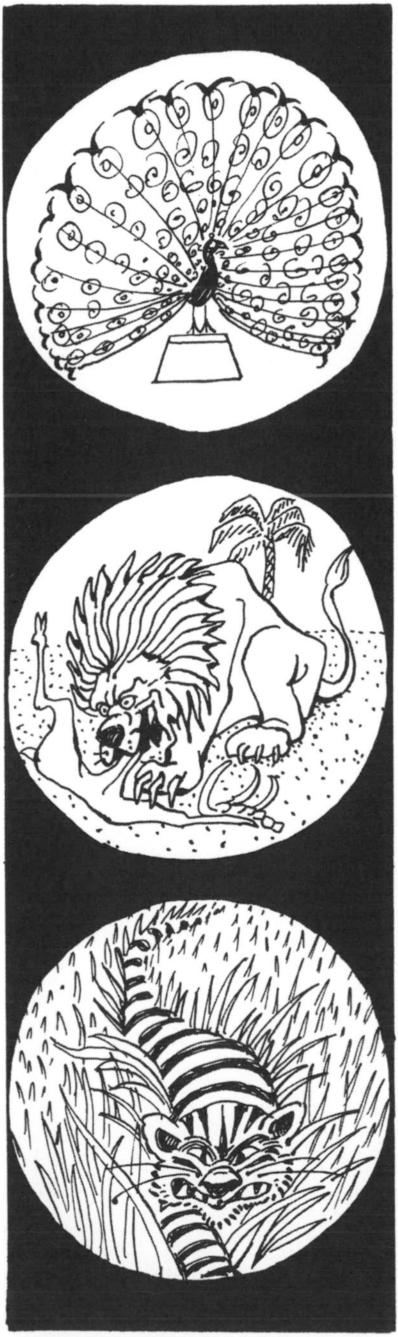

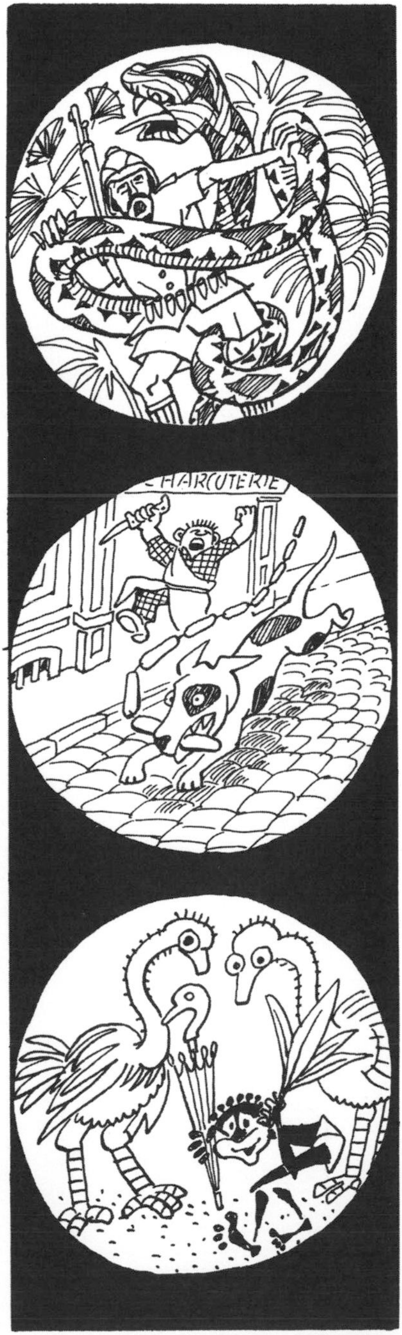

HARCUTERIE

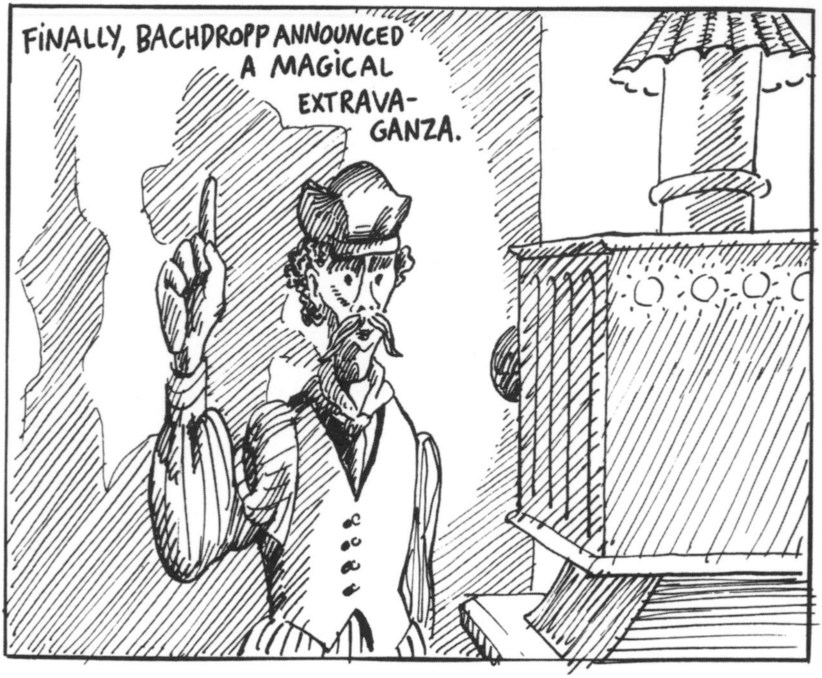
FINALLY, BACHDROPP ANNOUNCED A MAGICAL EXTRAVA-GANZA.

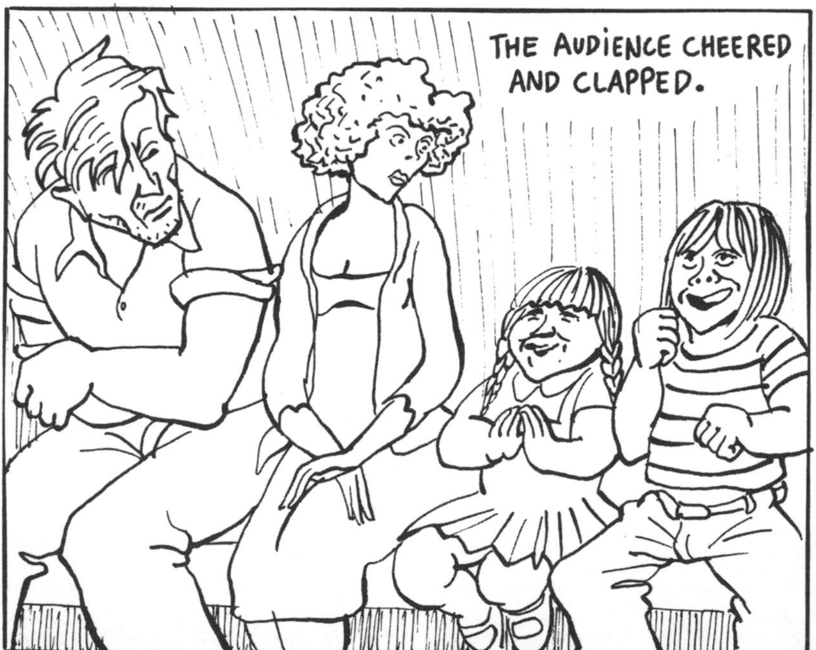
THE AUDIENCE CHEERED AND CLAPPED.

THE LEGEND OF KING JOLLY AND QUEEN GLEE

ONCE UPON A TIME THERE LIVED A KING
AND QUEEN WHO HAD BUT ONE SOLE AMBITION:
TO MAKE THEIR SUBJECTS HAPPY BY
ANY MEANS NECESSARY.

FOR INSTANCE, KING JOLLY COULD NOT BEAR THE THOUGHT THAT THE POOR HAD TO WALK ON THEIR OWN TWO FEET.

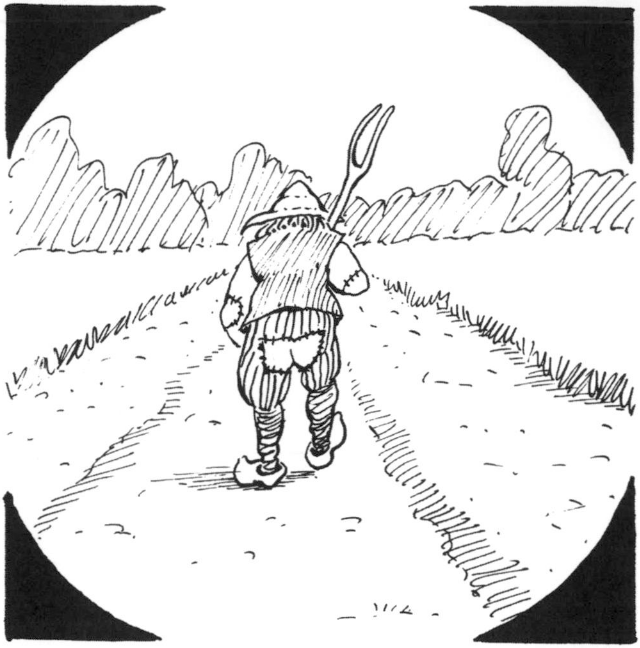

HIS KNIGHTS ROAMED THE KINGDOM AND, WHENEVER THEY CAME UPON A PEASANT ON FOOT, HELPED HIM WALK ON HIS HANDS INSTEAD.

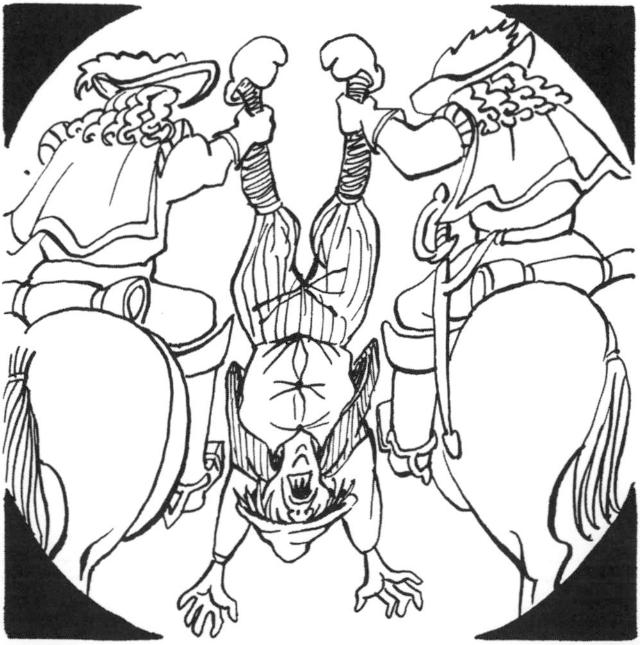

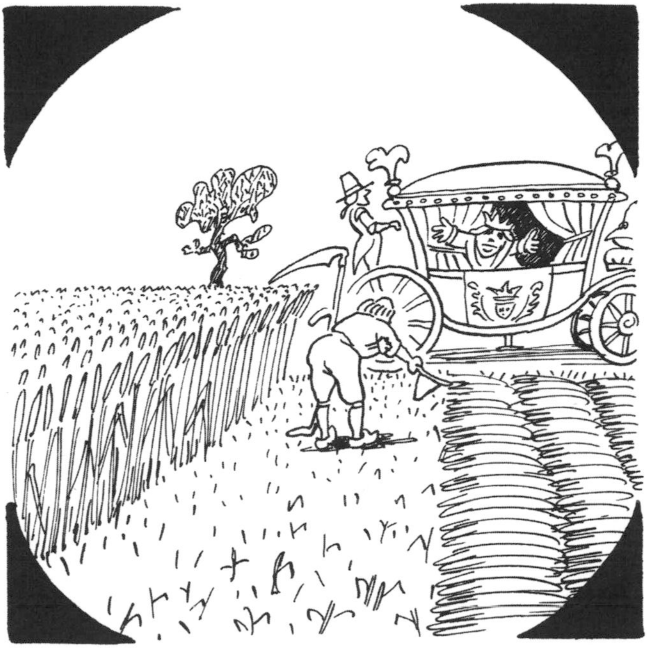

KING JOLLY, WHO LIKED SHADE IN THE SUMMER, FOUND IT UNJUST THAT HIS SERFS HAD TO HARVEST UNDER THE HOT SUN.

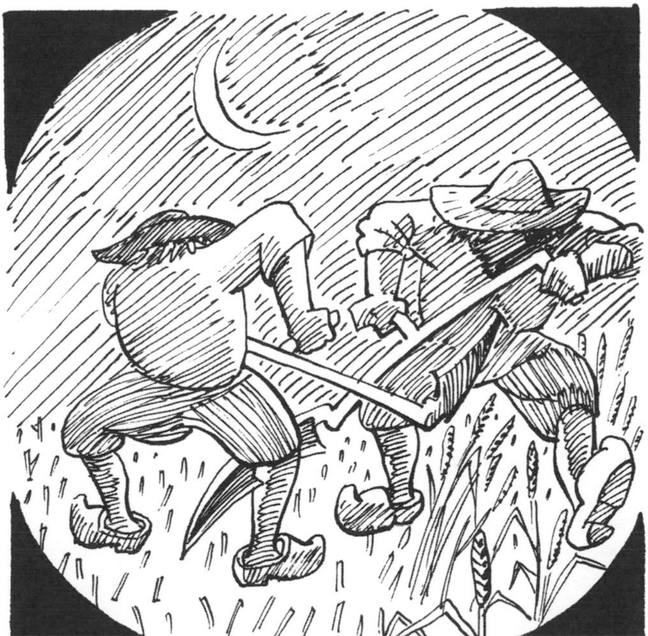

HE PASSED AN EDICT ORDERING HARVESTERS TO SLEEP ALL DAY AND REAP ONLY DURING THE DARKEST NIGHT.

AS FOR QUEEN GLEE, SHE HAD FIREPLACES BUILT IN THE FORESTS TO WARM THOSE GATHERING FIREWOOD IN WINTER.

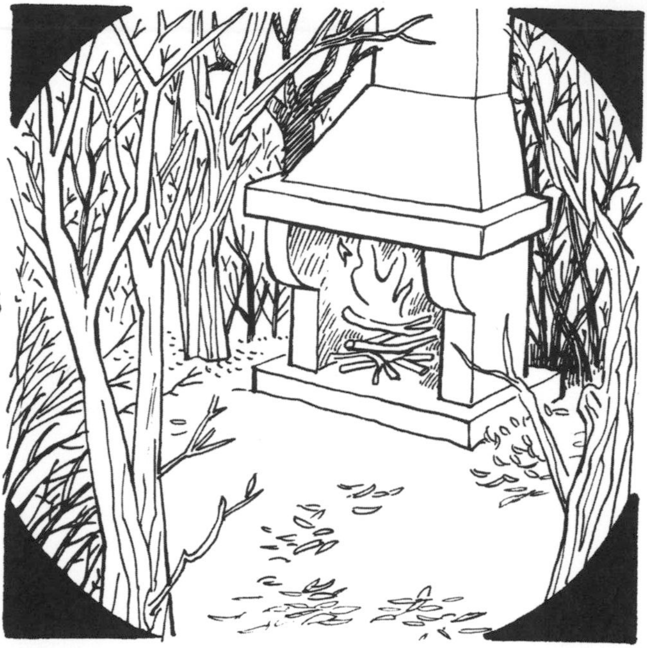

SINCE THESE FIREPLACES USED UP ALL THE FIREWOOD, PAUPERS HAD TO LEAVE THEIR FROZEN COTTAGES AND GO WARM THEMSELVES IN THE FOREST.

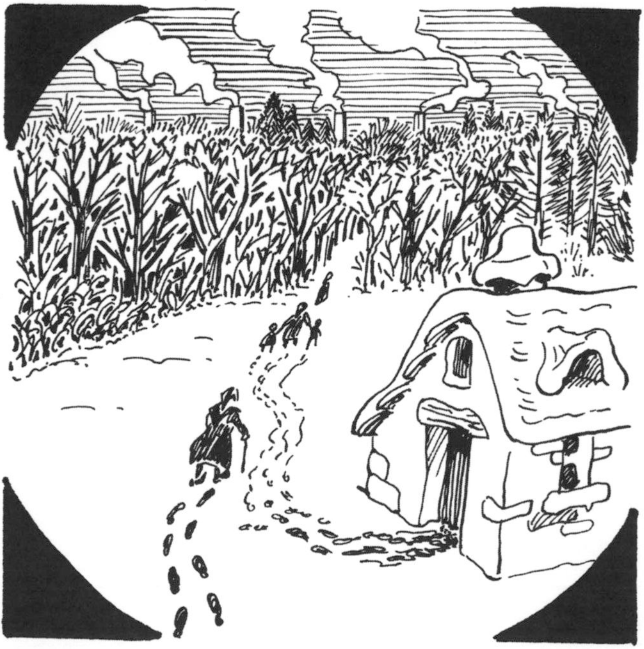

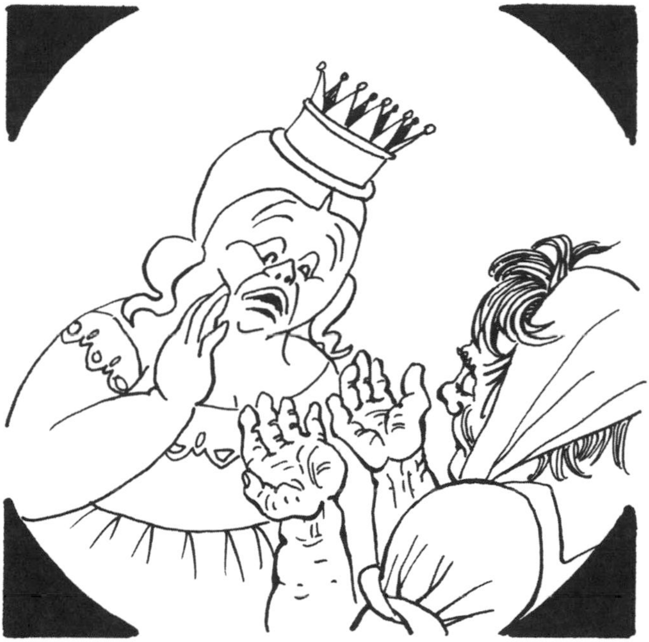

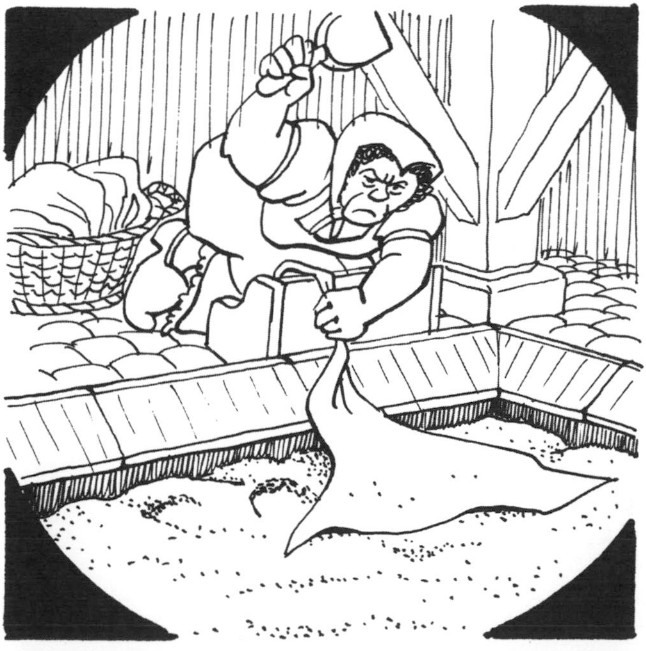

UPON LEARNING THAT COLD WATER WAS RESPONSIBLE FOR THE UGLY CRACKS SHE SAW ON WASHER-WOMEN'S HANDS, QUEEN GLEE HAD THE WASHHOUSE BASINS DRAINED AND REPLACED THE WATER WITH THE FINEST, MOST BEAUTIFUL SAND.

ABOVE ALL ANXIOUS THAT EVERY MARRIAGE BE BLISSFUL, KING JOLLY DECREED THAT EACH MAN TAKE TWO WIVES: A GOOD-NATURED HAG AND A BAD-TEMPERED BEAUTY.

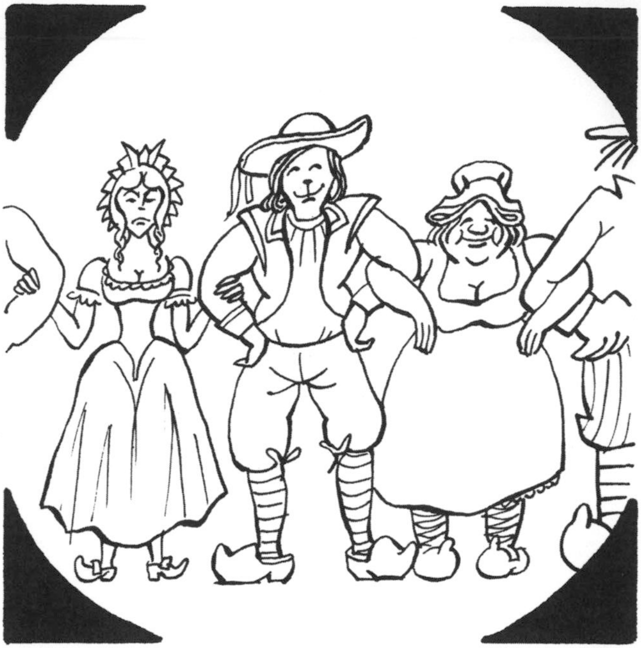

FOR THE SAME REASON, QUEEN GLEE DECIDED THAT EVERY WOMAN TAKE TWO HUSBANDS: A HARD-WORKING GROUCH AND AN AFFABLE IDLER.

THE KINGDOM WAS ONE BIG FAMILY.

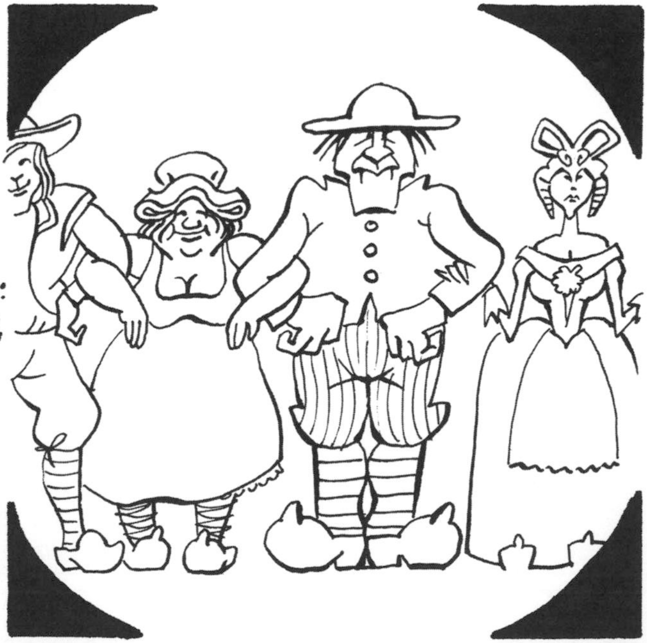

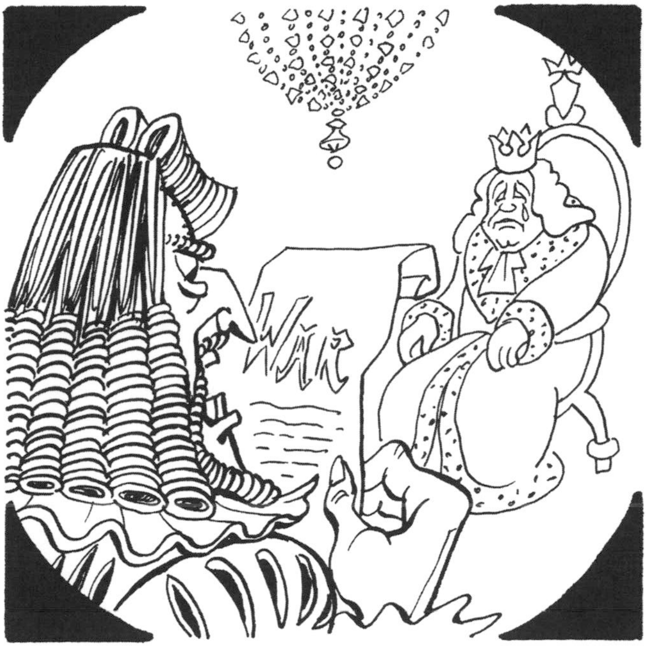
WAR

ALAS!
THIS HAPPINESS WAS NOT TO LAST

A NEIGHBORING REALM DECLARED WAR ON THE KING.

STRAIGHTAWAY, THE KING SENT A MESSAGE TO HIS SUBJECTS:

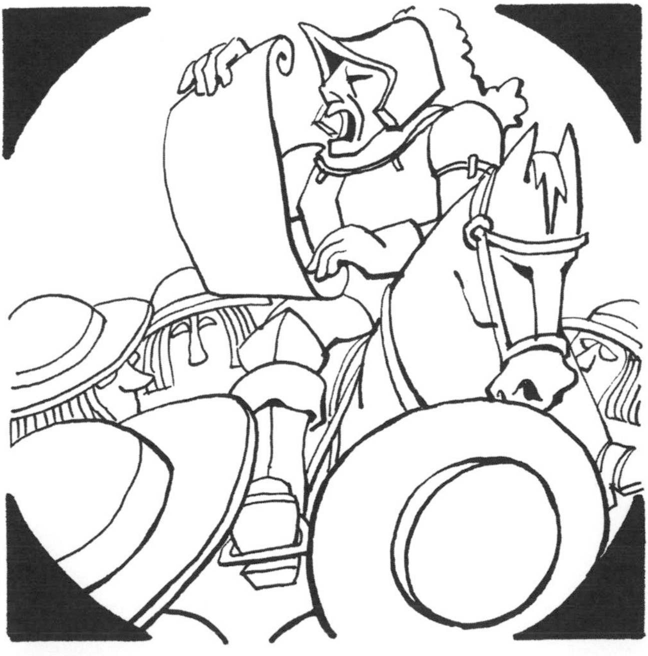

"BELOVED SUBJECTS, IN ORDER TO SPARE YOU THE HORRORS OF WAR, I SHALL SEND MY SOLDIERS TO TENDERLY SLIT YOUR THROATS."

THE PEOPLE DEEMED THIS DISPLAY OF LOVE OVERDONE.

THEY REVOLTED, AND A CONFUSING WAR FOLLOWED BETWEEN THREE PARTIES, EACH FIGHTING TWO OTHERS.

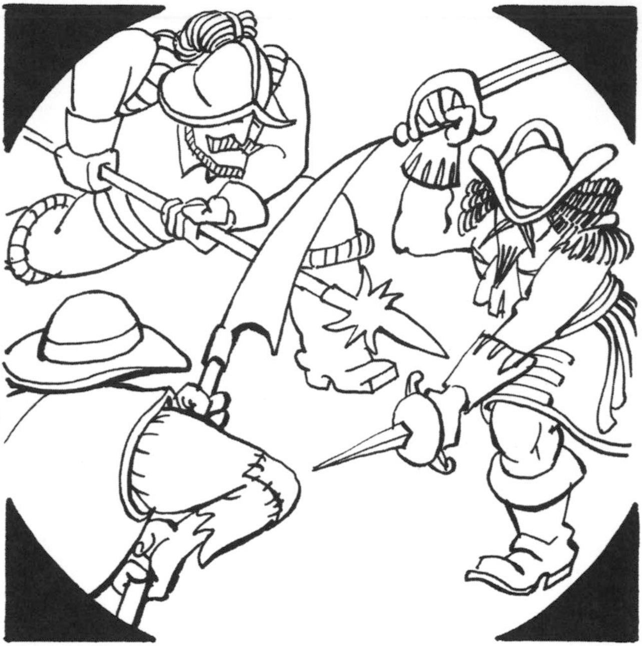

THE DEATH TOLL WAS CONSIDERABLE.

THE KING AND QUEEN THEMSELVES PERISHED.

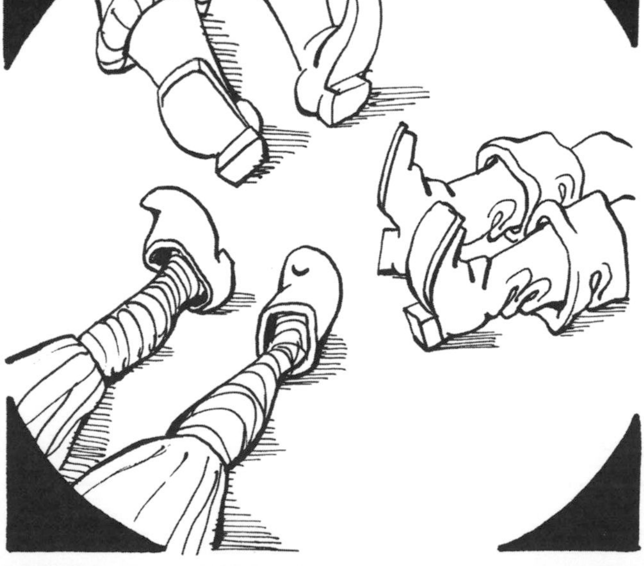

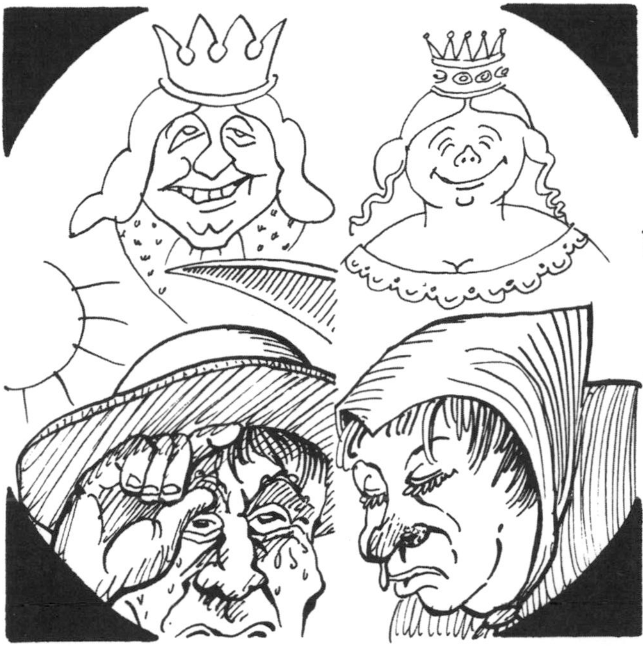

AFTER THE WAR, THE SURVIVORS RETURNED TO THEIR NORMAL LIVES— WALKING ON THEIR FEET, HARVESTING IN THE HOT SUN, WASHING WITH WATER— MOVED EVERY NOW AND THEN BY THE MEMORY OF THEIR FORMER RULERS.

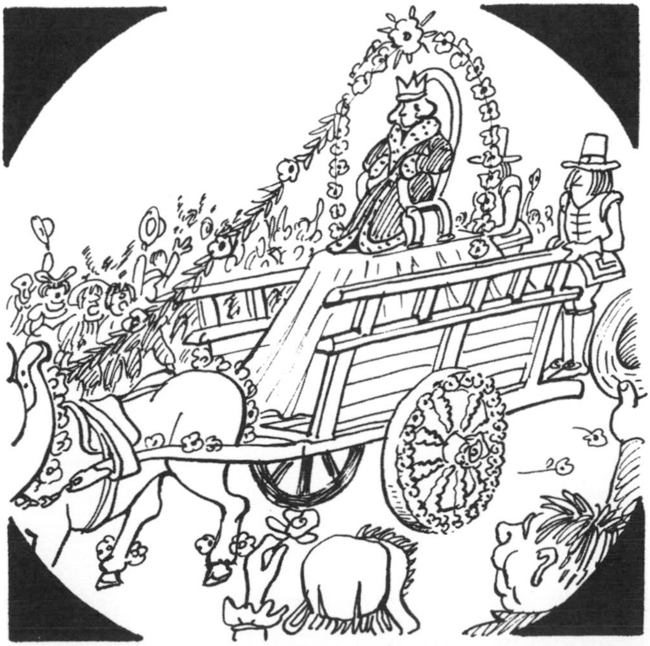

ON HOLIDAYS, THE PEOPLE WOULD PARADE PRINCE NICE, HEIR TO THE THRONE, ON A WAGON. THE REST OF THE TIME, THEY WERE CAREFUL TO KEEP HIM LOCKED AWAY IN THE PALACE.

WITH THE
PALACE DOORS
SHUT AND
BOLTED
BEHIND
HIM,
THE PRINCE
MADE HIS WAY
TOWARD
THE GRAND
STAIRCASE.

WHEN HE REACHED THE FIRST STEP, HE FROZE, AND THAT IS
WHERE THE PEOPLE FOUND HIM WHEN THEY CAME TO FETCH
HIM FOR THE NEXT HOLIDAY.   FOR SO NICE WAS PRINCE
NICE THAT HE DID NOT EVEN DARE STEP ON THE
STEPS.

THE SHOW ENDED WITH A COMICAL TALE,
"DUNDERHEAD IN THE ARMY."

IT WAS OVER. IT HAD BEEN BEAUTIFUL. ESPECIALLY THE COLORS.
THE SLEEPING CHILDREN WERE CARRIED OFF.
"I CHANGED THE SHEETS. THERE ARE FRESH SHEETS NOW, IF YOU'D LIKE"
OLD MOTHER LYFFE WHISPERED TO BACHDROPP.

AS I SAID, THIS ALL HAPPENED EIGHTY-SOME YEARS AGO
ON A WARM JUNE NIGHT. THE LILACS WERE BLOOMING.

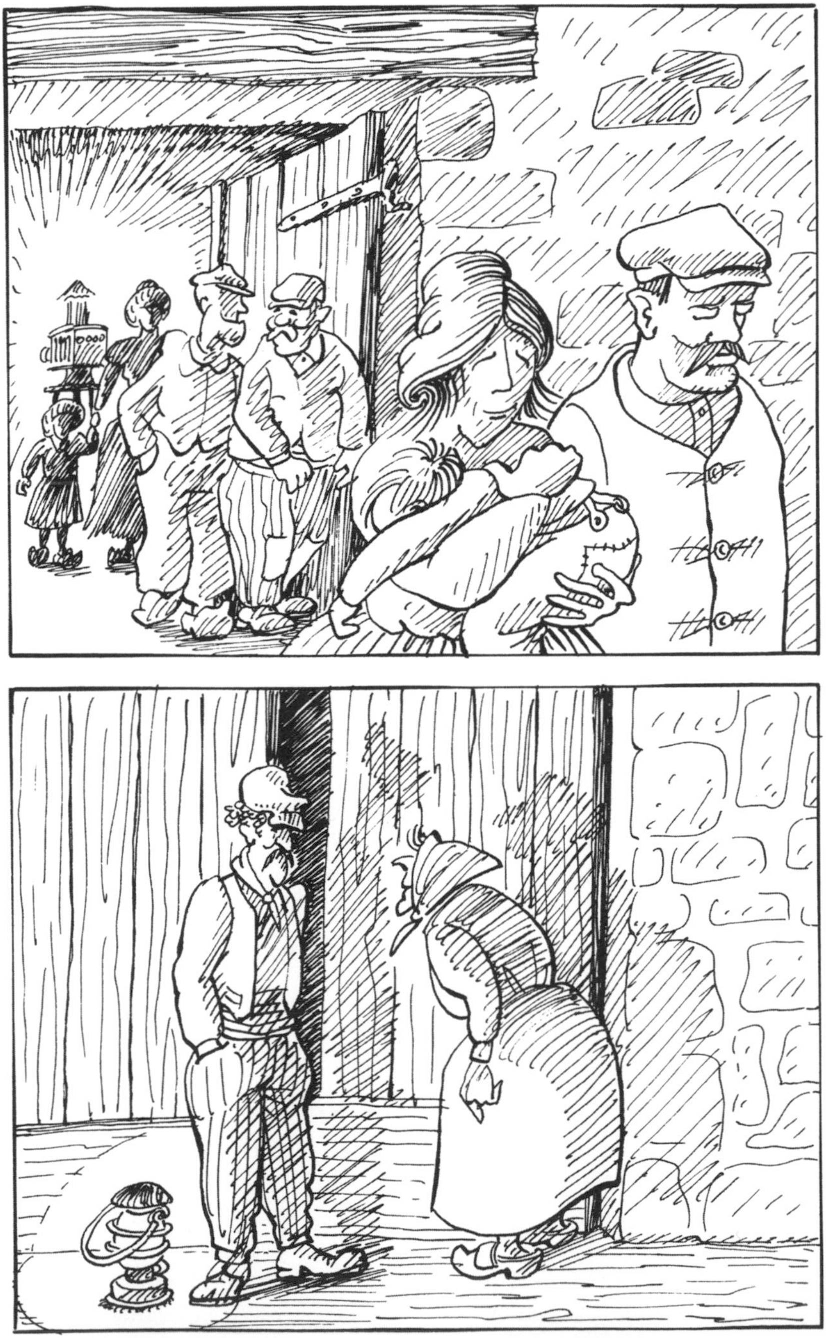

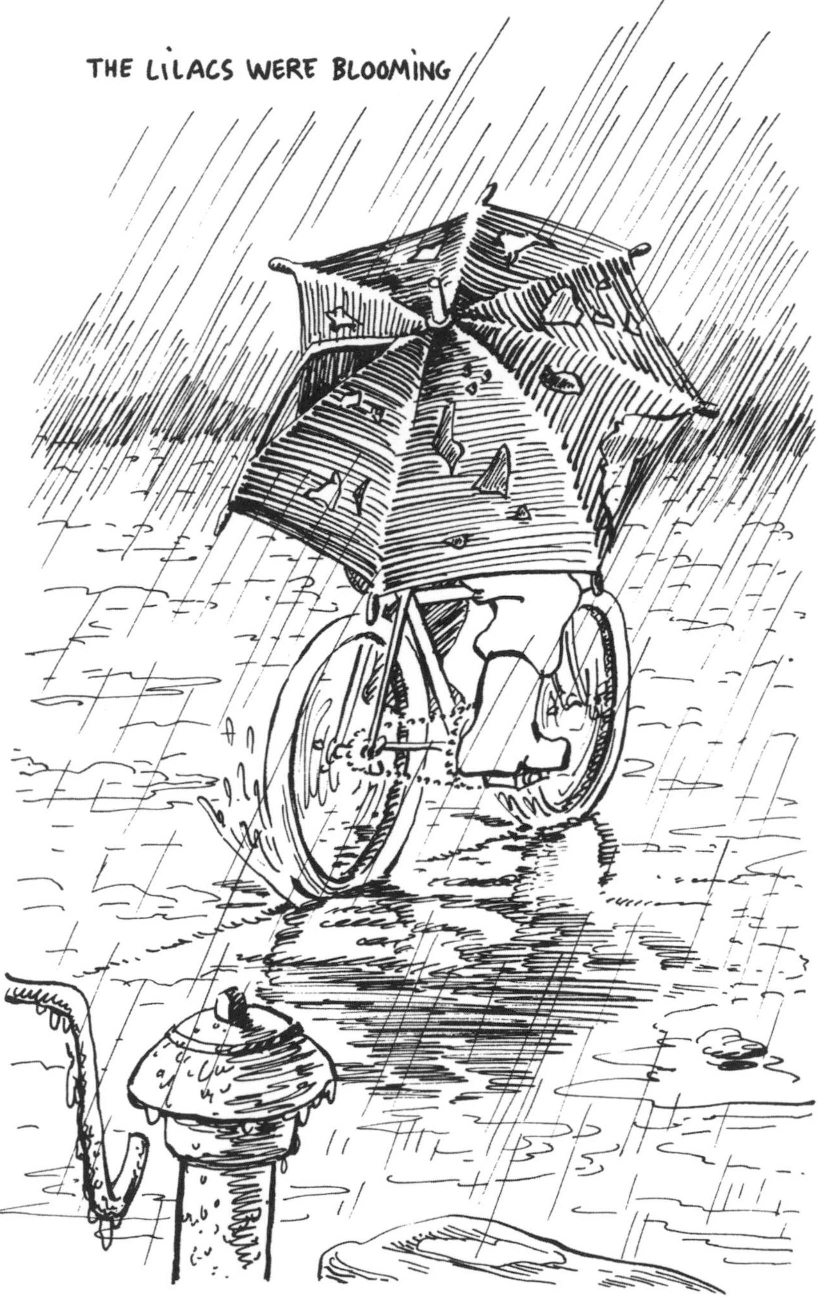
THE LILACS WERE BLOOMING

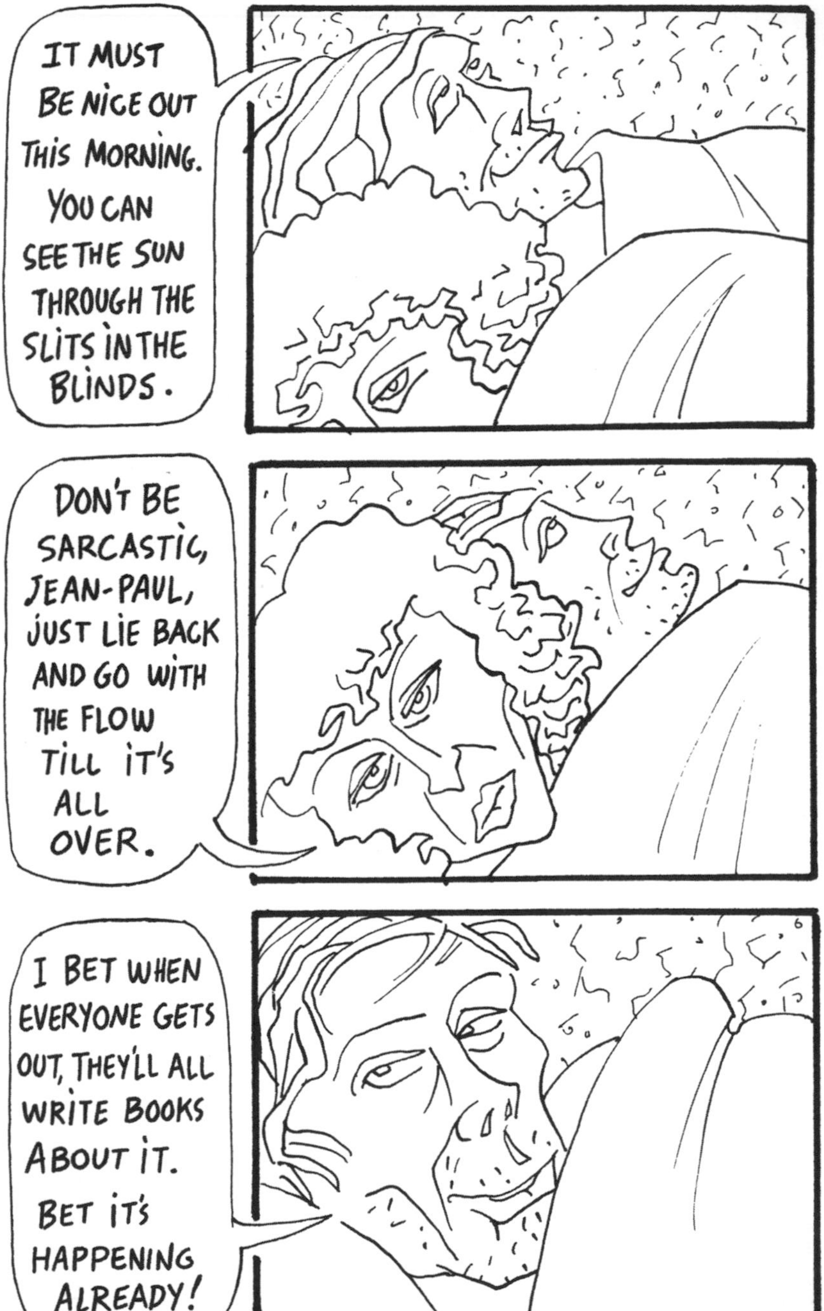
IT MUST BE NICE OUT THIS MORNING. YOU CAN SEE THE SUN THROUGH THE SLITS IN THE BLINDS.
DON'T BE SARCASTIC, JEAN-PAUL, JUST LIE BACK AND GO WITH THE FLOW TILL IT'S ALL OVER.
I BET WHEN EVERYONE GETS OUT, THEY'LL ALL WRITE BOOKS ABOUT IT. BET IT'S HAPPENING ALREADY!

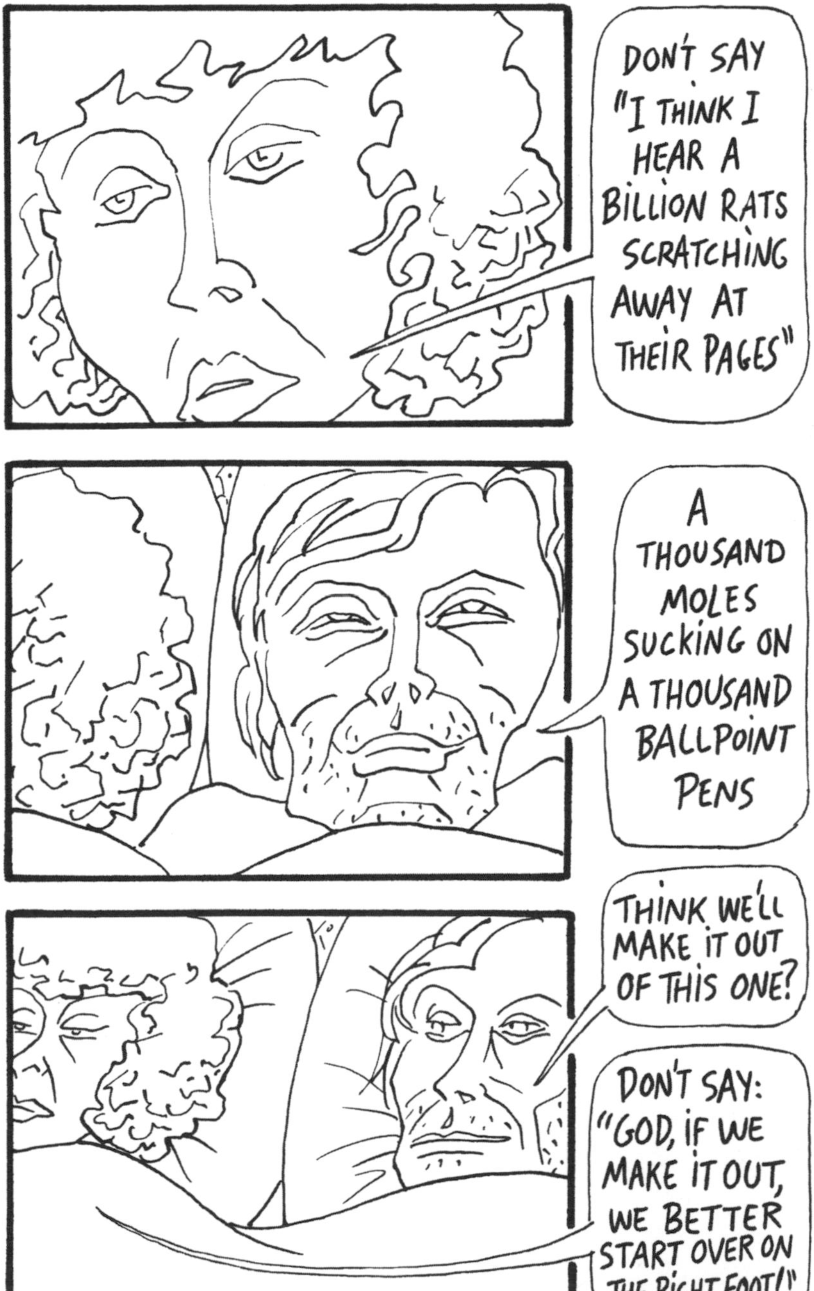
DON'T SAY "I THINK I HEAR A BILLION RATS SCRATCHING AWAY AT THEIR PAGES"
A THOUSAND MOLES SUCKING ON A THOUSAND BALLPOINT PENS
THINK WE'LL MAKE IT OUT OF THIS ONE?
DON'T SAY: "GOD, IF WE MAKE IT OUT, WE BETTER START OVER ON THE RIGHT FOOT!"

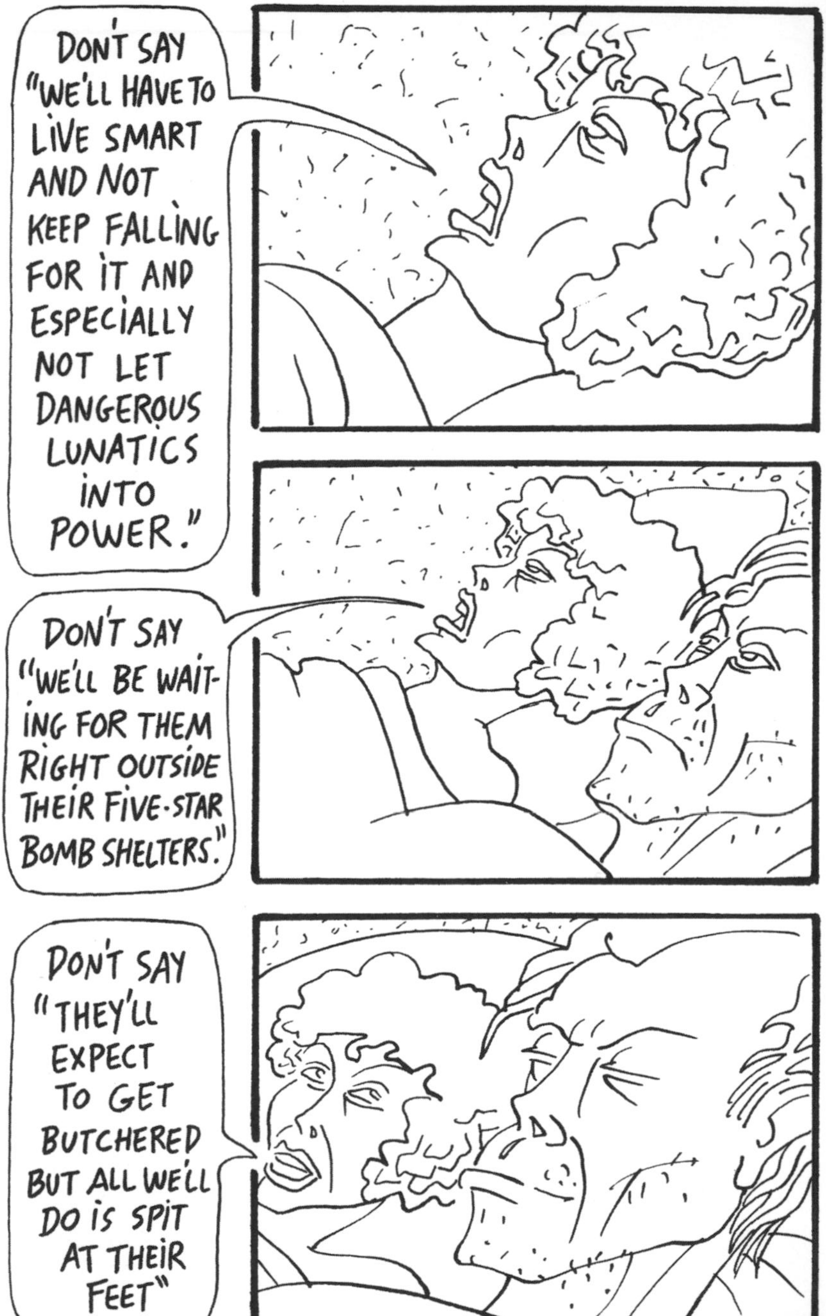
DON'T SAY "WE'LL HAVE TO LIVE SMART AND NOT KEEP FALLING FOR IT AND ESPECIALLY NOT LET DANGEROUS LUNATICS INTO POWER."
DON'T SAY "WE'LL BE WAITING FOR THEM RIGHT OUTSIDE THEIR FIVE-STAR BOMB SHELTERS."
DON'T SAY "THEY'LL EXPECT TO GET BUTCHERED BUT ALL WE'LL DO IS SPIT AT THEIR FEET"

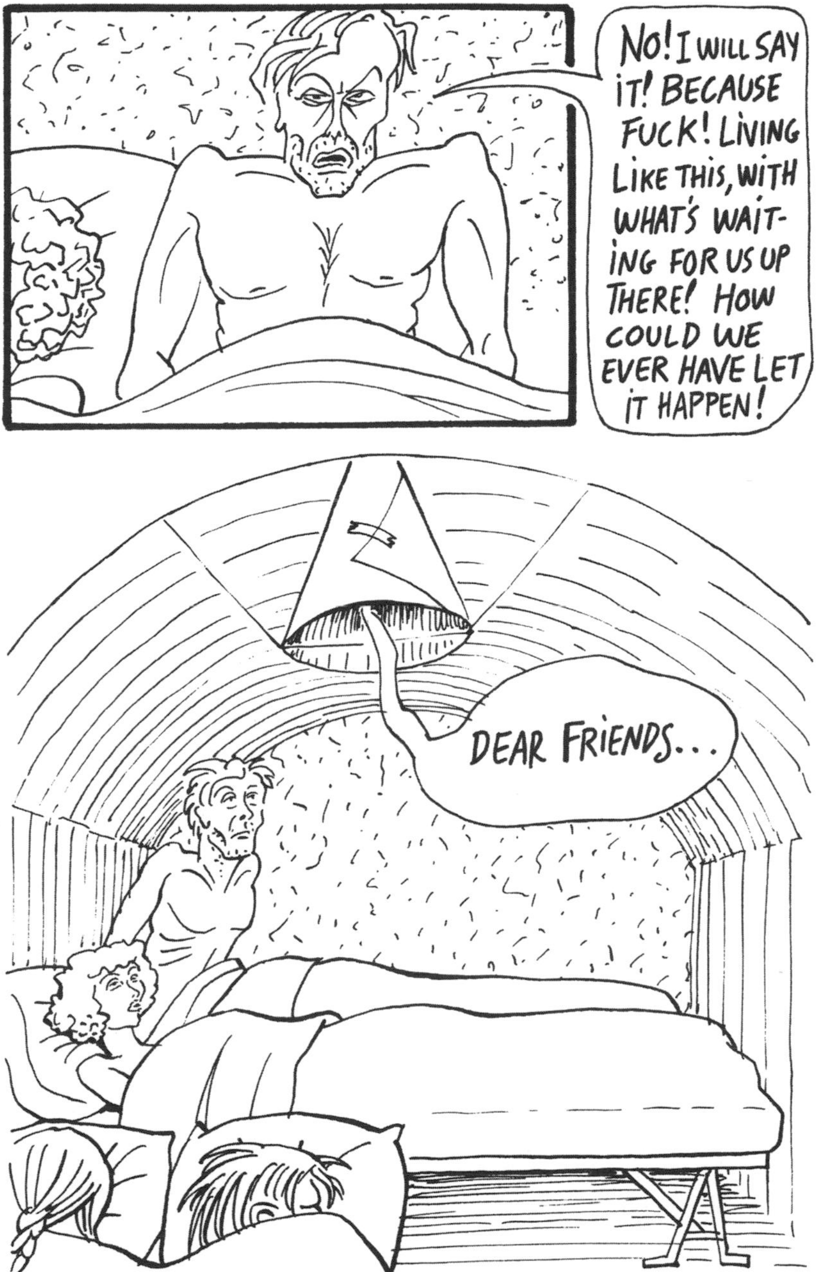
NO! I WILL SAY IT! BECAUSE FUCK! LIVING LIKE THIS, WITH WHAT'S WAIT-ING FOR US UP THERE! HOW COULD WE EVER HAVE LET IT HAPPEN!
DEAR FRIENDS...

. . .
TODAY MY LETTER WILL TAKE A CONFESSIONAL
TURN. BUT I'M NOT THE ONE SPEAKING.
THIS CONFESSION WAS GATHERED FROM
SOMEONE ELSE. LISTEN...

"I PAINT REALLY FAST.
SMARTASS FRIENDS MIGHT CALL ME 'POLAROID,'
BUT I DON'T HAVE ANY FRIENDS LIKE THAT.
WHAT INTERESTS ME IS BRINGING AN IMPRESSION
TO THE CANVAS, A GLIMMER OF A
LANDSCAPE, A CLUE, A PROMISING BEGINNING,
AND THEN SPENDING ALL DAY AND ALL NIGHT WITH ONE
EYE ON THE CANVAS AND THE OTHER ON A BOOK.
THEN, BACK TO SQUARE ONE!
THE BOOK AND THE CANVAS."

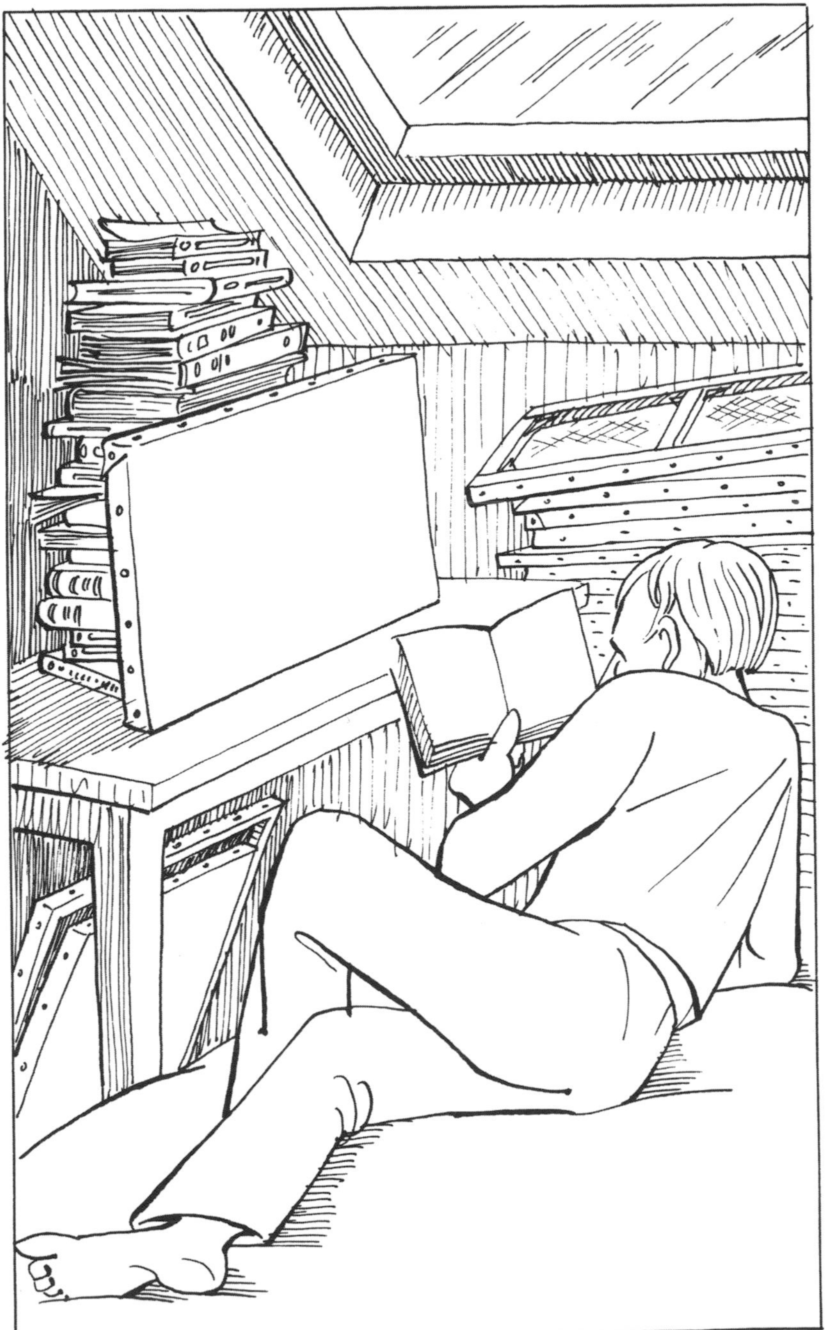

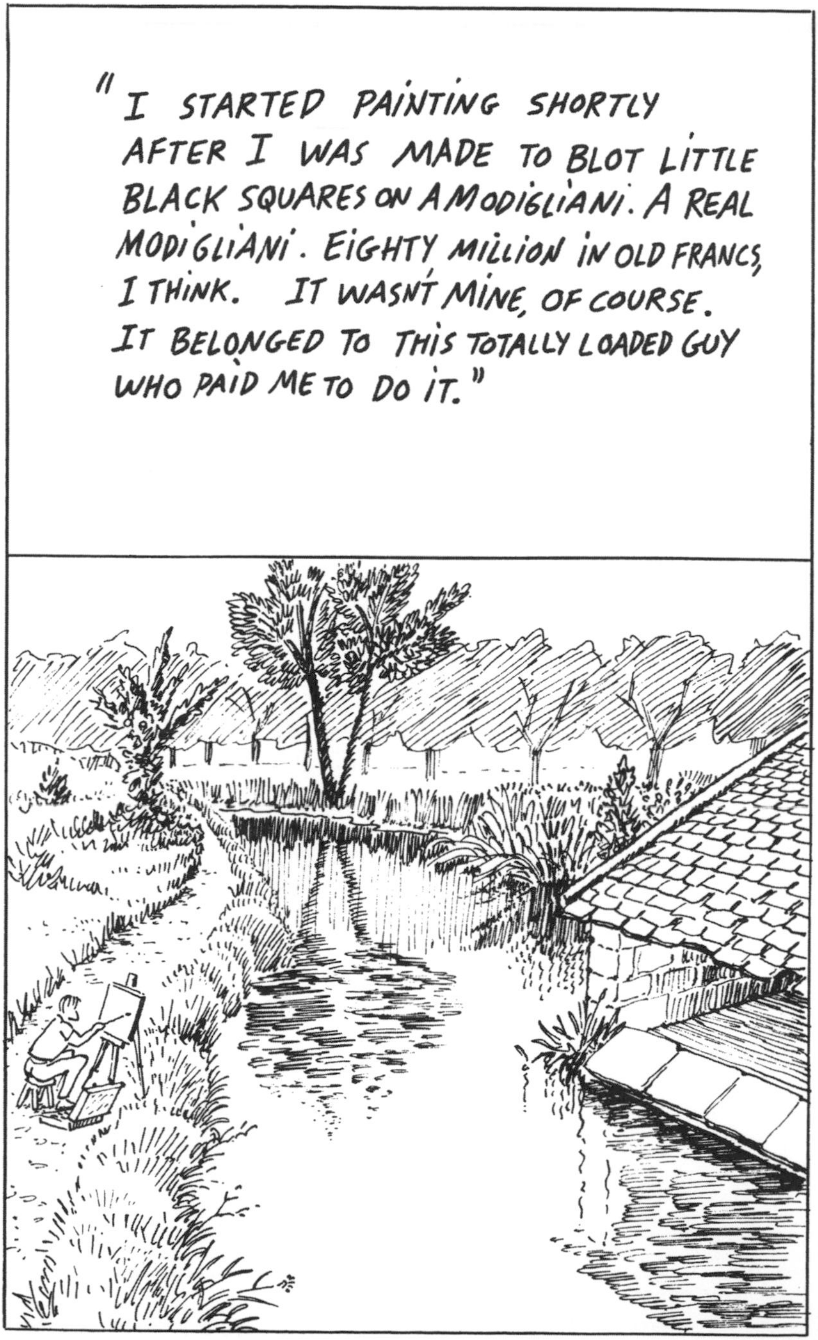
"I STARTED PAINTING SHORTLY AFTER I WAS MADE TO BLOT LITTLE BLACK SQUARES ON A MODIGLIANI. A REAL MODIGLIANI. EIGHTY MILLION IN OLD FRANCS, I THINK. IT WASN'T MINE, OF COURSE. IT BELONGED TO THIS TOTALLY LOADED GUY WHO PAID ME TO DO IT."

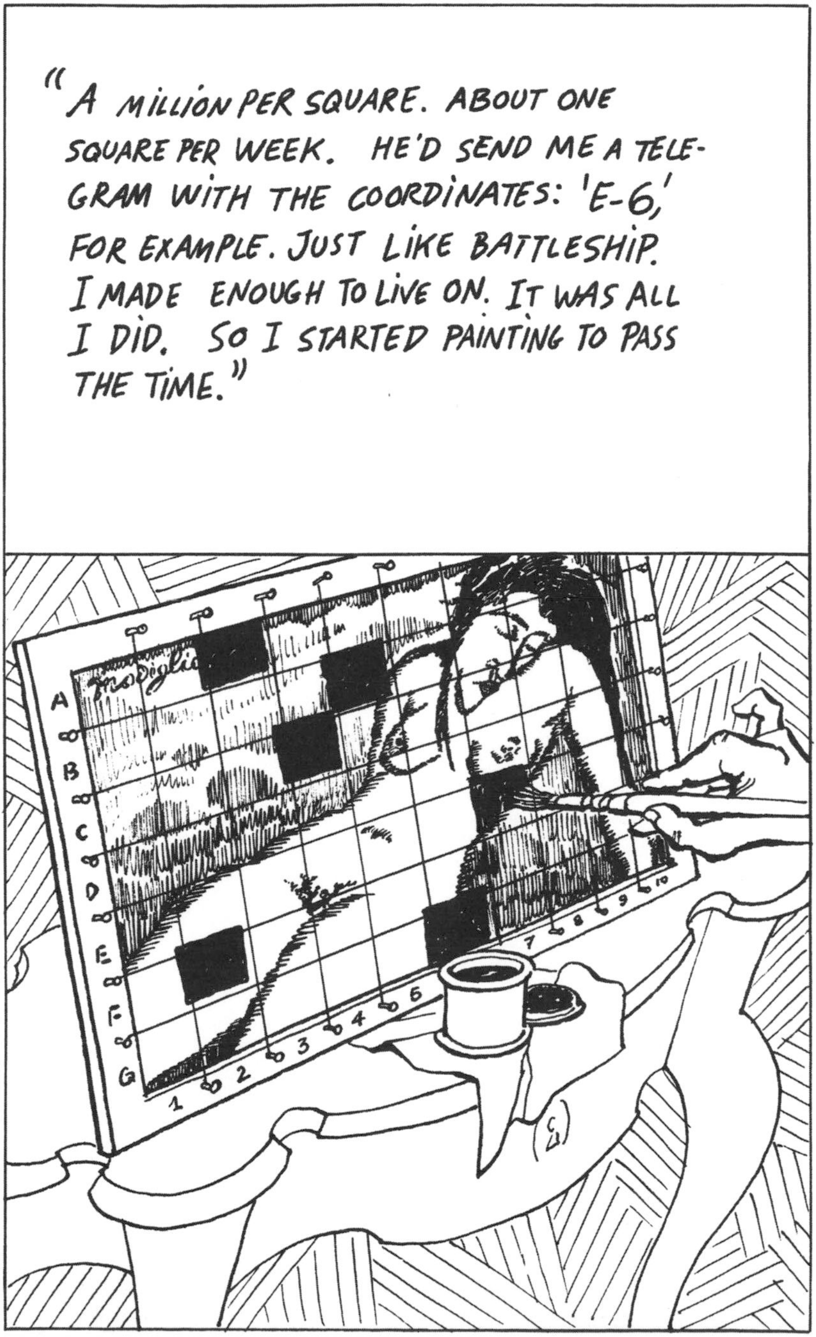
"A MILLION PER SQUARE. ABOUT ONE SQUARE PER WEEK. HE'D SEND ME A TELEGRAM WITH THE COORDINATES: 'E-6,' FOR EXAMPLE. JUST LIKE BATTLESHIP. I MADE ENOUGH TO LIVE ON. IT WAS ALL I DID. SO I STARTED PAINTING TO PASS THE TIME."
A
B
C
D
E
F
G
1
2
3
4
5
6
7
8
9
10

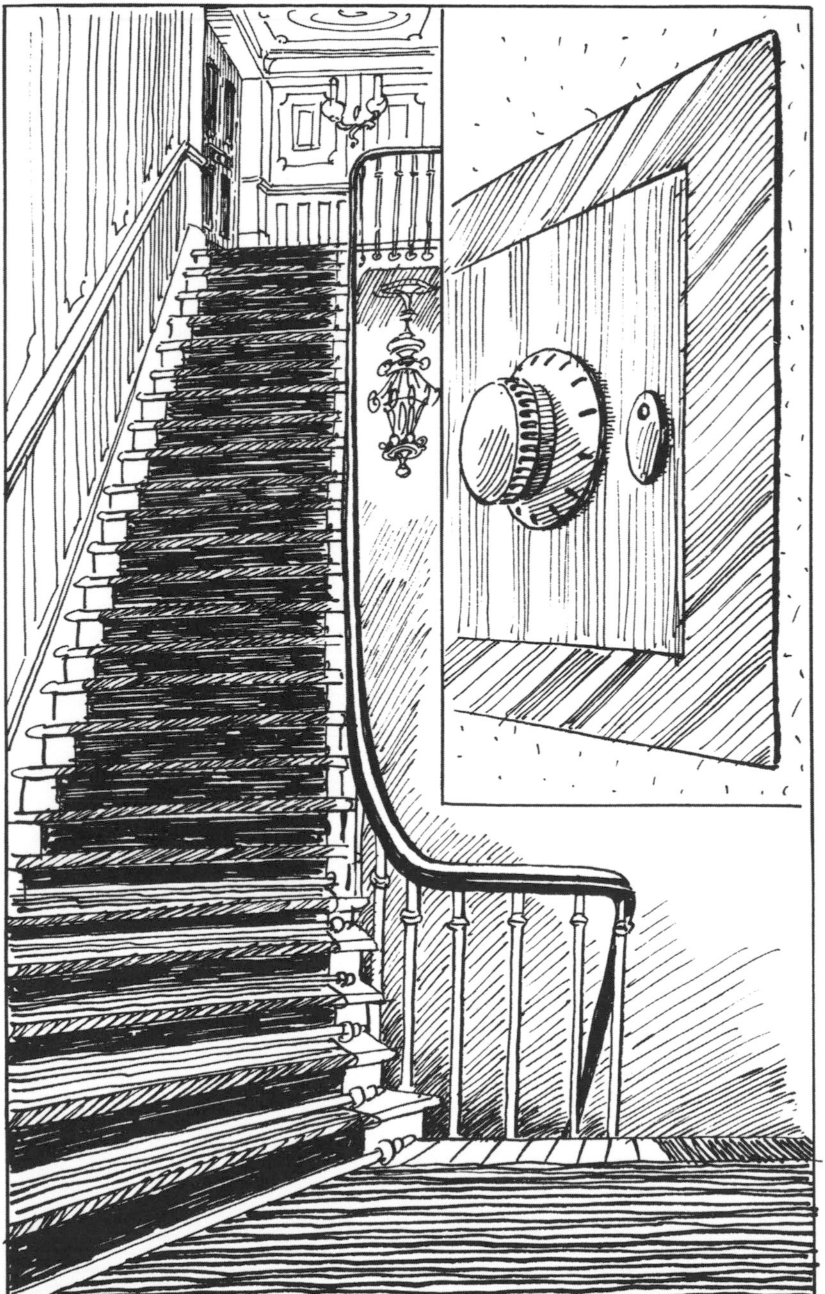

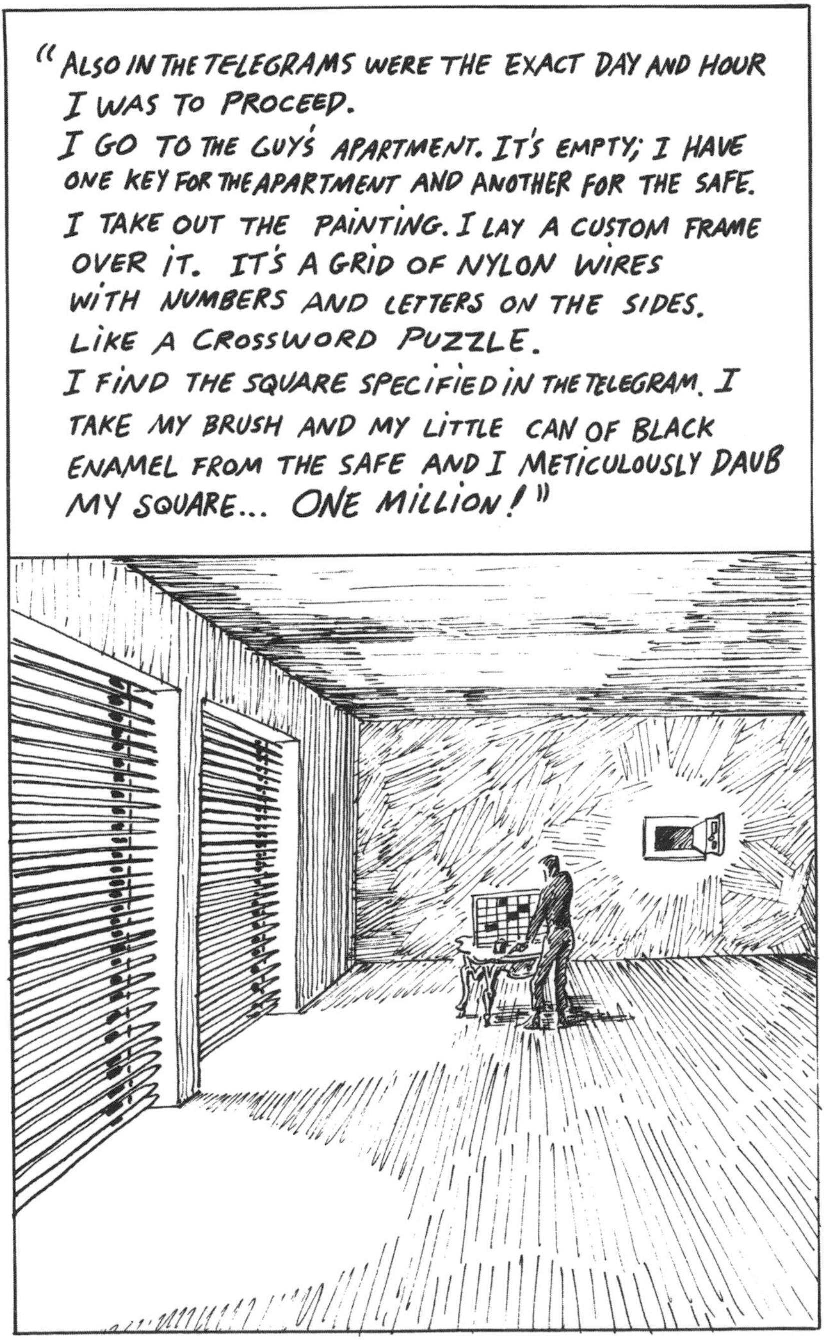
"ALSO IN THE TELEGRAMS WERE THE EXACT DAY AND HOUR I WAS TO PROCEED.
I GO TO THE GUY'S APARTMENT. IT'S EMPTY; I HAVE ONE KEY FOR THE APARTMENT AND ANOTHER FOR THE SAFE.
I TAKE OUT THE PAINTING. I LAY A CUSTOM FRAME OVER IT. IT'S A GRID OF NYLON WIRES WITH NUMBERS AND LETTERS ON THE SIDES. LIKE A CROSSWORD PUZZLE.
I FIND THE SQUARE SPECIFIED IN THE TELEGRAM. I TAKE MY BRUSH AND MY LITTLE CAN OF BLACK ENAMEL FROM THE SAFE AND I METICULOUSLY DAUB MY SQUARE... ONE MILLION!"

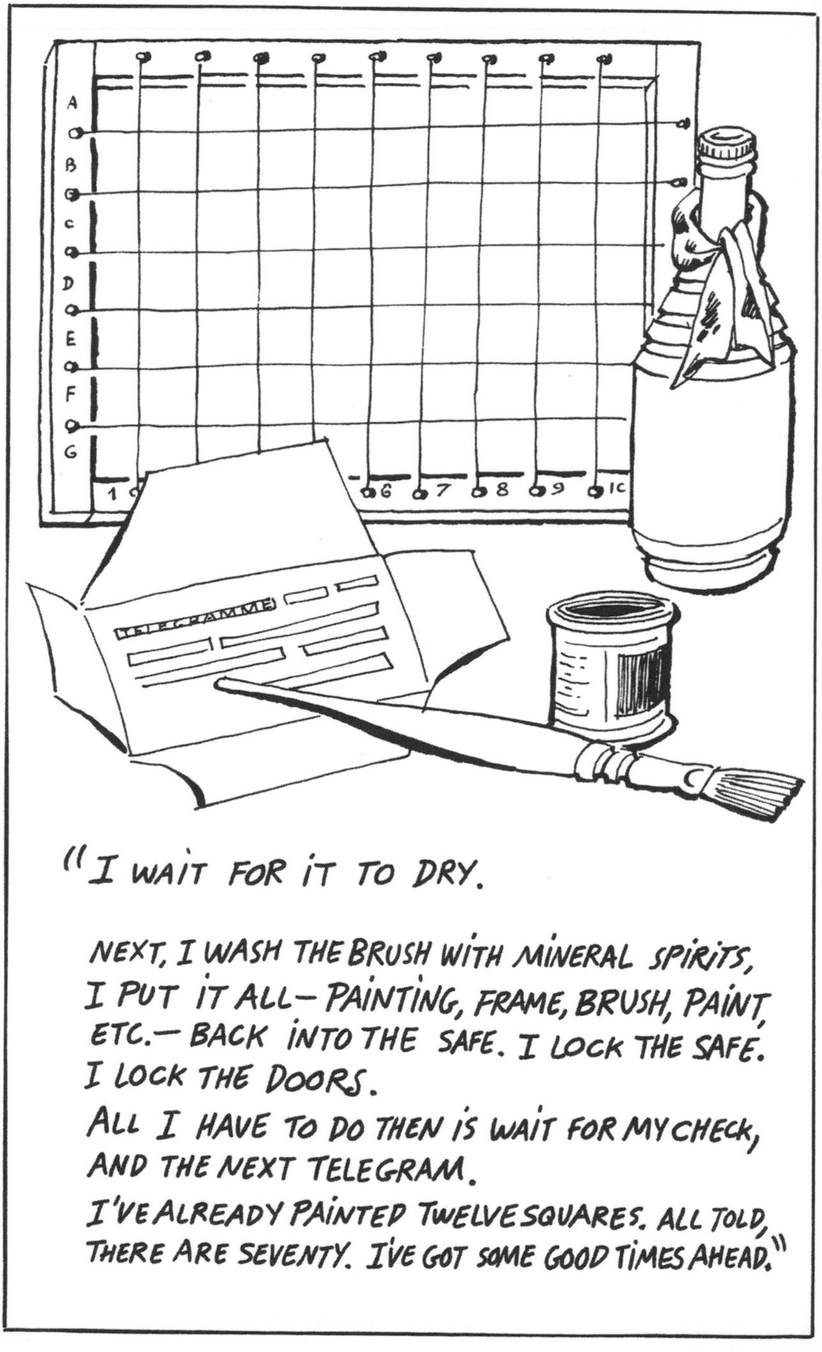
TELEGRAMME
"I WAIT FOR IT TO DRY.
NEXT, I WASH THE BRUSH WITH MINERAL SPIRITS, I PUT IT ALL— PAINTING, FRAME, BRUSH, PAINT, ETC.— BACK INTO THE SAFE. I LOCK THE SAFE. I LOCK THE DOORS.
ALL I HAVE TO DO THEN IS WAIT FOR MY CHECK, AND THE NEXT TELEGRAM.
I'VE ALREADY PAINTED TWELVE SQUARES. ALL TOLD, THERE ARE SEVENTY. I'VE GOT SOME GOOD TIMES AHEAD."

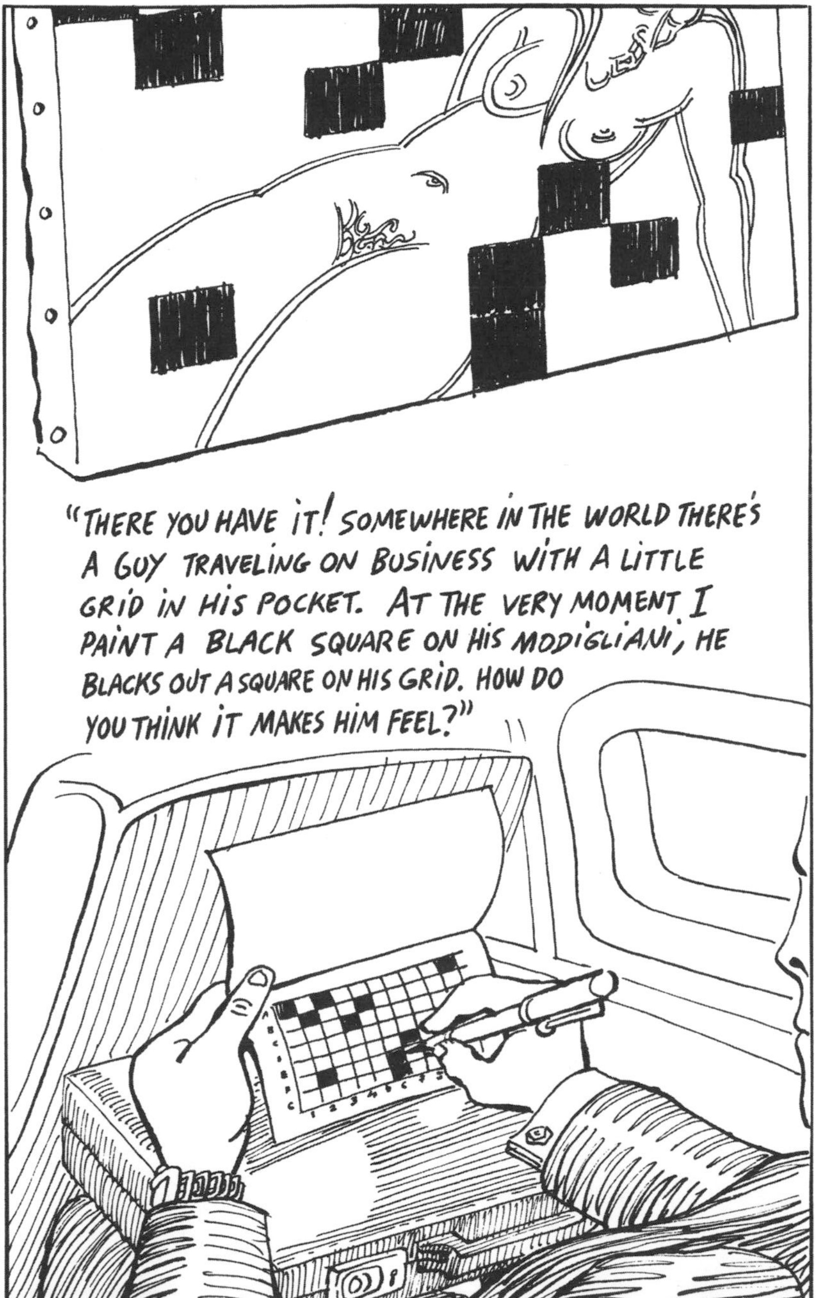
"THERE YOU HAVE IT! SOMEWHERE IN THE WORLD THERE'S A GUY TRAVELING ON BUSINESS WITH A LITTLE GRID IN HIS POCKET. AT THE VERY MOMENT I PAINT A BLACK SQUARE ON HIS MODIGLIANI, HE BLACKS OUT A SQUARE ON HIS GRID. HOW DO YOU THINK IT MAKES HIM FEEL?"

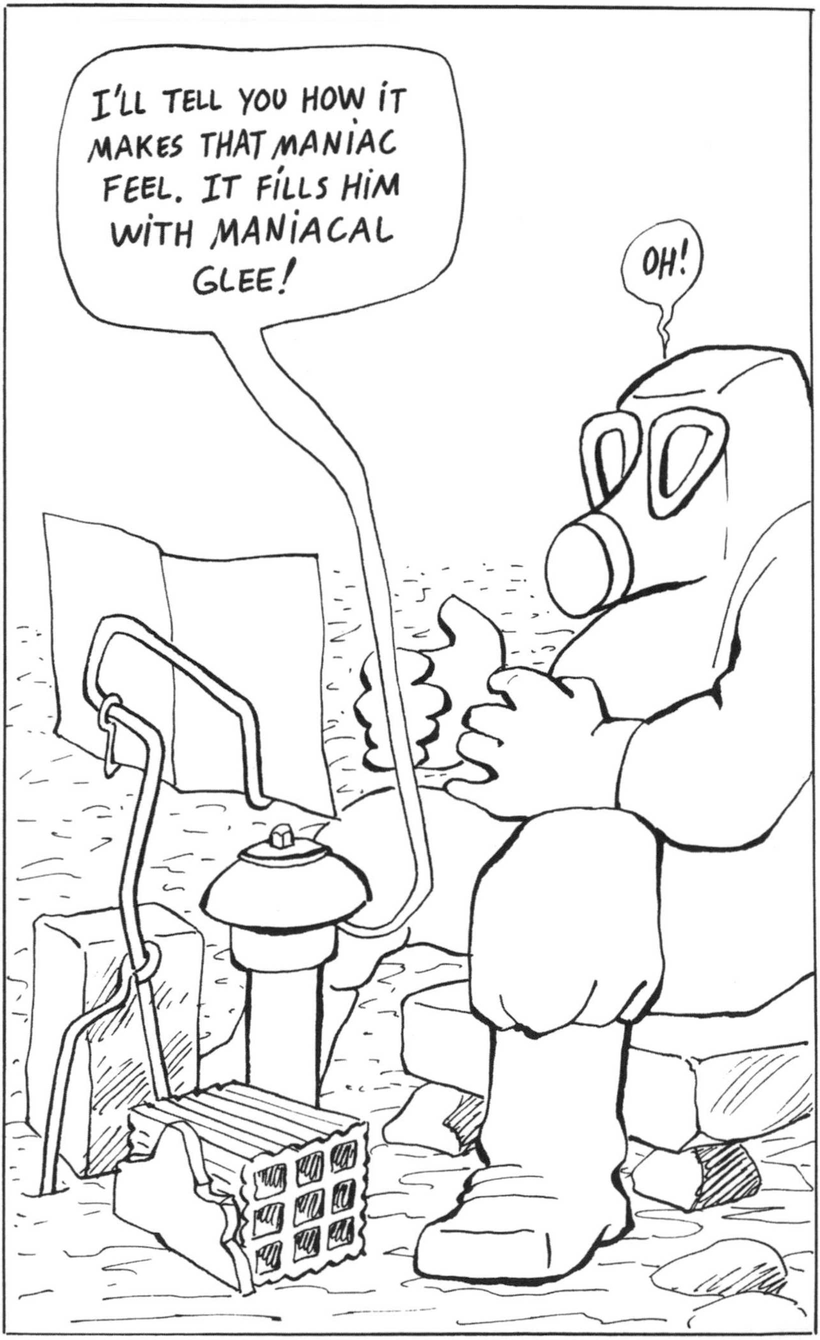
I'LL TELL YOU HOW IT MAKES THAT MANIAC FEEL. IT FILLS HIM WITH MANIACAL GLEE!
OH!

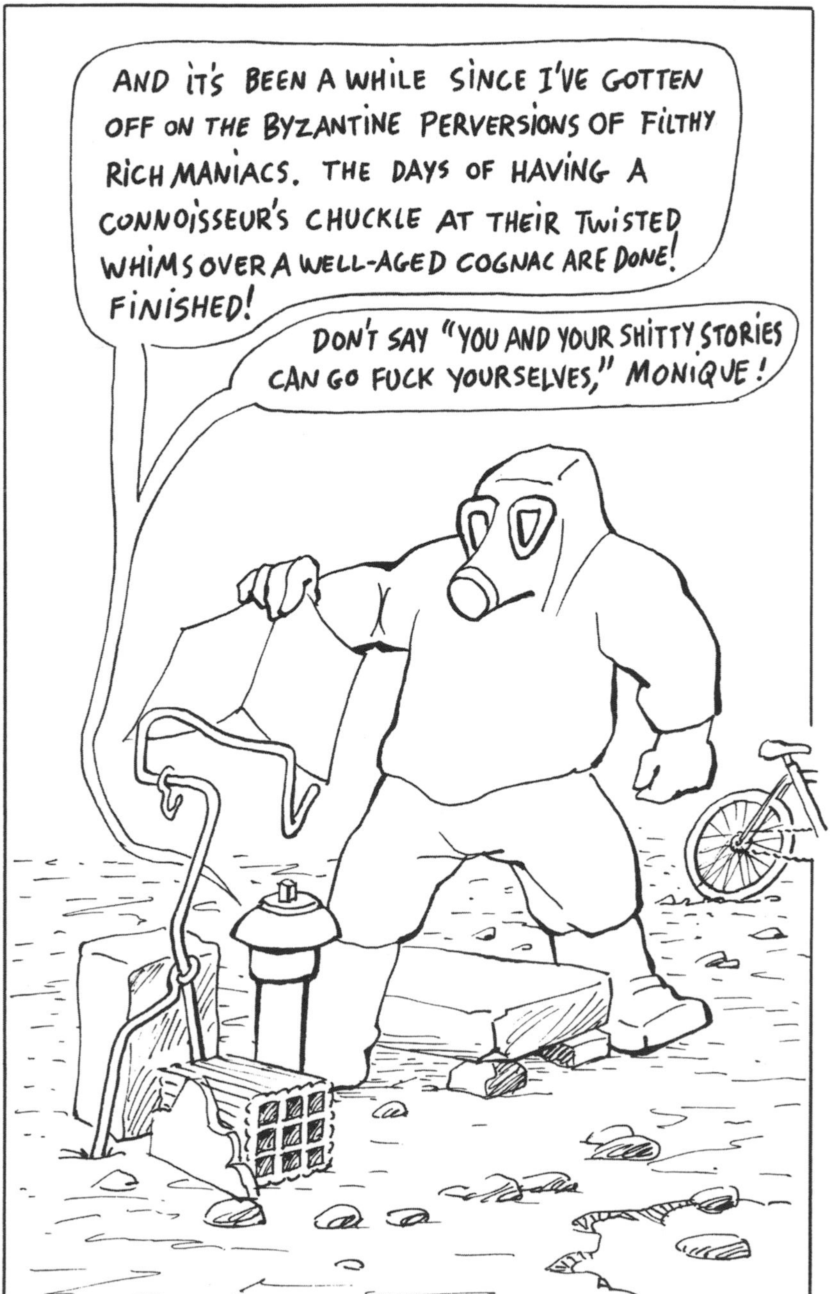
AND IT'S BEEN A WHILE SINCE I'VE GOTTEN OFF ON THE BYZANTINE PERVERSIONS OF FILTHY RICH MANIACS. THE DAYS OF HAVING A CONNOISSEUR'S CHUCKLE AT THEIR TWISTED WHIMS OVER A WELL-AGED COGNAC ARE DONE! FINISHED!
DON'T SAY "YOU AND YOUR SHITTY STORIES CAN GO FUCK YOURSELVES," MONIQUE!

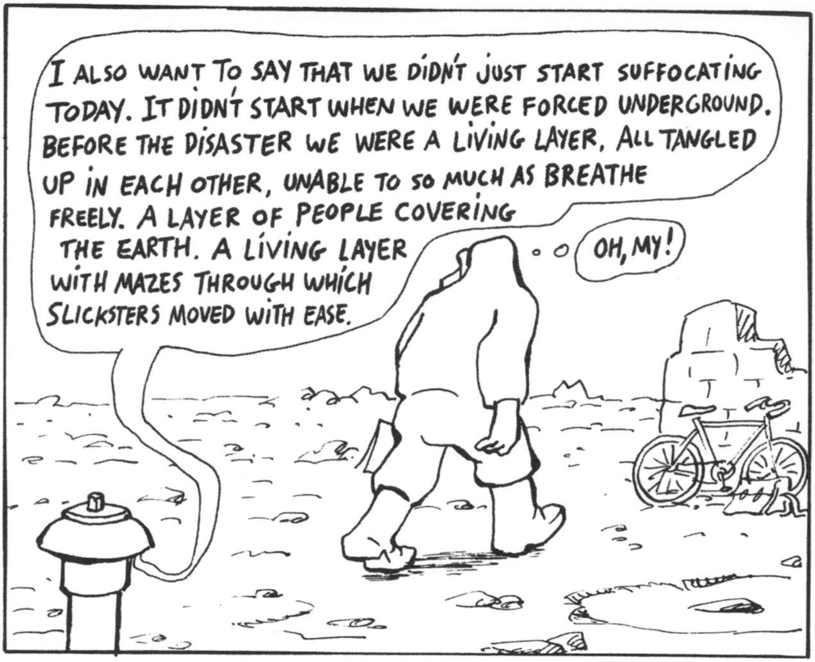
I ALSO WANT TO SAY THAT WE DIDN'T JUST START SUFFOCATING TODAY. IT DIDN'T START WHEN WE WERE FORCED UNDERGROUND. BEFORE THE DISASTER WE WERE A LIVING LAYER, ALL TANGLED UP IN EACH OTHER, UNABLE TO SO MUCH AS BREATHE FREELY. A LAYER OF PEOPLE COVERING THE EARTH. A LIVING LAYER WITH MAZES THROUGH WHICH SLICKSTERS MOVED WITH EASE.
OH, MY!

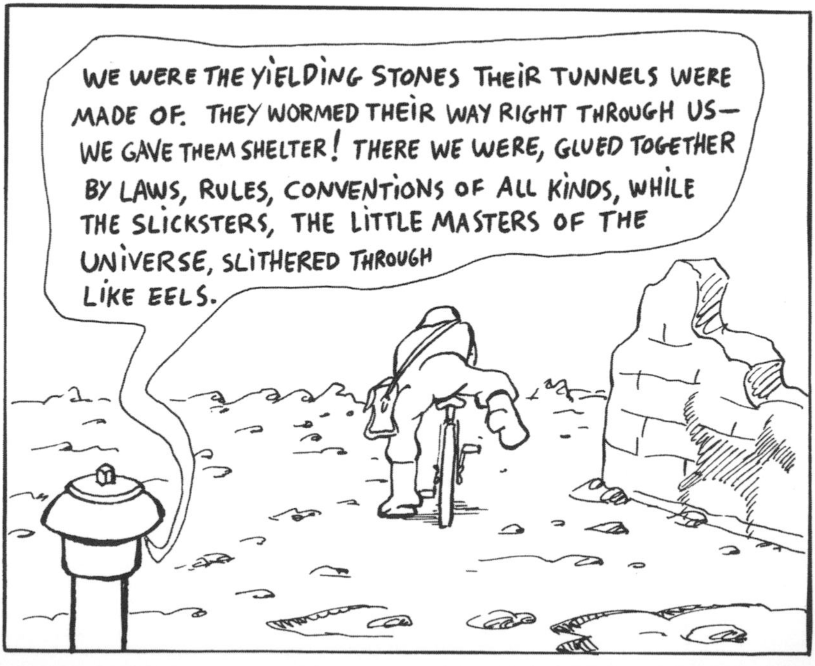
WE WERE THE YIELDING STONES THEIR TUNNELS WERE MADE OF. THEY WORMED THEIR WAY RIGHT THROUGH US— WE GAVE THEM SHELTER! THERE WE WERE, GLUED TOGETHER BY LAWS, RULES, CONVENTIONS OF ALL KINDS, WHILE THE SLICKSTERS, THE LITTLE MASTERS OF THE UNIVERSE, SLITHERED THROUGH LIKE EELS.

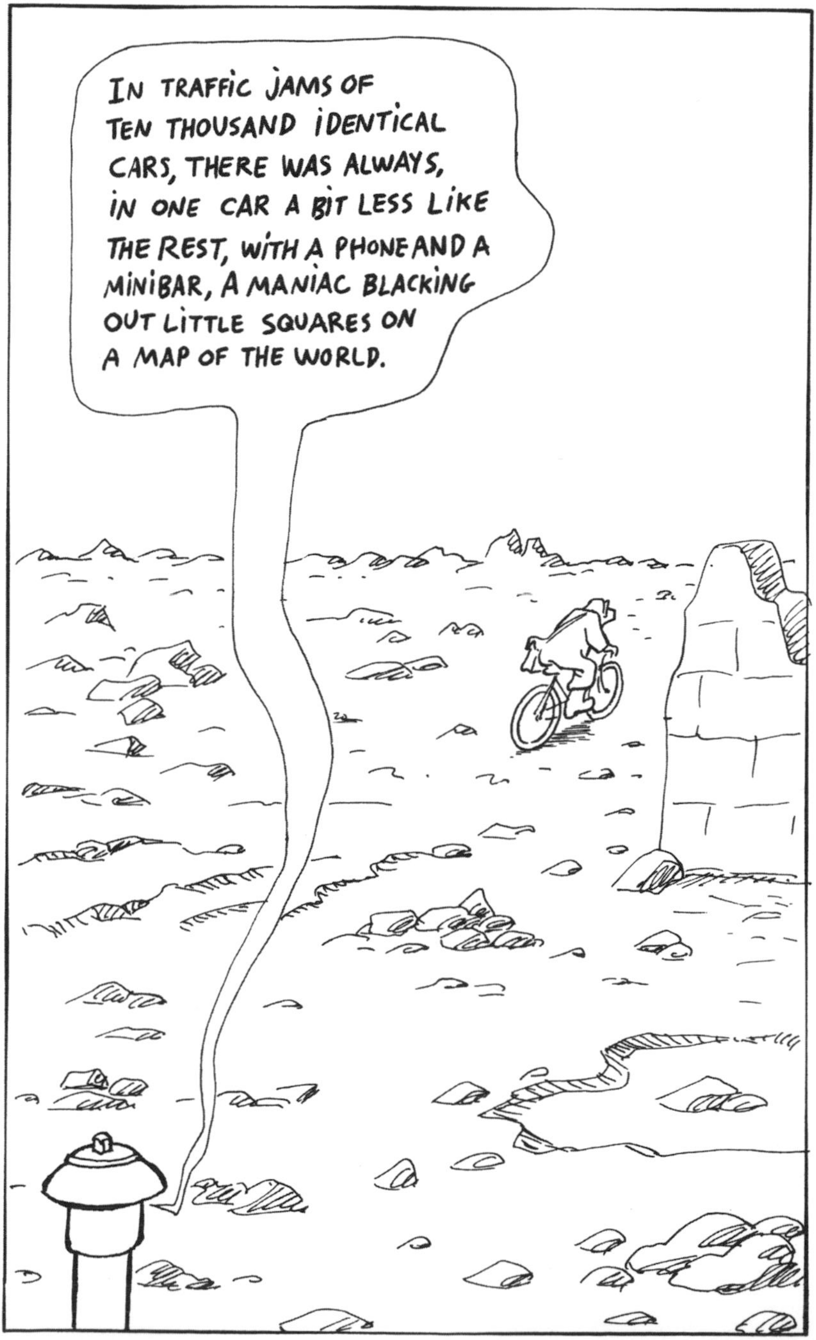
IN TRAFFIC JAMS OF TEN THOUSAND IDENTICAL CARS, THERE WAS ALWAYS, IN ONE CAR A BIT LESS LIKE THE REST, WITH A PHONE AND A MINIBAR, A MANIAC BLACKING OUT LITTLE SQUARES ON A MAP OF THE WORLD.

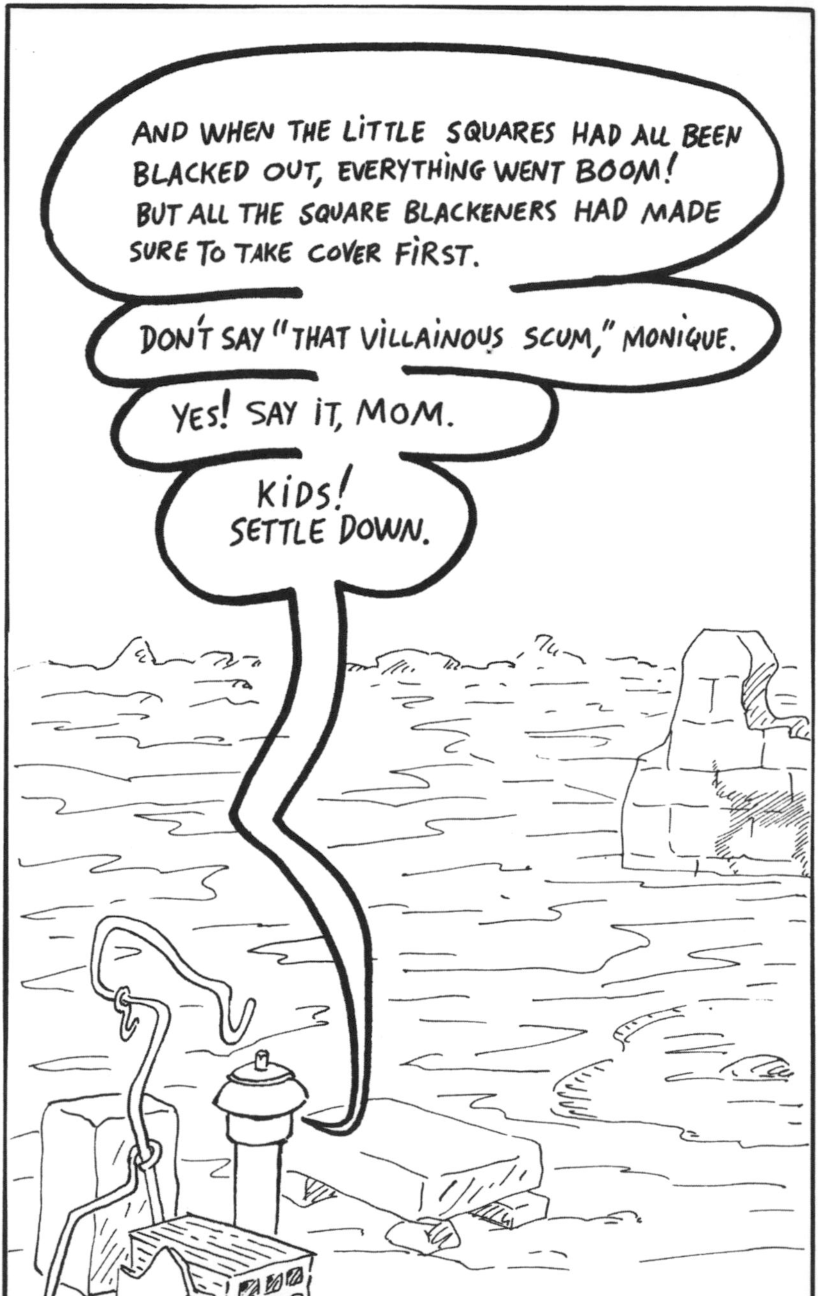
AND WHEN THE LITTLE SQUARES HAD ALL BEEN BLACKED OUT, EVERYTHING WENT BOOM! BUT ALL THE SQUARE BLACKENERS HAD MADE SURE TO TAKE COVER FIRST.
DON'T SAY "THAT VILLAINOUS SCUM," MONIQUE.
YES! SAY IT, MOM.
KIDS! SETTLE DOWN.

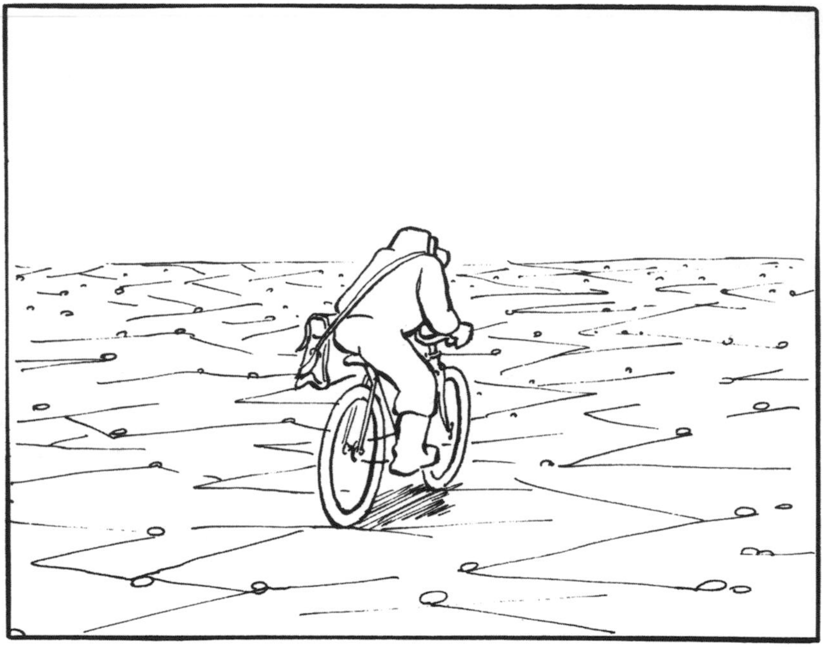

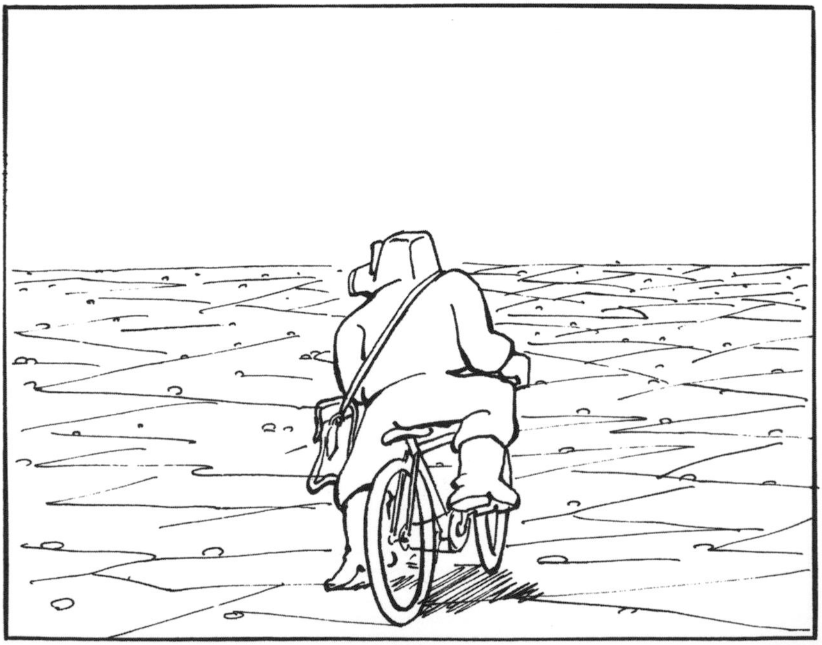

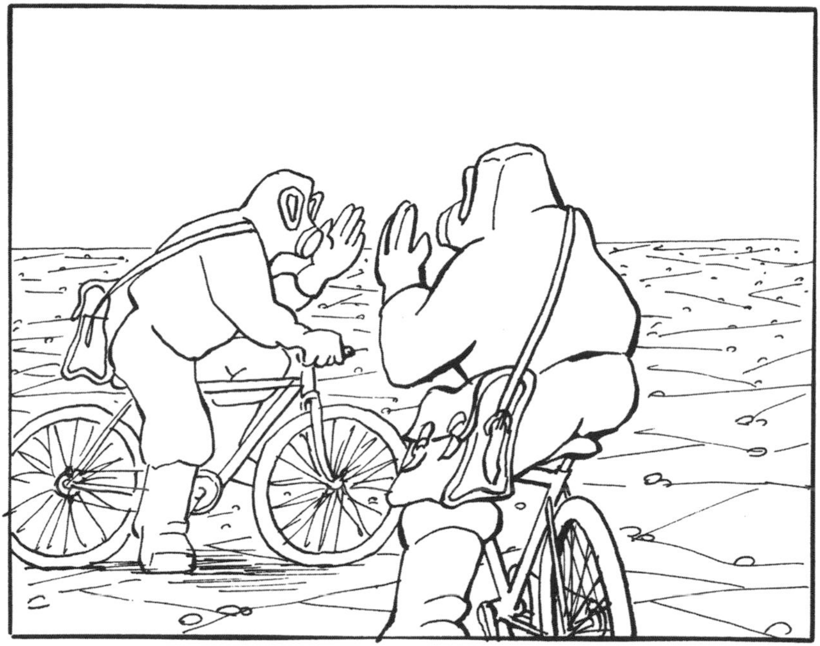

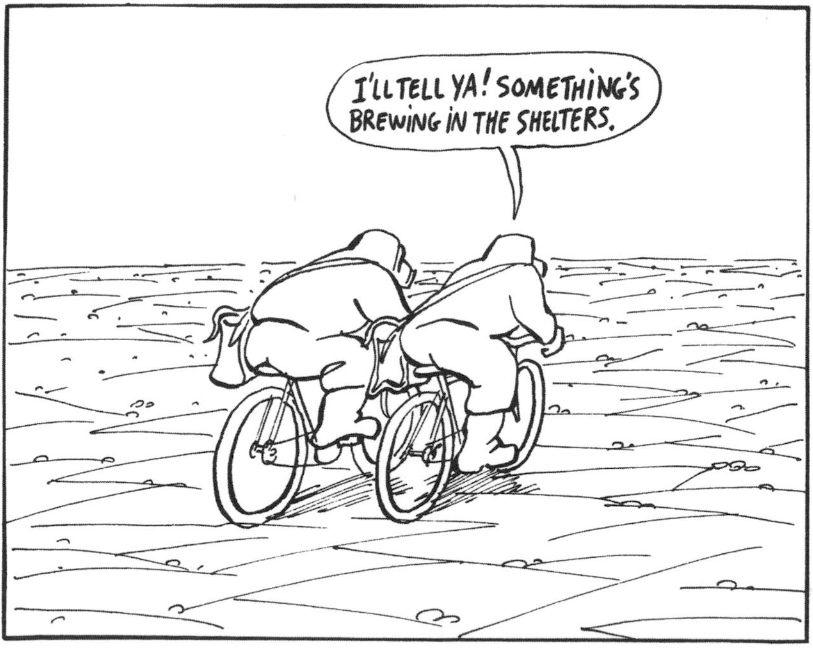
I'LL TELL YA! SOMETHING'S BREWING IN THE SHELTERS.

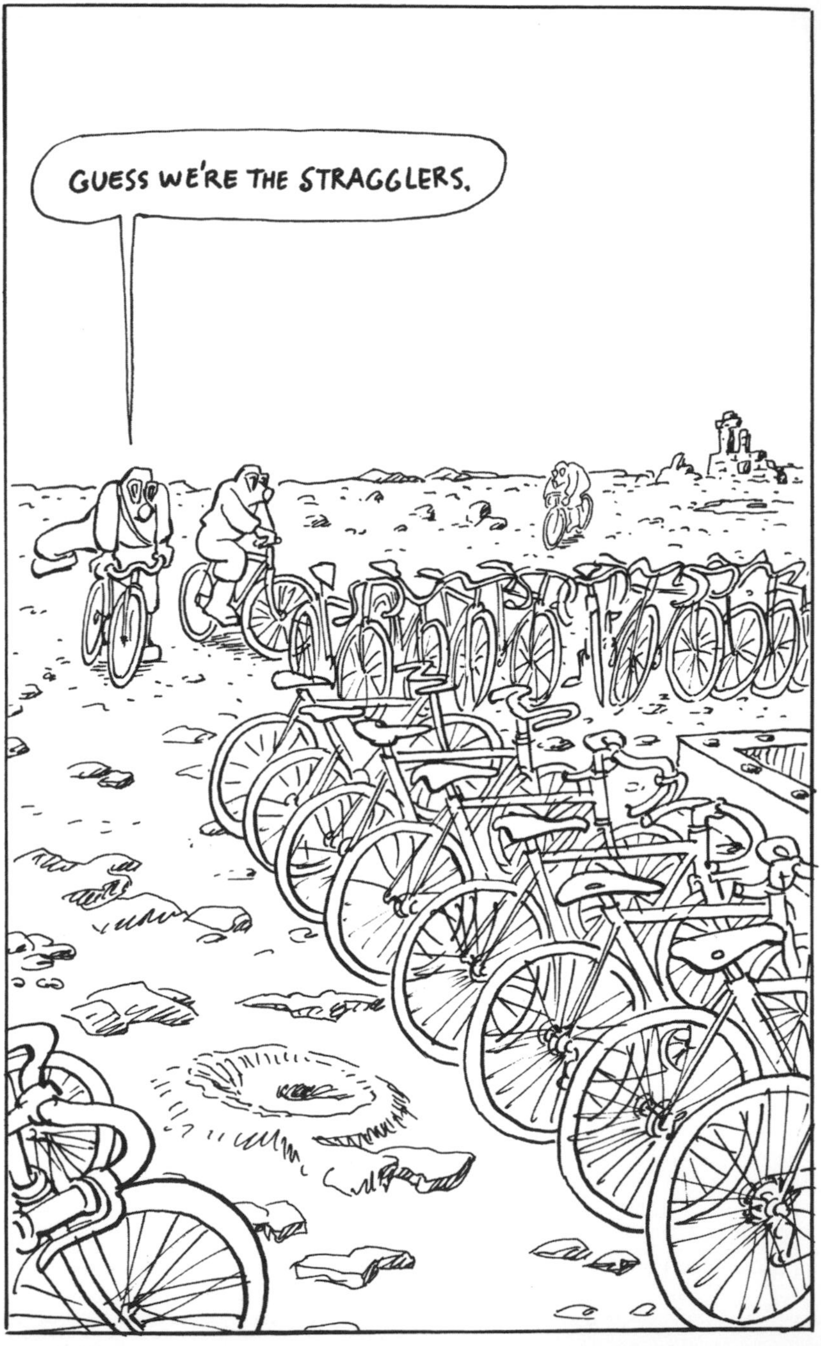
GUESS WE'RE THE STRAGGLERS.

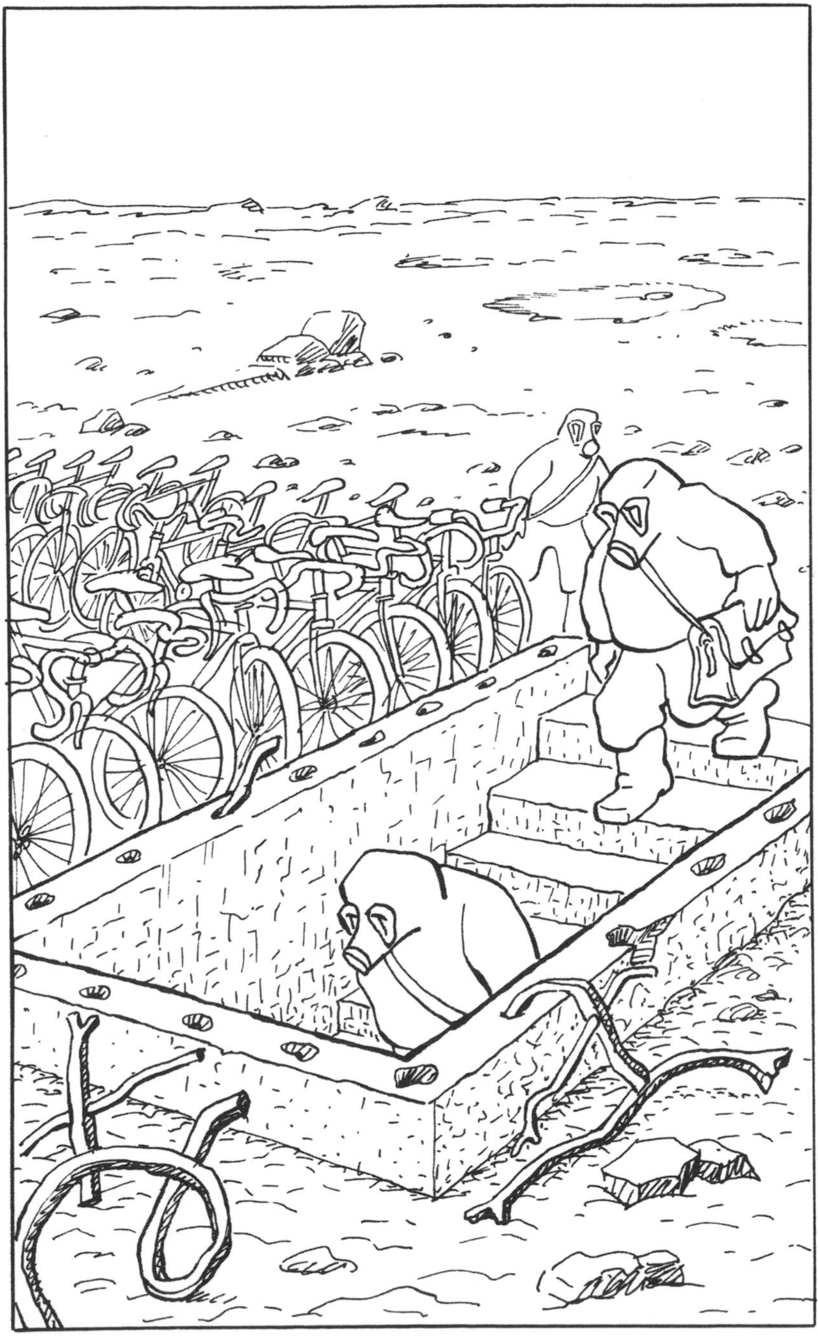

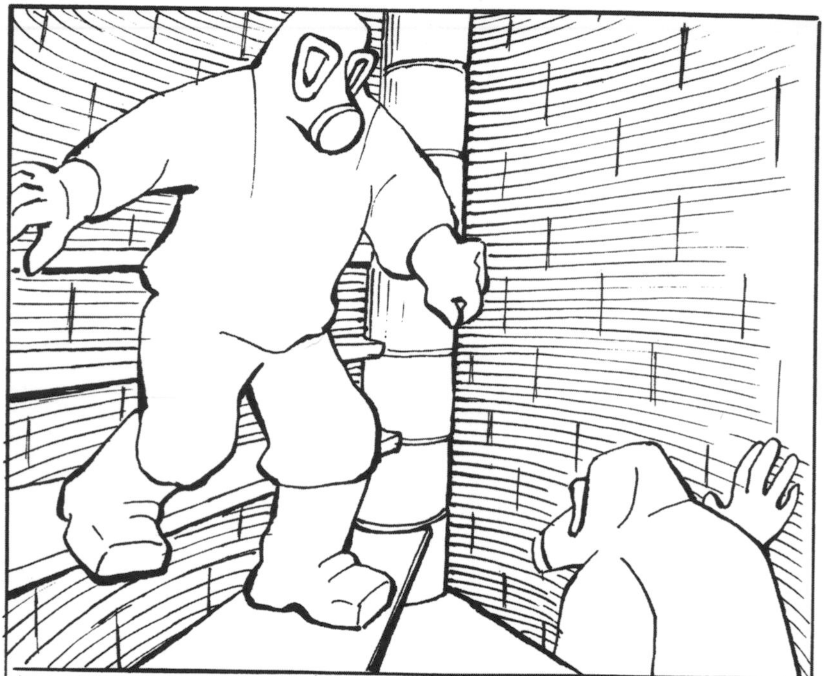

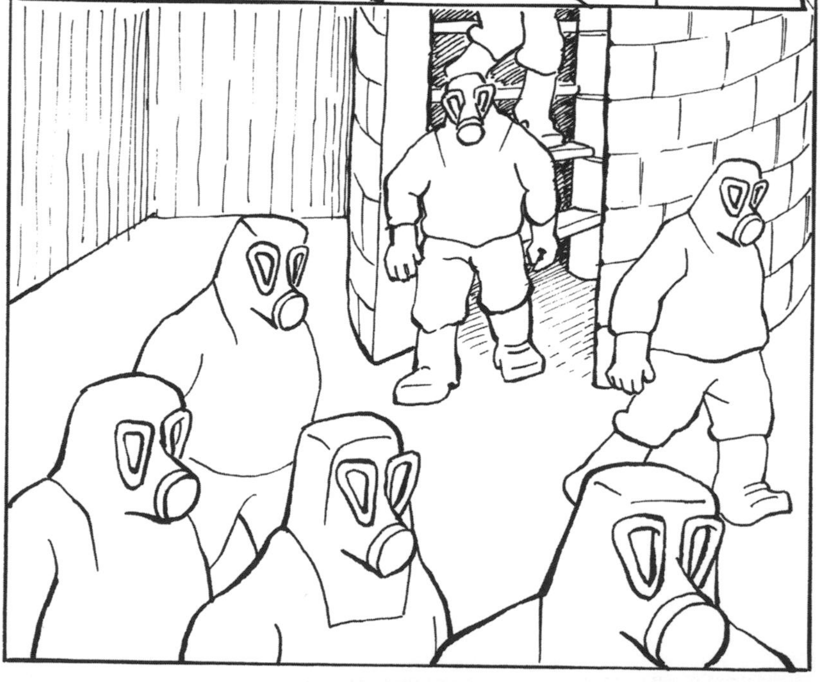

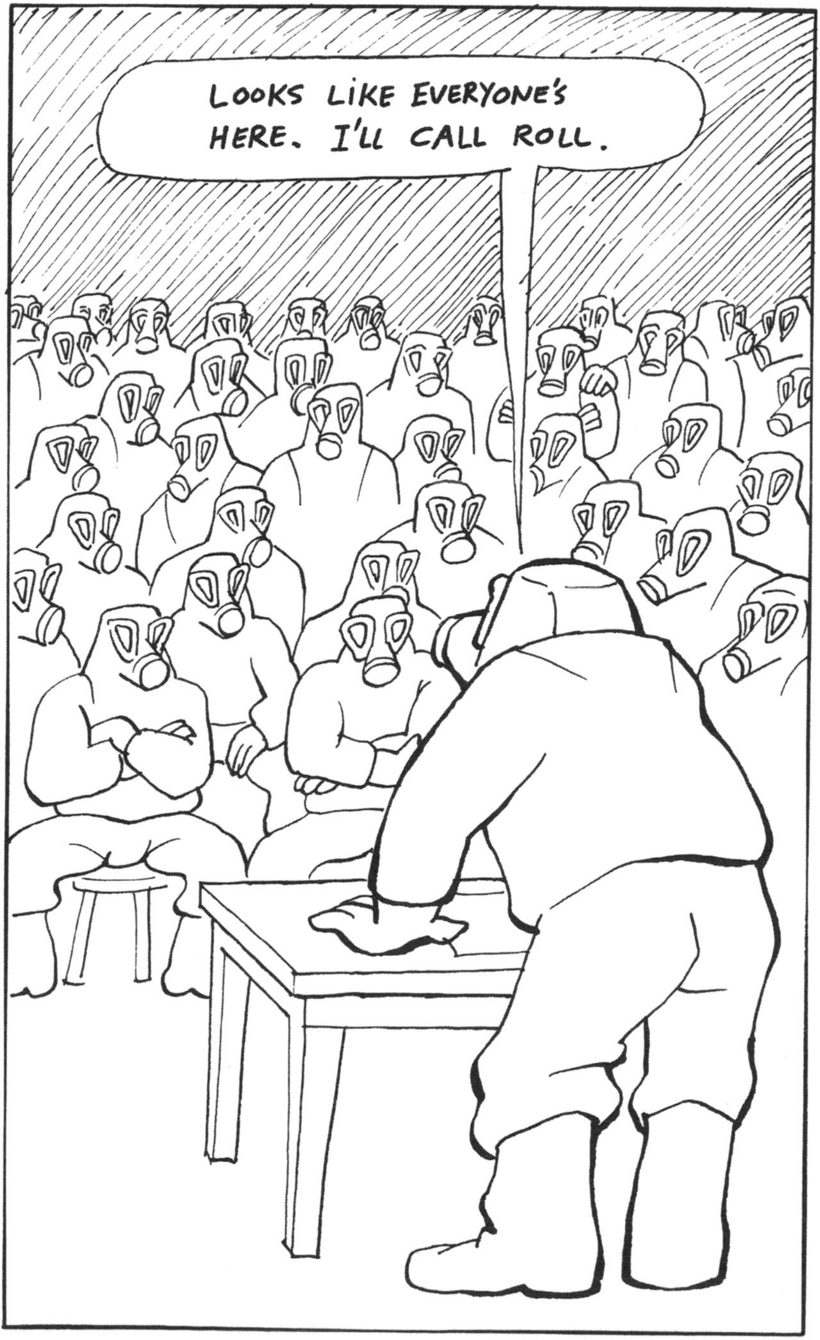
LOOKS LIKE EVERYONE'S HERE. I'LL CALL ROLL.

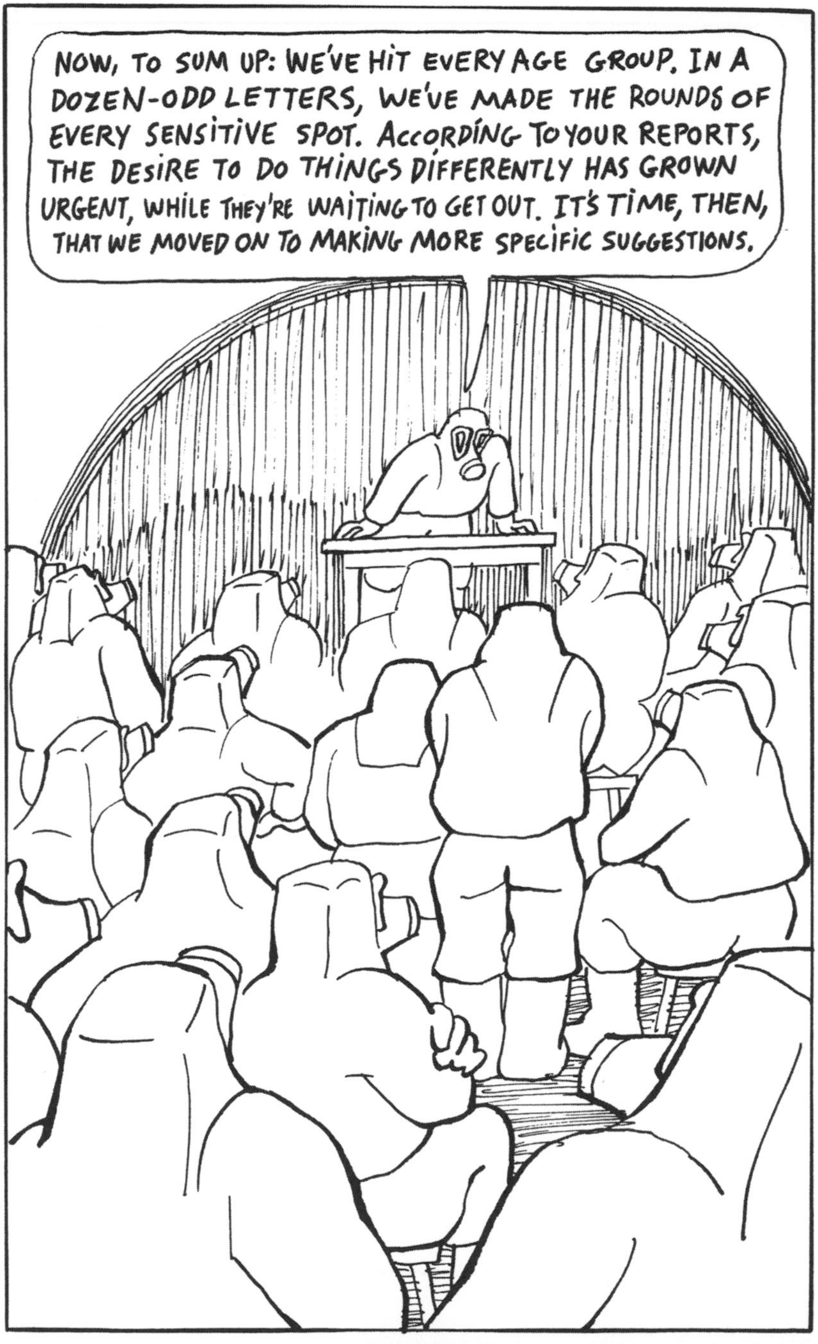
NOW, TO SUM UP: WE'VE HIT EVERY AGE GROUP. IN A DOZEN-ODD LETTERS, WE'VE MADE THE ROUNDS OF EVERY SENSITIVE SPOT. ACCORDING TO YOUR REPORTS, THE DESIRE TO DO THINGS DIFFERENTLY HAS GROWN URGENT, WHILE THEY'RE WAITING TO GET OUT. IT'S TIME, THEN, THAT WE MOVED ON TO MAKING MORE SPECIFIC SUGGESTIONS.

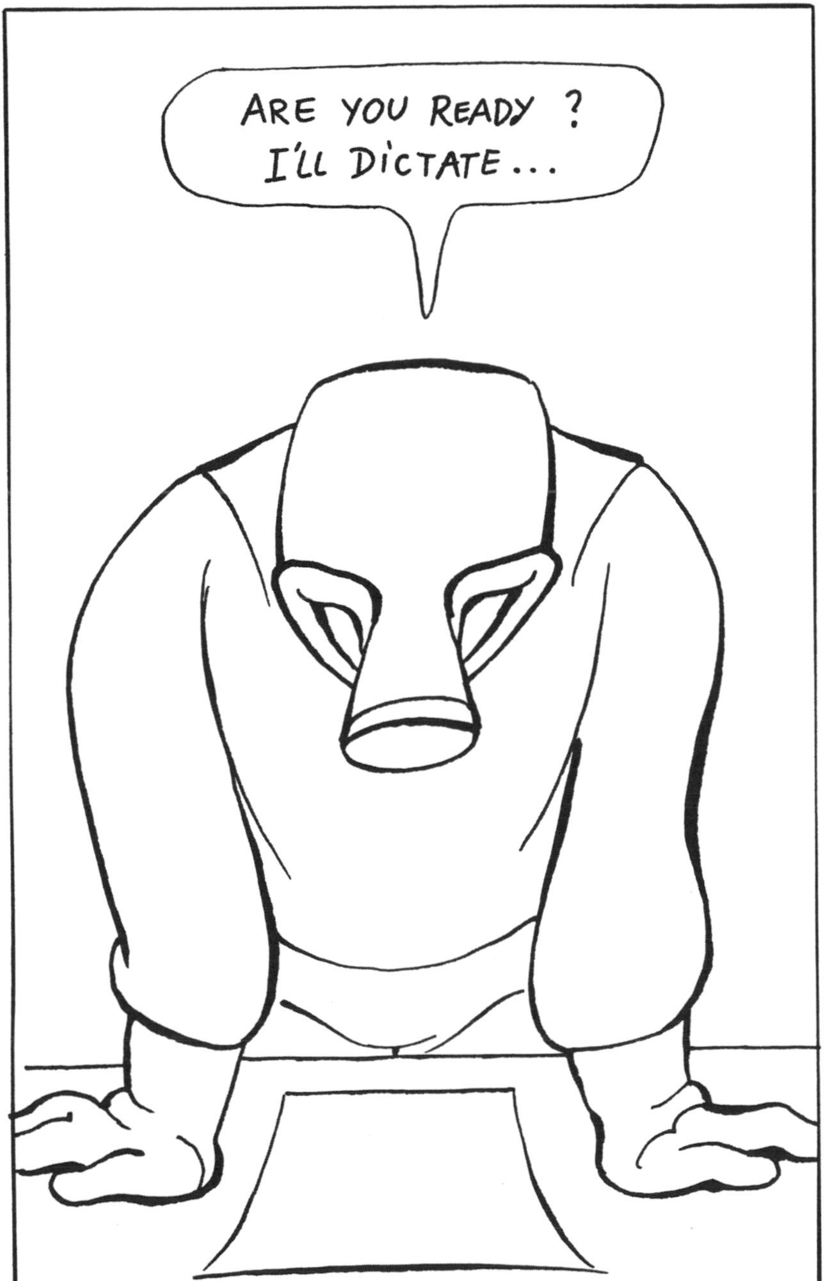
ARE YOU READY ?
I'LL DICTATE...

DEAR FRIENDS

...

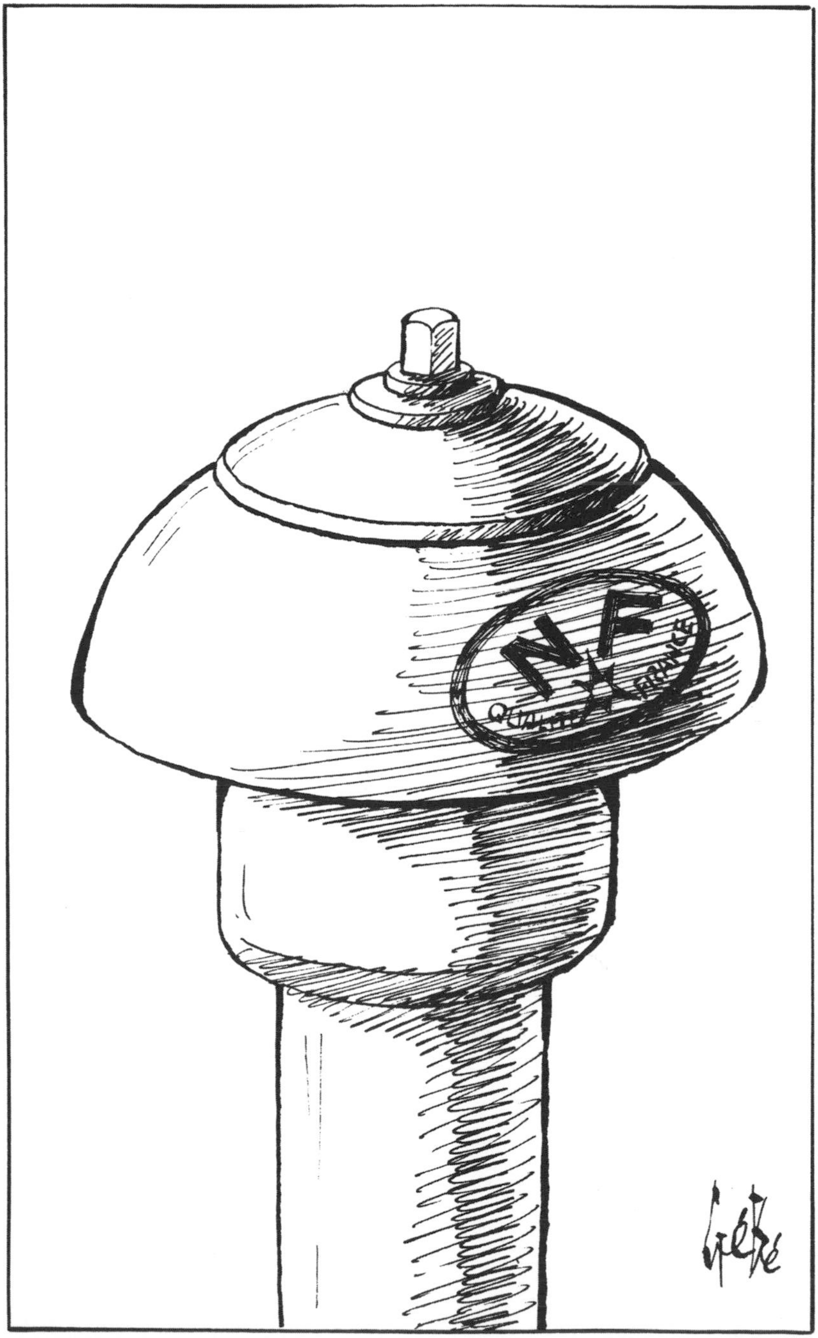
NF

ALSO AVAILABLE
FROM NEW YORK REVIEW COMICS

YELLOW NEGROES AND OTHER IMAGINARY CREATURES
Yvan Alagbé

PIERO
Edmond Baudoin

ALMOST COMPLETELY BAXTER
Glen Baxter

AGONY
Mark Beyer

PEPLUM
Blutch

THE GREEN HAND
Nicole Claveloux

WHAT AM I DOING HERE?
Abner Dean

PRETENDING IS LYING
Dominique Goblet

VOICES IN THE DARK
Ulli Lust

FATHER AND SON
E.O. Plauen

SOFT CITY
Pushwagner

THE NEW WORLD
Chris Reynolds

SLUM WOLF
Tadao Tsuge